The Concierge

by
Lora Lee Colter

Strategic Book Publishing and Rights Co.

Strategic Book Publishing and Rights Co.
12620 FM 1960, Suite A4-507
Houston, TX 77065
www.sbpra.com

ISBN: 978-1-61897-256-9

Disclaimer

This book, while inspired by some true events, is written
solely for enjoyment purposes in the context of pure fiction.
Names, places, and events are used fictitiously.

Dedication

For Chris, my beloved husband and soul mate, who inspires me with his wit and honors me with his heart. And for Cyrus, Calvin, and Chez' who make our world go around.

Acknowledgements

Thanks to Janet, my mom and biggest fan; to Diana, who supports me endlessly and is more like a sister than a cousin; and for you Linda, a never ending source of fun and inspiration to our family.

My heart is full of gratitude for caring family, friends, and neighbors. In a community like ours any dream is possible.

Darrell, I appreciate you showing me the Boiler Room again. It brought back a flood of memories!

Miracles and mysteries,

Life is full of lots of these.

Have faith and believe,

That good will prevail

And evil will recede.

Contents

Part I

Contents

Part II

Contents

Part I

1 – Moonlighting

I can't be late tonight! thought Ariel as she quickly clicked the mouse to shut down her computer programs with her right hand while simultaneously flicking off the overhead desk light with her left. After stashing papers and her laptop into the overhead cabinet, she grabbed her purse and coat and raced toward the outer office door that opened to the third floor skywalk high above the open atrium of Kaleidoscope Square. She scurried across the skywalk bridge staying well centered with eyes focused on the bank of elevators ahead. A slight glimpse of the marble floor forty feet below would create sweaty palms and shortness of breath. Heights had always been a problem for Ariel, but somehow despite her phobia, she always managed to reach the other side to safety in front of the glass elevators that quickly swooshed occupants to the polished ground level floor.

Ariel's high heels click-clacked across the gleaming marble as she scurried past Maude's flower shop on the right with showy floral arrangements in bright hues of purple, red, and yellow behind the sparkling glass with frosted letters. She zipped by the Sapphire Club where laughing, chatting patrons were getting a start on their Friday night happy hour, sipping their favorite concoctions.

Around the corner on the north side of the plaza was the bank of parking garage elevators. Impatiently, Ariel observed the lights above the scuffed, industrial elevator doors blink: three, two, one, and then the slow, weary doors parted with a creak. Ariel checked her watch. She had just twenty-five minutes to get to the hotel that would take thirty minutes to reach.

She squeezed in with others anxious to get to their cars and head out for their Friday night activities. The elevator chugged to the various levels of the parking ramp.

"Come on, come on," Ariel silently urged the slow-moving crate of steel. Eventually, the pulleys braked on level three, and the tired, heavy doors creaked open. Arial surged out into the cold air and headed to her usual parking spot, where her silver Nissan coupe waited.

Breathing heavily, little puffs of white vapor escaped her mouth. It was a typical cold January day in the Midwest, and thankfully, despite the forecast for snow, nothing yet had materialized. She yanked the car door open and slid into the seat reaching for her leather gloves on the console. The furry, soft lining felt good as she slid them over her bare hands. They provided welcome protection against the cold steering wheel.

She hastily started the ignition and flipped the warm air switch to high. Engaging the gearshift into reverse, she eased out of the parking space throwing the stick shift into first gear and then quickly to second. She smiled at the feel of the strong, smooth knob that conformed so well to her fisted hand. The maneuvering of the firm gearshift gave her a sense of comfort and confidence. The tires squealed a short distance on the cement then with a quick brake, she fell in behind the flow of cars following the arrow signs leading the way out. She began to relax just a little as she drifted in queue with the cars as they gently lulled around the spiral of the garage to the street below. Soon she would reach the lowest level to be delivered into the snarled traffic.

Gently pumping the brakes to fight the pull of gravity, she finally leveled out and reached the bottom of the garage where it was her turn to insert her prepaid parking card into the slot to lift the gate arm and allow for disposal out of the concrete structure. Traffic whizzed by on the one-way street and as a clearing broke, she surged out into the nearest lane and headed west toward Sixth Street to navigate north to I-35 West.

Ariel's thoughts reflected on her current life situation. While she was excited about her first, real job after college graduation, working for over a year with a promising start-up company, it delivered what Ariel considered a paltry salary that just covered the basic living expenses—nice but basic. Thus was one of the reasons for her race across town to her second more fulfilling part-time job at the Capitol Plaza Hotel.

Moonlighting helped provide her the extras and upgrades that she was sure she needed—a wardrobe of new clothes, shoes, accessories, and some fine beauty products to help sustain a single, working girl's lifestyle. She actually looked forward to another five hours of work at the Capitol Plaza Hotel on a Friday night. More than the supplemental income, it provided a superb social opportunity and surprisingly a chance to unwind behind the huge mahogany concierge desk. The sound of the soothing gush of the waterfall nearby offered a relaxing backdrop. And of course, as the job required, she assisted hotel guests with their inquiries, demands, and sometimes quirky personal requests. There was never a shortage of drama or excitement at the Plaza. Curious events were plentiful and lately, some interesting—no, make that bizarre—situations had fermented.

At the moment, Ariel's concentration returned to the task at hand and that was to get quickly and safely across town. Suddenly out of nowhere, some young, clueless guy in a faded red jeep cut in front of her and beat it to the entrance ramp of the freeway, nearly taking her front bumper with him. She pressed hard on the horn cursing his stupidity. In the rearview mirror, she saw her mauve hotel suit on the hanger in the back swing out wildly from the hook as she hit the brakes and brought the steering wheel hard to the right to ward off a collision. She sucked in a deep breath and regained composure as she merged left onto the entrance ramp to head west.

The mauve monkey suit, as she called it, was the only slight drawback to an otherwise fabulous and perfect part-time job. The pink, or officially mauve-colored, jacket and skirt with matching pink and white striped blouse wasn't nearly as flattering as the professional dress clothes she wore for her day job, not to mention that it was a nuisance to have to change into the required hotel uniform. However, it was a small price to pay for the overall enjoyment Ariel experienced once dressed and on duty.

As she shifted gears and edged into the traffic flow, the jerk in the jeep was up ahead sashaying from one lane to the other, as though his racecar style maneuvers would get him to his destination faster than everyone else. Traffic was typical for a Friday after work and undoubtedly the anticipated Friday night accident near Eighth Street in West Des Moines would occur. Nine times out of ten, someone failed to take into consideration the warning signs that the four lanes would soon merge down to three near the Eighth Street overpass. At the moment, it looked like traffic was still moving fine. Ariel kept her fingers crossed.

There was just something about Friday after a week of work that brought out the irresponsibility in people. For the married worker with a family, it was the anticipation of reaching home base in the suburbs to begin the official weekend with the neighbors, which caused driving a bit too fast in their quest for rest and relaxation. For the crazy singles, it was the pursuit to reach one of the latest hot spots in town. One such hot spot was Jimmy's, which just happened to be off the Eighth Street exit.

As traffic crawled past the exit ramp, Ariel felt a slight yearning for her friend Tori and roommate, Rachel, who she knew would be patronizing Jimmy's as usual. She thought about sending a text, however to avoid the risk of being involved in the latest Eighth Street collision, she decided to touch base with them later to catch up on the gossip and get the 411 regarding any interesting situations they might encounter that evening.

Jimmy's was known to some as the proverbial meat market, but for most it offered an opportunity to mingle with friends and unwind at the end of a long week. It was a super place for networking, both socially and professionally. It offered the pleasures of interesting people, the sensual smells of expensive perfume, Cuban cigars, musky aged oak, and even the smell of money. Ariel envisioned Tori and Rachel on the enclosed veranda in the thick of things, sipping on cocktails, eating hors d'oeuvres, and scanning the crowd for familiar faces or searching for some unknown person whose acquaintance they might like to make. Jimmy's served up a bewitching atmosphere where patrons felt special. The setting was conducive to all things magical and an evening there usually precluded other high energy venues around the town. Many an adventure typically began at Jimmy's.

Rachel was confident, polite, and sweet, with a gracious smile that could melt any heart. It was not surprising she had friends galore, and Ariel felt very fortunate to have her as a closest friend and roommate. The two had met through other acquaintances since moving to West Des Moines after college, both from small town Iowa farm communities. They had a common bond. This morning, Rachel had left for work, her blond hair pulled tight in a sleek, shoulder-length pony tail to show off earlobes sparkling with diamonds given to her by her on-again-off-again boyfriend, Steve. Tonight she was Steve-less.

Effervescent Tori was athletic and outgoing, with a hearty laugh and strong opinions. She had the ability to talk about the latest sports statistics with amazing recall, and never had trouble conversing with men because of this interesting gift of sports gab. However, to her dismay, her luck on the romance department was rather elusive, most likely due to the fact that men could sense she was overpowering and could belittle them with her sense of superiority.

With the 8th Street exit behind, Ariel focused on her destination, which was soon approaching. She had been maneuvering the mad dash from downtown to the west side for almost six weeks. The nice thing was that it wasn't an every night ordeal; it was just a couple of nights during the week and some weekend hours. And it wasn't just a job, but a real adventure. Ariel had learned a lot about the inner workings of the hotel after first starting as a banquet server just prior to the Christmas holidays and then unexpectedly landing in the concierge role, which was, in her opinion, a gem of a position. If the hotel was like a sundae, the concierge job was the cherry on top. Tonight marked the first night Ariel would fly solo as a concierge of the Capitol Plaza Hotel. She was excited! Of course, life isn't always as it seems and Ariel could in no way envision that her life's destiny was on a dangerously curious path.

- - -

2 – Six Weeks Earlier

Ariel's thoughts regressed to six weeks earlier. So much had changed in such a short time since her involvement with the Capitol Plaza Hotel and all its interesting associates and inhabitants. Unknowingly to her, the most dramatic events were yet to evolve.

It began innocently enough at the end of November, just prior to the winter holiday hustle and bustle, when extra staff was necessary to handle the nightly Christmas parties, office get-togethers and various banquet events. Ariel had zeroed in on the ad asking for seasonal banquet servers at one of the cities newest and hottest hotels. She and Rachel were enjoying a leisurely Saturday morning, sipping coffee and perusing sections of The Des Moines Register in their bright, sunny kitchen. With a wall of windows facing east, even the coldest winter mornings were pleasant when the sun was shining.

"Hey, Rachel, what do you think about this one?" she blurted out as she circled the small block of print under the Restaurant and Hospitality column in the newspaper. Her roommate was always supportive of her ideas and was aware she had been planning to get a second job. "This will be a great way to earn extra cash for the holidays, give me a chance to meet some new people, plus it will be fun mingling with people out celebrating at this time of year," Ariel gushed.

Rachel concurred. "Yeah, that sounds like the job for you, all right! Go for it," she encouraged Ariel. "I'll come visit you sometime and check out the hotel scene. It sounds exciting!"

"You know, I hate to say this, but if I can get this job, it would also be the perfect excuse to let Jake know I've decided we should go our separate ways," mused Ariel.

"How do you think he'll take that news?" Rachel threw her a sideways look.

"I'm guessing not well, although he may not be too surprised after the last few weeks we've been having." Ariel sighed, elbows on the table with her chin resting in cupped hands. She gazed back at her friend with a look of apprehension. She had decided her boyfriend, Jake, was turning out to be a source of concern and frustration and contemplated whether to sever ties with him and move on with her life. *A part-time job would be a great excuse to tie up my evenings and not be available for his company,* she thought.

Although they had dated about eight months, his unpredictability, moodiness, and instability started to take its toll. He had a rather dark past and as she learned more about his history, the more cautious and uncertain she became about wanting any part of his future.

"Well, it's definitely time to make a change," Ariel stated with confidence. "I'm going to call the hotel and set up an appointment."

"Good for you. I wish you luck and when you deliver Jake the news, just make sure I'm not anywhere nearby!" Rachel threw Ariel a look of concern.

"Thanks, and don't worry, I won't, but I will fill you in on the gory details," Ariel grimaced and then smiled.

Ariel was grateful she had found such a great friend and roommate. They had shared a duplex on Plum Tree Lane for about a year in a small bedroom community just west of the metro. The duplex was perfect, just the right size for two, although it had a one-car garage. With two cars, in their agreeable manner, they established a weekly rotation. The entry from the garage was a small hallway with a laundry room and a bathroom on the right and the cheery kitchen at the back and to the right. To the left of the kitchen was a very open great room with a high ceiling and an open staircase leading to an upper level where they each had their own bedroom and full bathroom.

Merging their individual possessions had worked out nicely as they had similar tastes leaning toward modern-contemporary. The kitchen table was a metal and glass top style with chairs of pewter and rich coal fabric offering an urbane mix. A trio of ornamental ceramic vases—two yellow and one black—were centered on the table. A bright red sectional L-shaped sofa fit comfortably in the great room and faced a flat-screen TV above the fireplace on the north side. To the east, a nice view of the back patio and small yard was visible through the sliding glass doors. A square glass coffee table positioned in front of the sofa held a small stack of magazines and a huge 4-wick candle that typically flickered at night. For the most part, the roommates were sparse on embellishments for their living quarters and both agreed "less-is-more." A large abstract art mural in shades of red, yellow, black, and white filled the west wall to the right of the front entrance and gave a nice splash of color against the caramel colored walls.

The women enjoyed their cozy and well-kept living quarters. They were content and life was good.

---

3 – The Capitol Plaza Hotel

The time had arrived for Ariel's interview at the Capitol Plaza. Conveniently, it was a brief drive from the duplex on Plum Tree Lane to the hotel on University Avenue. With only two turns, five stop lights, and a total of about ten minutes between the duplex driveway and the parking lot, it was an easy jaunt. *Another plus to the job,* thought Ariel.

Ariel reached the hotel parking lot destination and the minute she turned off the ignition, the warmth that had begun to accumulate in her car quickly dissipated. Without the reliable circulation of heat, her snug cocoon was no match against the cold bitterness outside her trusty transportation. Despite the sunny skies, it was deceivingly cold. She lingered for just a moment sizing up the tan stone exterior complete with the huge red sign shouting *Capitol Plaza Hotel* across the top. She had driven by this place many times since its construction began on the edge of town about a year ago, and in fact had even hung out at the high energy dance club, Paradigm, a few times after it opened, but had never given much thought about working here.

Something stirred within her and Ariel felt a new chapter of her life might be about to unfold. It was inexplicable and while self-instigated, there was something she sensed was out of the realm of her own control. Little did she imagine that seasonal employment would evolve into a more long-term and exciting position, nor could she ever dream that the Capitol Plaza would catapult her mundane existence into a life filled with excitement, paranoia, suspense, and eventually downright terror.

She wrapped her wool scarf around her neck a little tighter and opened the car door, stepping out onto a patch of packed snow and ice. For the most part, the lot was clean and clear, but piles of snow from previous flurries had been scraped and deposited along the outer perimeters of the vast lot. She didn't believe in wearing heavy snow boots—didn't need them for her day job due to the series of indoor skywalks connected to the parking ramps and downtown businesses, which provided protection against the winter elements. However, snow boots were tucked in the back seat during cold winter months just in case. Winters in Iowa were unpredictable and you just never knew when they would be needed. Admittedly, there were times when Ariel's feet were overly exposed in winter, all in the name of fashion. On harsh cold days, she wore boots of fashion but not of warmth. Even if she wasn't committed to keeping her feet warm, she was always faithful in wearing her black leather gloves. At the present, her gloved hands were clenched tightly to her notebook that held her resume.

She headed toward the building and was ready to tackle an interview for a banquet server position and to meet some new people. *This should be a piece of cake. I've had plenty of experience in restaurant service during college working as a waitress and bartender. Also, since it's a temporary, part-time job, I'll survive even if I don't get hired,* she thought.

The cobbled brick drive in front of the hotel allowed for guests to temporarily park and unload their gear and necessities. Bellmen dressed in wine-colored uniforms, sporting gold name tags, were the on-duty escorts equipped to handle even the most cumbersome of luggage. Guests to the hotel were greeted and ushered through the massive revolving glass door, or were escorted through one of the traditional glass doors flanking either side, depending on a person's preference for passing from the outside elements into the comfort and safety of the strong fortress-like structure.

Ariel approached the grand entrance covered by a high carport roof and immediately felt reprieve from the cold as the wind subsided, blocked from the north. She circled behind an open-trunk Cadillac, engine running and beside which stood a pudgy, red-faced man, sagging under the weight of his bags. His middle-age wife, with her heavy pile of blond hair was moving her hot pink lips and ordering her husband to get her makeup bag from the back seat. The husband shot her a scowl but lumbered his way around the trunk toward the back car door as a bellman approached to provide some assistance.

In front of the Cadillac, an SUV was running and inside were two fun-loving couples, organizing to unload, apparently on a road trip or vacation. Ariel smiled inwardly and mentally noted that on any given day, a variety of personalities would disembark here and likely there would be some interesting encounters on the job.

The boxy black letters spelled out *Howard* on his gold nametag. Howard had a grinning round face, upon which perched a nimbus of gray hair that circled the bald spot on his head. Behind his wire-rimmed glasses were kind eyes that welcomed Ariel. He gave her a friendly nod. The pleasant, elderly man with the burgundy wine-colored suit had similarly black gloved hands as hers. He opened one of the side doors, and gestured her inside. "Welcome to the Capitol Plaza," he greeted her as she entered the vestibule.

"Ah, it feels nice in here—like an oasis." With the warm air circulating through the small area between the outside doors and the lobby doors, Ariel quickly warmed. She returned Howard's greeting as he ushered her on through to the lobby.

The spacious ten-floor hotel was comprised of a large, open atrium with a beautiful, gushing waterfall that magically poured out of the fifth floor to a small pool below. Light streamed in through the glass dome structure on the rooftop, and beams of light coruscated off the glass elevators and sparkled on the chrome tube-like fencing that circled and defined the inner atrium. The deep, jewel tones of blue, green, and berry in the carpet lent a cheery, peaceful feel to the place. Ariel stood for a moment taking in her surroundings.

To the right, tucked back into a corner subdivision was a dimly lit but open lounge area. The section was defined with the same shiny tube-like fencing around the outer perimeter. Little strands of yellow lights outlined the raised floor platform and followed around the two steps that led to the bar. It was a cozy area with low, mirror-topped tables surrounded by heavily cushioned chairs and couches. At the present time the lounge was quiet. One bartender was behind the bar and was meticulously wiping shelves and bottles. A sense of pride was displayed in his orderly behavior and it was a nice feeling to observe someone immersed in his work and enjoying it at that.

Across from the wide, carpeted walkway that meandered around the lounge, and in a wide, open area to the right of the atrium was a cheery family style restaurant called The Garden Spot, which boasted a huge buffet table in the center. Several uniformed waiters and waitresses bustled about, clearing table remnants and cleaning up after a busy Sunday brunch shift.

Continuing down the walkway past the lounge and

heading to the northern doors of the hotel was Paradigm, the dance club that Ariel was familiar with, although on past visits she and her friends had always used the outer doors that were nearest to the club. Adjacent to Paradigm was a fine-dining restaurant of which Ariel had vague awareness based on previous comings and goings from the dance club.

The expansive front desk was to her immediate left where Ariel paused to ask about her interview with the Banquet Services Manager. The boxy black letters on his gold nametag identified him as Malcolm, a handsome, well-groomed black man whose skin looked as rich as the deep mauve suit jacket he wore.

"Hi, my name is Ariel Sterling. I'm here about the banquet server position."

"Ah, sure, let me page Mr. Blackstone to the front," he responded in a strong baritone voice. "Typically, I'd send you around the corner to Human Resources but no one is on duty in that department on Sunday. Mr. Blackstone will probably invite you back to the banquet area to talk. Excuse me a second," he said as he stepped away. He quickly returned. "He'll be right out in about five minutes. He's just finishing up some business."

While waiting, Ariel glanced toward the direction Malcolm had pointed when speaking of the H.R. department and marveled at the beautiful, massive, mahogany desk at the end of the lobby area. Seated behind the desk was a blond-haired woman, in her late thirties, wearing a mauve suit jacket. She was concentrating on some sort of project, her head bent over a piece of white tag board. She appeared to be carefully writing with an assortment of calligraphy pens. Ariel stepped a bit closer and saw the sign *Concierge* in a gold plaque displayed on the desk.

The concierge stayed focused and engrossed in her work,

half hidden and protected by the dark wooden desk that separated her from the rest of the enormous lobby and atrium area. A jutting divider wall in conjunction with the desk made a small right angled area for the woman to maneuver. Beside her on a lower smaller desk was a computer and sophisticated looking phone system, with buttons blinking and identifying the various lines in use throughout the hotel stations. To the right of the divider wall was a glass door that informed visitors of the Sales Office—hours of operation Monday through Friday, 7:30 a.m. to 6:00 p.m. and 9:00 a.m. to 5:00 p.m. on Saturdays. At the present time it was dark and quiet.

Further to the right of the Sales Office and behind the sparkling waterfall were two elevators hidden behind this curtain of water. Just opposite the elevators was an entry to the women's and men's restroom lounges. Ariel took a quick opportunity to visit the ladies room to check her hair and makeup prior to meeting Mr. Blackstone. The outer lounge door gently swung open and she was startled at first to see her reflection in a wall-sized mirror ten feet from the entry. Two comfy lounge chairs with a table between offered a place to relax or wait on a friend. She deposited her wool winter coat and binder on one of the colorful patterned chairs and proceeded through the next door into the restroom. A bank of pink stall doors were all slightly ajar and seemingly beckoned to the black marble sink parallel on the opposite wall. Small overhead chandeliers were strategically situated for maximum lighting. It was empty. Not much action in the hotel on a Sunday afternoon, she decided.

Ariel gazed in the mirror, satisfied with the reflection that returned—pinstriped navy pants and a complementary pale blue sweater; around her neck a double strand pearl necklace rested. Her medium length, highlighted blond hair was feathered around her face and her dark brown eyes scrutinized her fair skin. She rifled through her Coach purse for her makeup bag and found a rose-colored lipstick and lip

Lora Lee Colter

pencil to trace and redefine her full lips. Suddenly, Ariel felt a vague, prickly sensation trickle down the back of her neck. She slowly turned to be absolutely certain she hadn't been mistaken about being alone. All the stall doors were open and there was definitely no one else in the restroom. *Hmm, that was strange,* she thought and quickly realized she better get back to the front desk before Mr. Blackstone came for her.

---

4 – Joining the Hotel Family

To Ariel's delight, Mr. Blackstone didn't spend much time asking detailed questions about her resume and seemed satisfied with her past restaurant affiliated accomplishments. He had escorted her to the banquet and convention area through a door, over which was displayed a large sign, identifying that they were in the Grand Ball Room. They conversed at a table while workers swarmed about, rolling round-topped tables across the floor to properly position them for upcoming dinner parties scheduled for the evening. The ballroom was grand with crystal encrusted chandeliers suspended high above the activity below. The eight, ornately cut, multifaceted glass energy sources reflected dazzling colors of light and angled in all directions, as if with seeing eyes. There was an omnipotent quality to their presence. The interesting thing Ariel discovered about the ballroom was that it could magically be transformed from a massive 12,000-square-foot area down to eight smaller, more intimate, yet functional spaces. With just a push of a button hidden doors would scroll out to form appropriate dividers for any given occasion.

Mr. Blackstone instructed her to report for work beginning Friday evening and Ariel was thrilled and excited to become a temporary member of this hotel family. "This should really be fun. I know I will enjoy it, especially at this time of year," Ariel enthusiastically gushed. To serve the mass of partygoers all celebrating in the fervor of the holiday season would hardly seem like work. *After all, how difficult could it be to distribute plates of food around the ballroom tables, drop off drinks, and pour coffee,* she thought.

Thinking back to her time in college waiting tables, she figured her skills would easily return.

In his soft-spoken yet energized manner, Mr. Blackstone politely requested that Ariel follow him to the laundry room where he would provide her with a banquet uniform. "If you'll please follow me this way," he gestured while explaining that today, he would not have time to provide a tour of the kitchen and back working area, but promised Ariel when she reported to work Friday evening he would familiarize her with that department.

Ariel followed on his heels toward the rear ballroom doors, observing his backside. His rear end was rather round for a man, but it matched his round front side—both belly and face—so it suited him. He wore black slacks cinched tight at the low hanging waistline where the upper roll met the lower roll. His short, busy legs seemed to work extra hard just to maneuver along, but there was a spring to his step that suggested there must be some muscle hiding under those slacks.

They exited into a very wide hallway that ran parallel to the outer ballroom wall along the length of the hotel. Ariel was surprised to observe how spacious the outer working perimeters were. The floor was the color of brown brick and looked as if it had just been freshly mopped. In fact, sure enough, there sat a big yellow industrial-size bucket on wheels with the handle of a mop sticking out, the dirty brown water settled under floating flecks of paper, dust balls and other unidentifiable particles. Mr. Blackstone glanced at it and muttered something about John not quite finishing up with his duties.

After walking about twenty feet, the two approached a small, windowed office on the right. Mr. Blackstone stuck his short stub of a thumb up and with a quick couple of jabs directed them toward the office. "Let's stop here for just a second and I'll grab a couple of forms that you need to complete."

Above the door was a sign that read *Convention Services Director*. The walls of the small office were painted yellow. The chipper yellow color was an attempt to exude some sense of cheerfulness to an otherwise drab environment. Although glass windows looked out into the rather dreary hallway, there were no windows to the outer world where sun and nature could stimulate and sooth the senses. All stimulation from this office locale had to be derived from actual activities occurring within the confines of the corridor. Inside was a desk weighted down by an assortment of paper piles, folders, coffee mugs, and framed photos of smiling family faces. On the wall near the desk hung clipboards securing banquet request forms. Schedules and other informational sheets dangled from big rings on hooks.

Mr. Blackstone gave Ariel's application a toss on top of his desk where she wondered if it might just disappear over the course of a day or two. He bent down and dug out some forms from the three-drawer filing cabinet for her to sign.

"You'll need to fill these out and turn them in to H.R.; just bring them back on Friday," he instructed.

"Sounds good," Ariel responded in her cheery voice as she placed the papers in her binder.

"Okay, let's head down the hall to get your uniform." They proceeded out of the office toward the laundry room and Security Office, which were located in the same back corner of the hotel near the employee entrance. As they approached the back hall area, Ariel noticed through a glass windowed office that a lanky, dark-haired guy in a navy blue uniform was leaning back on his chair with long legs stretched out, black rubber-soled shoes resting on the desktop.

"Looks like Randy is real busy today," joked Mr. Blackstone. "These security guys sure have it rough. There are four of them. Usually, two are on duty at a time unless it's a slow Sunday; then just one of them takes care of things. Their primary job is to monitor this back employee entrance and hotel camera systems, control the hotel keys and locks, engrave and assign employee nametags, and stuff like that. I don't believe they've ever had to handle anything too high security yet, anyway," Mr. Blackstone laughed. "When you report to work, you'll come in this entrance here by the Security Office and punch the time clock. Security guys may not always be in the office but you can always spot their navy blue suits cruising the hotel. A couple of them are real jokesters so don't take anything they say too seriously."

"Oh, don't worry about me. I can handle it. I grew up with ornery brothers," Ariel assured him.

Randy glanced up as he heard their voices and lifted a forefinger as a small gesture of recognition then quickly refocused on his matter at hand. They passed the Security Office and in another ten feet reached brown, wooden double doors. On one of the doors was posted a sign: *Employees Only*. Mr. Blackstone pulled the right door open and inside was a huge laundry facility all abuzz with a row of commercial-size washers spinning, swishing, and splashing and dryers humming and tossing white, pink, and burgundy linens. Three women were engaged in keeping up with a never-ending flood of dirty sheets, towels, tablecloths, and napkins. Although barely discernable, a radio was delivering the sounds of oldies but goodies and amazingly, the ladies seemed content with the process of sorting, loading, unloading, folding, and storing their inventory. The women glanced toward the two newcomers but didn't seem too interested and continued with their tasks.

Across a rod the length of the left wall hung uniforms covered in plastic wrap, neatly sectioned by color. The majority of uniforms were burgundy, representing the banquet and waiter/waitress staff and bellhops. There was a small section of navy slacks and jackets, which Ariel had recently learned were for the security guards, and there were dark gray slacks, mauve-colored jackets and mauve skirts, attire for the crew behind the front desk and for the concierge. Mr. Blackstone eyeballed Ariel, sizing her up. He twisted his lips together and speculated on a size that would fit.

"Hmm, size four?" he questioned.

"I think I can squeeze into that," laughed Ariel. He stretched up on the toes of his black wing tips, his stubby legs just a smidgen too short and he shuffled through the burgundy section in search of a size four.

"Ah, here we are." He struggled to lift the suit off the rod. As his hand yanked up, his head simultaneously jerked back. Ariel was afraid he would pull a muscle and winced slightly as she watched his struggle.

"Can I help?" she offered.

"No, no, I've got it." After three tries he had freed the unyielding wire hanger and handed the garment over to her. "There you go, young lady. Now you'll need to report for duty no later than 5:00 for your first shift."

"No problem," Ariel replied with confidence. Internally, she envisioned the harried race she'd have from her office downtown to the west side.

"I'll make sure you get a proper tour of the kitchen. We'll go over some basic guidelines and there will be the usual prep work." He slid his stubby fingers through his wavy brown hair and pushed his dark-framed glasses up on his nose. He drew a breath of air and went on to further explain that several big parties were scheduled for Friday evening and that a few other new servers were coming on board for the most robust season of the year.

"Come on, I'll take you back up to the atrium." He opened the doors to exit the stuffy, noisy laundry room. The doors shut softly and it was quiet again in the back hall. Randy hadn't changed positions. His navy slacks were still parallel to the floor and his black-soled shoes still rested on the desk. He was staring through the glass window of the Security Office into the outer hallway, with the phone stuck to his ear and a far away look in his eyes. After they passed, his gazed trailed Ariel with guarded curiosity.

Mr. Blackstone motioned to the right and a few steps later, pulled open one side of a double door. They were greeted with the bright, cheery colors of the atrium carpet, and they were back in public territory.

"As you can see, this corridor runs alongside the ballroom. See these signs jutting out from the three side doors that exit into the hall? We have the Magnolia, Maple, and Willow rooms on this south side. These are the entrances that guests are directed through if the ballroom is sectioned into smaller components. On the north wing is a similar corridor that connects three separate entrances to the rooms: Michigan, Ontario, and Erie."

"It sounds like trees on the south and lakes on the north," Ariel surmised.

"Yep, it definitely makes it easy to remember," confirmed Mr. Blackstone.

They continued along the azure and turquoise carpet splashed with lily-pad-shaped greens and dots of burgundy berries that eventually meandered around a corner signaling the approaching open atrium area that joined the front entrance of the Grand Ballroom.

"Well here we are, back where we started. I'll see you on Friday. Be dressed in uniform and report to Michigan; it's the farthest back on the north, near the kitchen. I'd have to double check but I believe that is the Peard holiday party. Mayor Peard and his wife throw a good bash every year. Honestly though, we have so many parties and events coming up, it's hard to keep them straight. It is one crazy time of the year so be prepared for a workout."

"Oh, I can't wait. It's just what I'm looking for," Ariel beamed.

He extended his doughy hand and Ariel reciprocated the gesture with a firm squeeze.

"Thank you so much for your time, and see you Friday."

"You're welcome." He quickly departed and ducked inside one of the massive doors to the Grand Ballroom. Ariel paused for a moment gazing again at the atrium and surroundings, this time from another angle. This place was enormous but was logically designed and appeared to be very functional, not to mention absolutely beautiful.

Relieved that the interview went well and was over, Ariel pulled on her wool coat and gloves, and wrapped her scarf around her neck. She headed toward the front doors with her size four, burgundy uniform folded across the crook of her arm. When Howard saw the uniform, a broad grin spread across his face.

"Guess I'll be seein' you around here, huh?

"Yes, I'll see you if you're working Friday night."

"Ah, but of course, I'll be here as usual," Howard replied with a gleam in his eye. He politely gestured her out the door.

---

5 – Banquet Festivities

Friday night arrived. The banquet room to which Ariel was assigned was radiant and aglow in the soft twinkling lights of the colossal chandelier overhead, its strands of prism-cut glass cascading down from the ceiling while candles flickered and danced atop mirrors on the white clothed tables. Glistening silverware was perfectly aligned around the table edges with gold-rimmed plates nestled in between the forks, knives, and spoons. Each setting was flanked by crystal goblets out of which fanned red cloth napkins. It was a beautiful and festive display down to the finest detail and ready to greet the guests who would soon arrive. A similar scene repeated itself throughout the conjoining banquet rooms, each a secret getaway unto itself.

Little did anyone suspect the crystal glass beauty above was not as it appeared; rather, covert and dangerous *eyes* were lurking. An omniscient presence was embedded amidst the innocuous, cheerful setting.

The back hall and kitchen quarters were the nemesis of the calm and peaceful dining room. You could count on it. And unless you experienced it firsthand, you would never believe the chaos that ensued the minute you crossed the barrier from the oasis into the storm. Behind the scene was pure energy, a sort of controlled chaos. All efforts were to orchestrate the perfect banquet performance, several times over in one night. The communication had to be flawless, starting with the sales ticket, written up weeks in advance, which detailed exactly what entrée, side dish, dessert and drinks would be served including when and how they would be delivered. The room arrangement, too, was planned according to the reservation, ranging from banquet style to full service sit down including specifications on décor and other amenities. The food preparation and delivery must be timed to perfection and served with graceful speed.

The air in the kitchen was thick and heavy, redolent with a vast combination of smells—sumptuous food, steam from the dishwasher, body odors from the kitchen help that had been slaving all afternoon, co-mingled with the scents of freshly showered and groomed wait staff arriving for their shifts.

Ariel received a quick rundown of the evening's game plan upon arrival and was directed to join the crew. There was much to do: scoop up bowls of butter and sour cream, prepare plates of salad greens, fill pitchers of water and ice, and fetch carafes of wine from the bar. Mr. Blackstone was bustling about, beads of perspiration dotting his upper lip and semi-circles of sweat outlining the underarms of his once crisp, but now wrinkled shirt. His sports jacket was draped over the chair in his back hall office until necessitated for guest engagement.

At 6:30, guests began to arrive for the Peard party. Eager to begin a festive evening, mingling and swapping pleasantries, they were dressed in glitz and glam. The room was aglow with soft lights and the soft buzz of conversation filled the air. The bartender and his liquid offerings quickly became the center of attention. Gin and tonics, expensive scotch, and martinis were concoctions of choice. Glasses of red and white wines were plucked off trays and beer flowed freely into frosty mugs. The party had begun. As cocktail hour progressed, as expected, the decibel level rose. Finally a ping, ping, pinging sound of knife to glass signaled the exuberant throng to seek out a seat at the dinner tables.

William Peard was mayor of the small neighboring town in which Ariel and Rachel lived and he and his spouse, Linda, frequented the Capitol Plaza regularly. Their Christmas party was one of the most elaborate events of the season, and they genuinely enjoyed sharing their wealth with their friends and neighbors. Bill, as his close friends called him, was politically connected and enjoyed serving and protecting the people in his community.

From high above, covert dome unit cameras blended in with the chandelier base. The wide-angle lens, with its electronic iris, adjusted to the various lighting situations and tracked all movement and activity within the confines of the room below.

In the back hallways, the energy level accelerated as the wait staff assigned to serve the Peard party congregated for last-minute orders shouted out by Mr. Blackstone. "It's show time in Michigan," he bellowed. "Everyone ready? Let's lock and load!"

Ten waiters including Ariel circled the salad prep area and each hoisted a huge tray of twelve plated salads and filed into Michigan. Others claimed trays with baskets of bread and butter, sour cream and pepper mills and fell in line. With timed precision the salads and condiments were delivered with the synchronicity of a fine Swiss watch. The same process was duplicated for the main entrees and dessert service.

By the end of the evening, Ariel had that buzz of high energy, bordering on exhaustion. Most of the staff had that same adrenaline rush that required some serious unwinding. A sense of restoration was taking shape in the kitchen as dirty dishes were transported through the dishwasher, pots and pans were scrubbed by a couple of muscled, tattooed, and pierced kitchen workers who had a greasy shine from many hours in the steaming wash area.

"Party at The Cove," someone yelled through the kitchen clatter.

"Oh yeah, oh yeah," one of the servers chanted in a sing-song voice as he threw his apron into the dirty laundry pile.

The Cove was a hangout just down the street and around the corner from the hotel, a common venue for the late-night crowd. Because hotel staff was not allowed to patronize Paradigm, the hotel's club, many would navigate to The Cove after their late shifts were over. It allowed for some bonding and relaxation after a hard night's work.

Ariel chose to pass on The Cove option, however at a future time might like to get to know some of her co-workers better by joining them after a shift. It had been an exhausting first evening. She was ready to head home and wind down. She still hadn't worked up enough nerve to deliver Jake the news about starting a part-time job and possibly wanting to end their relationship. It jangled her nerves to even think about it.

Ariel had informed Jake she was spending time with the girls tonight. This was not a fabrication, as Rachel had arranged a jewelry party and had invited several of their girlfriends to their place. She and Rachel shared a weakness for jewelry and their favorite sparkling baubles were made by their acquaintance Lu, who had a real knack for jewelry design. *Artistic Works by Lu* was growing into a wildly successful business, which they supported with unabashed abandon. She was looking forward to viewing Lu's latest creations. Also, no doubt, the margaritas were flowing and she couldn't wait to partake in the female camaraderie that awaited her.

Although it was getting late, Ariel was sure many of the girls would still be hanging out at their place and she looked forward to seeing them. She could use some girl talk and was excited to share her experience of the first night at the hotel, as well as strategize with Rachel and Tori on delivering her news to Jake. She and Jake had a date night scheduled for the following evening, and it would be a good opportunity to enlighten him with her latest thoughts about their relationship, as well as inform him of her new job. Her girlfriends would help bolster the confidence she needed to prepare for that bumpy encounter.

- - -

6 – Jake

Ariel's heart beat in rapid fire, her palms were sweaty and mouth a bit dry as she and Jake headed out for a customary Saturday night dinner at a favorite restaurant. She really didn't know of a good time to break the news, but was determined to get it over with tonight. Rachel and Tori had offered their creative suggestions the previous night ranging from just a quick announcement to a long drawn out yarn of how they had had many great times but it just seemed they were growing apart. After much deliberation, Ariel opted for a two-step approach, the first of which was to announce her new job, which in turn would automatically lead to step two—that they would have less time to spend together and eventually go their separate ways.

Jake clenched his teeth and his jaw drew taut and his usually glittering blue eyes appeared just a shade darker as Ariel announced her plan to work at the Capitol Plaza through the holidays. It was interesting and somewhat startling how quickly his expression could fluctuate. One minute his eyes were dancing like sparkling sapphires and the next they were narrowed with a cast bordering on navy blue.

"What do you mean you'll be working on the weekends?" They stared at each other across the basket of fragrant hot bread, Ariel swirling her glass of cabernet, the ruby red legs drizzling inside the sparkling bulbous chamber, and Jake tightly clenching his pilsner half-full of amber brew.

Stammering a bit, Ariel attempted to convey her rehearsed speech that she hoped would sound like a logical decision. "I . . . I just thought it would be a great opportunity to earn a bit of extra money for the holidays." The truth of the matter was that in addition to earning some extra "fun" money it would be the perfect way to wean them apart before she had to tell him in no uncertain terms that they would be better off parting ways.

They had enjoyed each other's company several evenings over the course of the past eight months in this charming and established neighborhood restaurant. In earlier times, their conversations were friendly and light-hearted, however as details and personalities begin to unfold, as they do in a relationship, Ariel gradually began to realize his vibrant, kind exterior was threaded with unstable, tightly wound knots of negative energy that snapped and sizzled at unexpected times.

There were mood swings, accusations, lies, denials, and a peculiar past all tucked underneath a surface image of polish, confidence, enthusiasm, and innocence, intertwined with apologies, outings, and unexpected gifts. It was taking its toll and Ariel had been rehearsing her exit for several weeks. She fully expected this conversation to provoke an episode.

"You know, this is so typical of you to think about yourself and to not even have consulted me ahead of time," he accused. "What if I don't want you working extra hours? As it is, you already work too much at your day job." Ariel winced but forged ahead.

"For heavens sake, it's just temporary for a few weeks and then I'll be done. It's not a big deal." Jake shook his head no with a decisive, short, side-to-side motion. He shot Ariel a stern look and tossed down another swill of his beer.

Fortunately, as luck would have it, the waitress appeared with plates of crisp, fresh salad greens drizzled in scrumptious house dressing. Smiling, she offered cracked pepper for the salads and more focaccia bread.

"Yes to both, please," Ariel responded with marked enthusiasm. Jake merely nodded and forced a non-convincing smile. They silently forked at the leafy greens as thoughts turned inward.

Jake was a few years older than Ariel and grew up on the north-side of town, or as one would say, on the wrong side of the tracks. His mother was a sweet, nervous, religious fanatic, subservient to his father, and afraid of her own shadow. His father, at times, displayed temper tantrums that could elicit shock or amusement depending on how you chose to view the situation. Shock because it was hard to believe a grown man could act like a three-year-old and amusement because it was comical to watch a grown man act like a three-year-old.

It was apparent to Ariel that Jake didn't fall too far from the family tree. On the one hand, he proclaimed a strong faith in God, instilled by maternal teachings; however, by most standards, it was a dysfunctional relationship at best, and he had plenty of occasions to demonstrate ways in which he strayed from any type of religious foothold. It was easy to see how emotional instability germinated from an unbalanced family life and grew ripe feeding on the insidious neighborhood that molded his early childhood development.

Surprisingly and admirably, he had managed to a certain degree to break free from his unfortunate and bleak beginnings and had carved out a nice business for himself as a general contractor. He knew a lot about the construction business, having knowledge of not only the construction process, but also electrical and plumbing installations as well as the finer aspects of commercial design. The money rolled in and he spent it without much thought.

Their contradiction in financial styles was one aspect of their relationship that would never mesh—he was an avid spender and she preferred to be more cautious with money. This, along with their own strong personalities and differences in upbringing, would always cause them to struggle. Ariel was perceptive enough to understand that a committed and successful relationship required certain commonalities intertwined with trust and respect. In the long term, this relationship wouldn't fly.

In the beginning, Jake's predominant mood tilted toward the happy-go-lucky end of the spectrum and the Jekyll and Hyde transformations didn't manifest until after Ariel's heart strings loosened just enough to feel involved. The trust and respect had begun to erode and she questioned just how far Jake might push the envelope if she ever crossed him. So, the relationship would teeter along until the natural course of fissures and faults became too great, causing it to splinter by little fragments and unravel on its own, or until which time she could decisively sever the ties with the impression that somehow it was really his idea.

Ariel recalled things Jake revealed that she honestly wished afterward she didn't know. Although she decided it was better to learn of his life's encounters sooner than later. Jake's deepest emotional destruction came from serving in the Gulf War and seeing firsthand the ravages and horrors of carnage and brutality. His brief but harrowing encounter with imprisonment undoubtedly left deep scars in his mind that would never quite heal. He most related to war movies and in particular an old movie recounting the true story of young men captured and detained in a Turkish prison for trying to smuggle hash out of the country. Ariel couldn't be sure if some of the stories that he shared were true or just fabrications. He once told of a past courageous adventure of sneaking packets of drugs from South America through the local airport during the days when security was very insecure. Ariel imagined him getting away with this risky business because he had relatives who worked as baggage handlers and many of the airport personnel were familiar and comfortable with his easy smile and conversation. His twinkling blue eyes and aura of confidence easily masked the deception of hiding things in secret compartments of luggage and clothing. It's hard to believe these activities could have ever gone undetected, but long before 9/11, things were different.

Ariel was in the process of slicing a little round tomato remaining on her salad plate.

"You know, I can probably take a break from you for a few weeks," Jake suddenly declared.

"What?" Ariel snapped back to the present. "You mean it? You're okay with this situation and us seeing a little less of each other?"

"Yes," he delivered a slow, even statement as he fingered the bread basket searching for another wedge of warm soft dough hiding under the cloth napkin. "Actually, there is a lot going on with me right now that you don't know and probably wouldn't understand. Plus it sounds like you don't give a damn about working on a relationship considering you've taken on another commitment." Ariel was flabbergasted. Her mind raced and swirled; it bifurcated. What was he hiding and how could this be easier than she imagined?

Their dinners arrived. Her appetite evaporated despite the beautifully presented smoked chicken pasta dish before her.

She stared at the steam rising from the plate. She felt a wave of uneasiness surge through her.

"What in the world are you talking about? So are you going to tell me what's happening?" she asked cautiously. "Is it your health, your family, your business? What is going on? I'm a little scared."

---

7 – Jake's News

Jake's voice lowered and he cleared his throat. "Well, for now I'll just say, I'm filing for bankruptcy and moving out of my house."

"Wow," Ariel said just a bit too loud. She could hardly believe it. On the one hand, she felt a strange sense of loss, but at the same time felt a wave of relief wash over her at the realization he had bigger fish to fry than dealing with her new job.

"Where are you going to go?" Ariel questioned, puzzled.

"I'm not sure yet. I've got a lot of rubble to sift through, but I might be heading to California sometime after the first of the year. I actually have a buddy out there who can take me in until I get on my feet again."

"So how long has this been coming? It seems so sudden. I mean, I had no idea. When were you going to tell me?" Ariel countered, shaking her head at what she had just heard.

"Hey, too many questions, sweetheart!" he responded in a condescending voice as he held up his hand as if to back her off. "I've been thinking about my lousy situation for some time now."

"So maybe that explains why you've been so moody lately?" Ariel speculated. "You never gave me any indication that things were anything but great. Why not?"

"Listen, I didn't tell you this so you could condemn me and besides didn't you just surprise me with your latest announcement—a job at a hotel that will put you in the company of God only knows who?" His navy eyes looked at her threateningly.

"You know, isn't it actually a bit ironic that we each shared news suggesting we need some space and time to sort through things? Can we just leave it at that and get through the rest of the evening in a civil manner? How does that sound?" Ariel offered. Jake didn't respond.

They both sat in brooding silence, stirring their pasta and forcing bites of the flavorful, warm but now deflated in value, meal. Ariel absorbed the news that had been delivered and Jake contemplated the depressing and dire situation he was faced with along with the vision of her schmoozing—in his mind anyway—at the hotel. Somehow, they managed to work through the main course. Apparently the waitress had heard an earful because she approached their table with caution to clear away plates. And although she most likely knew the answer, she asked anyway, as was customary, as to whether either cared for dessert. "We have some enticing options," she chirped in a high decibel trying to sound cheerful.

"Just the check would be great," Jake quickly requested.

The drive back to the duplex was marked by silence. Ariel replayed in her mind Jake's latest news. As far as she knew, he was successful and established. However, in retrospect, there may have been clues that it was all smoke and mirrors. He obviously had a lack of discipline and understanding of finances; therefore, he would never be able to stabilize and enjoy a comfortable sense of monetary accomplishment for the long haul. The fruits of his labor were squandered on many short-lived indulgences. A twinge of guilt stabbed at her heart knowing how many times Jake spoiled her with dinners, extravagant outings, or gifts. She could clearly see now that he was generous to a fault, enjoyed living for the moment and was not at all concerned about saving for a rainy day. He defined hedonism. Ariel, on the other hand, believed in a long-term financial plan and could envision a day far in the future where decisions made today would affect the outcomes of tomorrow. Despite this, she did understand that life had to be lived to the fullest on a daily basis, so she tried hard to balance enjoying today and saving for tomorrow.

As Jake pulled into the driveway, he spoke in a controlled, almost robotic manner. "I'm going to call you in a few weeks. You are not just going to disappear out of my life."

Ariel agreed that he could get in touch. "Take care of yourself and thanks for the dinner. You know, you can be a very kind person. I hope everything works out for you and I mean that." She leaned over and gave him a quick hug before hopping out of the car.

The Sunday night after the date, Ariel hashed over her and Jake's conversation with a very supportive Rachel, who was as shocked as Ariel about the bankruptcy situation. They were sitting on their red sofa with plates of cheese, crackers, and fruit and their favorite soft drinks spread out in front of them on the glass coffee table for a casual Sunday evening meal. The four-wick candle flickered.

As Ariel explained to her roommate what Jake had told her, she realized that he had actually said "one of the things" that he was going through and something about "things she probably wouldn't understand." She concluded that there was much more to the story, although it probably was just the amount and extent of his debt plus the mounting pressure that he referred to. "I can't imagine what he must be going through, but somehow he will manage to end up smelling like a rose. He just has a knack for finding the next opportunity, plus he has some pretty good connections." Ariel shook her head and continued, "I can't fathom why he had to get himself into this quandary other than I guess he was living beyond his means. He had me fooled."

Although Rachel obviously didn't know Jake as well as Ariel, she had been impressed with the lifestyle he exuded. "He sure seemed to have it all and I figured he was pretty stable," Rachel added.

They continued analyzing the situation and shared a variety of conversational topics into the evening as they enjoyed their light meal and watched shadows dance on the walls as the candle light grew stronger and the night closed in on their comfortable and innocent world.

Two weeks evaporated in a flash. Between her primary day-job, sprinkled with the hectic nights of hotel banquet services, the season progressed, one holiday party after another. It had been a bit of a blur and Ariel was exhausted yet exhilarated with her busy life. There hadn't been a word from Jake; he hadn't called or even sent a text. Undoubtedly, he was as busy as she had been. Along with working long hours on his latest building projects on the city's new southwest side development, he was probably ducking bill collectors and racking up attorney fees—not a pleasant situation.

Funny how ambiguous feelings can be: the last time they were together, she was quite decisive that he was history. Now after a break, she felt a yearning to find out what he had been up to and to share some time together. No chance of that! She was busy today running errands and would soon have to get ready for work. Tonight, the hotel was going to be packed as one of the busiest nights so far this season. It was the last Saturday night before Christmas and the place would be *rockin'* with a multitude of festivities and a variety of partygoers.

- - -

8 — Mystery Date

It was approaching 4:00 p.m. as Ariel wove her car through the hotel parking lot to the back corner, found a spot near the employee entrance, and made a dash for it. The sky held a hint that snow was on the way. Warm air greeted her as she pulled open the windowless back doors and parted the hanging air strips just inside. She quickly punched her time card just past the Security Office and glanced at the navy suits who were engaged in hearty laughter and *manversation*. Apparently one of them had just wrapped up a whale of a joke.

Over the period of a few weeks, she had come to know all of them to some degree. Tonight, all four would be on duty—Sean, Ed, Chuck, and Randy. What a foursome. Around the hotel, they were known as SECR (secure)—the acronym that spelled out the initials of their first names. Currently, Sean, the youngest of the crew, was in the doorway leaning on the door frame; serious Ed was standing, arms folded, near the wall of camera monitors, his eyes darting back and forth between the group and the activity on the security screens that monitored the front desk, two public side entrances, employee entrance, and the Grand Ballroom. Randy assumed his most common position, shoes propped on the desk leaning back on two chair legs. The only one missing at the moment was easy-going Chuck. He would arrive later when things were in full swing. Ariel gave them a wave of acknowledgement and turned on her heel as she slid her time card into its holding slot. She hastened down the long, wide hallway toward the kitchen at the opposite end of the hotel.

Mental preparation and focus were necessary because it was going to be an arduous evening of synchronized manual labor. As Ariel approached the Convention Services office, Mr. Blackstone burst out, his short arms waving wildly as he shouted toward the kitchen doors to Jill, the Server Captain, trying to get her attention for something important before she disappeared. Despite Mr. Blackstone's best efforts, not every event came off flawlessly. There were times when things went off track. Somehow the communications were dropped and a room wasn't quite ready or there weren't enough staff assigned to a particular function. Tonight was not a night for oversights as all employees and staff would be utilized to the fullest capacity. There were no backups in the wings.

Other banquet staff also arrived at four o'clock, and the second stop after clocking in was to check assigned room locations and learn of the party requisites. Ariel congregated with others outside the Convention Services office and scanned the posted party listings, anxious to find out her fate for tonight. She was hoping for *lakes* not *trees* as the rooms on the north were much closer to the kitchen and required less manual work than those on the south. Luck was on her side tonight as she scored Ontario, the second closest to the kitchen, in between Michigan and Erie. Others groaned as they learned they would be working in Willow. It presented the most hardship from a service delivery perspective as it was the farthest distance from the kitchen. The haul back and forth was a grind. The Maple and Magnolia rooms weren't much better.

For the first go-around of the evening, the Grand Ballroom was partitioned off to accommodate six individual party rooms. Each would display a festive holiday theme, some more elaborate than others. Events of some sort would begin as early as 5:30 p.m.; others would start later and not wrap up until long after midnight. There would be a point where, as two parties concluded, the wall panel would be opened to transform the two smaller rooms into a larger room, reconfigured and reset for the next event. In addition to the Grand Ballroom area, there was another small meeting room off the hotel's south public entryway that had a maximum occupancy of twenty-five and could be converted to dining if necessary. Tonight, that room would be needed twice over with an early party starting in an hour and a half for a group of senior citizens and later a small party would be prepared for 7:30.

Banquet housemen and set-up staff had been hard at work earlier in the day moving tables and chairs, juggling props, and installing dance floors and bar stations. It was a laborious process. Once all the furniture and equipment was in place, the rooms were ready for phase two—decorations and table settings in tandem with condiment prep work in the kitchen. Ariel and the other servers along with Banquet Captains were responsible for phase two. Typically, a good two hours was necessary to finish the rooms and to be ready for the arrival of the guests. They were always under the gun and no one had time to loaf.

Some celebrations were very formal with several courses, other dinners less formal with three-course meals, and other arrangements were set so guests could mingle and simply graze from a variety of unique appetizers, hors d'oeuvres, fruit, vegetable, and cheese trays. The entertainment ranged from speakers to hypnotists to big bands. It was always interesting to find out what might transpire.

Ariel learned that the festivities in Ontario for Meredith Publishing would commence with a social hour of light hors d'oeuvres and drinks followed by a four-course meal to include soup, salad, choice of prime rib or Chicken Kiev, and followed by dessert. Her team was lighting the final candles on the table tops as the first few guests began to appear. The service bartender was set up in the corner of the open area arranging glasses and bottles. He flagged her over to ask a favor. "Looks like I'm low on premium vodka. Will you please track down Bud and get me a back-up bottle? I don't want to run out."

"Sure thing, I'll be right back as soon as I can," Ariel promised.

She exited Ontario to search for Bud, the Beverage Manager, who would likely be in the vicinity of one of the hotel bars. The wait staff lovingly referred to him as "Bud-lite" because he peaked at a mere 5 foot 6 inches and weighed in at just under a buck fifty. He guarded the liquor in the hotel with his life. All bars and parties had strict bottle inventories and he kept a close count of every case of wine, every keg and bottle on the premises. She headed down the north hall past Erie and into the pre-convention area in front of the Grand Ballroom. Ariel had never seen the hotel so heavily occupied. Surely they were pushing the maximum occupancy load tonight. The open atrium was a sea of people milling about and searching for familiar faces prior to heading off to their individual room locales. Large signs, one near the front desk and one on the south side entrance, provided information by party name to aid the search process for those in need of direction.

Ariel cut through the Garden Spot toward the vicinity of the open lounge and Paradigm club. She scanned the area and spotted Bud just departing the open lounge bar. In his usual style, he was striding off to his next destination. She quickened her pace to catch him before he got away. After explaining what was needed, Bud circled back to the bar and the bartender tossed him a full frosted bottle of clear liquid with a goose on the side. He scribbled a note in his inventory log book.

"Thanks, Bud," she called after a quick hand-off of the bottle. She was on a mission to quickly deliver the goods to Ontario as promised.

Just as she emerged out of the Garden Spot, out of the corner of her eye, she saw him. She did a double take. Unbelievable! There in the pre-convention area, just outside the Grand Ballroom was Jake, and he was with someone! They were all smiles, dressed to the nines, and ready for a night of pleasure and carefree fun at *her* hotel. As hard as it was for Ariel to admit, she couldn't help but be mesmerized by the beautiful creature hanging on his arm. The young woman was dark skinned with dark brown, almost black, glossy hair sleeked back into a very long and luxurious, ponytail. A sparkling silver band gathered and cinched strands of hair off her slender neck in a clasp at the back of her head. On the arm not clutched to Jake appeared to be a diamond bracelet refracting light as the woman gestured with her hand while happily chattering to another couple with them. She wore a short black dress open at the back with shiny, black high heels elevating her off the floor. Her ponytail brushed Jake as she tossed her head in loud laughter.

Ariel ducked into the ladies room closest to the north hall before Jake had a chance to see her and darted into the nearest stall. She felt nauseous. She stood there clutching her forehead, thumb and forefinger on her temples and hoped that she wouldn't vomit.

"How dare he do this!" she muttered through clenched teeth. She knew she had to gain composure and forge ahead with her head held high.

In an instant, another wave of nausea washed over her as she realized Jake, the woman-creature, and the other couple just might wind up in Ontario. That would be the most awkward and embarrassing situation imaginable. The name Meredith Publishing didn't ring a bell as anyone who Jake might be associated with, however it could be a group with which that woman was affiliated. Ariel could only hope and pray that that would not be the case. She had to get moving. Realizing the bottle of vodka was clenched tightly in her hand, she wondered how that would appear as she walked out of the restroom so tucked it inside her jacket until she could be sure no one was looking. She peeked out around the corner of the restroom entryway and scanned the crowd. She spotted the foursome still milling about, talking with others who would soon be migrating toward their respective locations.

Head bent low and turned away from the crowd, she scurried off toward the north hallway to reach Ontario and drop off the vodka she had fetched for the bartender. She drew in a deep breath and proceeded to the kitchen pandemonium to render assistance to the vast responsibilities at hand. The various service teams were partnering with pantry chefs to plate up lettuce salads and fill bread baskets. Before long, her crew would load hot bowls of French onion soup onto trays. She had to maintain self-control, but her head was spinning. She could not get the picture of Jake and his mysterious date out of her head. In a robotic fashion, she joined the motions of her work buddies as they performed their duties. There was still time to calm her beating heart before the dinner began. Social hour was in full swing. *Shoot, she should have swilled some of the vodka to calm her nerves when she had the chance,* she thought half-jokingly.

- - -

9 – Excitement in the Air

Very soon it would be time to return to Ontario and she anticipated what would happen if Jake and his friends were there in the room. She felt jittery but told herself she would just be polite yet distant and deal with it in a professional manner. When the command to "move out, Ontario" was ordered, she snapped to attention. They were ready to roll with the baskets of bread and soups. She shouldered a large tray and got in line. As they filed through the doorway of Ontario, Ariel held her breath and darted furtive glances around the tables looking for Jake and the black ponytail. It took a bit of time for her eyesight to adjust to the dim soft lights compared to the harsh lights of the kitchen. By now, most everyone was seated, aside from a few stragglers near the bar and a few women entering from their recent trip to the powder room. So far, so good! No sighting of Jake and the chick. Whew, she began to breathe easier and relax as she confirmed with a more thorough scan of the room that they were not present. She was extremely relieved.

The guests of Meredith Publishing all seemed to be enjoying themselves. Soup bowls and bread baskets were delivered. The rest of the courses fell into place and by the time desserts and coffee were to be offered, Ariel's curiosity and anger heightened. She desperately wanted to coordinate an espionage sting to gather some more information on her revolting boyfriend, or actually her ex-boyfriend.

Back in the kitchen, she pulled aside a couple of her server friends. One was working the south side in Maple and the other was working Erie next door. "Hey, you guys, I need to know if you've noticed a dark-haired girl with a really long, thick ponytail. She's wearing a black dress and is with a guy wearing a dark gray suit and red tie."

"Why?" they both chimed at the same time.

"Never mind, I don't have time to explain right now." Neither had seen the girl, but said they'd keep their eyes open.

Ariel grabbed two pots of coffee and headed out of the kitchen. She circled tables pouring coffee for those who offered their cups. Once the pots were empty, she dashed back to the kitchen and started the machine for two fresh pots. While the coffee brewed, she whizzed back to the door of Michigan to take a peek. It was thinning out—looked like their party was about over. No ponytail. She backtracked down the hall past Ontario and Erie toward the pre-convention area to scan the atrium and main lobby—nothing. Back in the kitchen, she got word that for sure the mystery woman with the ponytail wasn't in Maple. With the north side cleared and Maple confirmed as a negative that left only Magnolia and Willow as to where they might be, unless they had already left the premises. She sure hoped not because she had a score to settle.

In Magnolia, tables were being moved and a portable dance floor was in the process of being assembled. The wall between Magnolia and Michigan was being retracted and a band was setting up. The Brickman party in Magnolia was not only doing dinner, they were celebrating into the late night hours with a rock band of Des Moines origin, Corkscrew, now known around the world. The party organizer just happened to be a sister of the drummer so she finagled the band to perform a special limited show, since they were off tour and back in town for the holidays. As expected, word slowly leaked out and not only would the Brickman party enjoy the entertainment, but others within the confines of the hotel would sponge off this once-in-a-lifetime opportunity to see one of the hottest rock bands in history up close in an intimate setting.

The fact that Corkscrew was performing at the hotel required SECR—Sean, Ed, Chuck, and Randy—to be on high alert. Additionally, an off-duty police officer was contracted to help keep the crowd from getting too unruly. Initial attempts to keep the secret under cover were successful, however word spread like wildfire once the band made their preliminary appearance and began testing equipment and making sound checks. "Did you hear that Corkscrew is performing? Did you hear Corkscrew is in the hotel?" people buzzed. "For real, are you serious?" others expressed with hopeful skepticism. Hotel employees were talking and guests were talking. The excitement generated.

Meanwhile, as the band organized and prepared for their gig, local TV and radio stations were beginning to broadcast special reports of a blizzard sweeping east across Iowa and that it was expected to hit the metro area hard within the next hour or so at around 10:30 or 11 p.m. All the flat-screen TVs around the hotel —in the open lounge, behind the bars, and near the concierge desk—were scrolling memos of the impending snowstorm approaching. On one channel, a weather reporter in his most serious tone was delivering grave declarations that travel was shutting down on Interstate 80 east of the Nebraska border and that the system was widespread, stretching from Kansas to North Dakota and quickly moving east. "In the Channel 13 viewing area, we can expect ten to fifteen inches of snow with strong winds creating white-out conditions. At this present time, travel is not advised on I-80 West and in time, travel across the state will likely be restricted," the reporter warned.

Wiser, older folks, hearing the news, took heed and began to navigate toward the coat check area to retrieve their winter wraps in order to beat the crowd and hence beat the brunt of the storm. As many people were evacuating the hotel, wanting to reach their homes before being stranded by the blizzard, others milled around the TV screens, mesmerized by the latest reports. They peered out the glass doors to watch the snow swirl and accumulate. Their approach was to just wait and see, not thinking too far beyond the moment, not fully grasping the severity of the situation ahead.

Then there were those who embraced word of the storm with glee. They sensed excitement in the air, the kind that stirs any time a natural act of God or disaster occurs—hurricanes, floods, tornados, fires, and the like. If they are out of harm's way, their tendency is to take pleasure in the wonderment of nature and the possible danger it elicits. The promise of being stranded with strangers evoked its own sense of exhilaration for the folks with this mindset. Finally, there was the group holed up in the room in which Corkscrew was organizing to perform and hadn't a clue about what was going on outside those four walls.

Ariel heard the news reports on the kitchen radio, as she made trips back and forth from Ontario delivering bus tubs of dirty dishes to the dishwashers. She thought of her boots in her car and thought that she'd better get them before it was too late. She decided just as soon as the tables were cleared, she would dart out to grab them. She figured it was best to be prepared as she wouldn't be leaving for another hour or so and the snow might really pile up before then.

More importantly, though, she wanted to peek on the south side and see if she could spot her prey anywhere. As soon as the last heap of dishes was delivered to the conveyer belt in the dish room, she raced toward the kitchen doors and burst into the wide back hallway, not bothering to retrieve her coat from the employee closet. About halfway down the long hall, she could see a few guys that appeared to be in rock and roll garb along with two of the security guys near the open doors through which band equipment had just been hauled into Magnolia/Michigan.

Ariel was accustomed to seeing bands in the hotel and around town in various venues, but she was totally caught off guard to catch a peek of the band from Des Moines that had made a name for themselves and were now famous around the globe. She paused long enough to say hi to Sean and Ed and to make some small talk with them. "How's it going guys?" It was a subtle excuse for an up-close and personal opportunity to rub elbows with members of Corkscrew. She tried not to gawk at the rockers standing within just a few feet of her. They were tattooed and pierced—authentic and artistic specimens of the rock scene.

"We're helping the band here get organized," boasted Sean. "Ariel, this is Jimmy Florence and Spike Booth." He puffed out his chest and introduced them to her.

Ariel stretched out her hand to give them each a good handshake. "It's really, really great to meet you," she gushed. "I love your music. You're super awesome." She turned to the security duo and said, "I hope you are taking good care of them while they're here."

They assured her they were. Other servers traveling down the employee back hall slowed down wanting a piece of the action. A few of them stopped to get in on the opportunity to meet and greet a couple of members of the band. Jimmy and Spike were very patient with the extra attention they were attracting. Ariel stepped to the side and got a glimpse inside the doors of this end of the ballroom.

Two other band members and some assistants making adjustments to the microphones and guitars were visible through the backside of the stage area upon which sat the drums, equipment and speakers. Around the perimeters of the dance floor people were gathering at tables and in chairs. A sighting through the gap between two of the big speakers on stage caused Ariel's heart to jump and her breath to catch in her throat.

Straight across the room at a table near the dance floor was her target. The couple looked happy, content, and smug to be in a comfortable and enviable position, ready to enjoy the show along with their friends. On the one hand, Ariel was still experiencing the jubilation she felt to be in the brief company of the band, but on the other hand, she was seething with what she witnessed in the ballroom.

Afraid that her knees would buckle, she turned back toward the group and politely excused herself. "Nice to meet you both," she said as she quickly stepped around the huddle near the doorway. What a combination of emotion she felt— euphoria and anger all muddled together. Definitely a weird sensation, she decided. She hustled down the hall and quickly the anger won out over the euphoria. Her mind raced to come up with a strategy to corner Jake. She was ready to hand him his head!

In the Security Office, Chuck was in a man stance, legs slightly spread apart with arms crossed, facing the camera screens as they flashed shots of the various hotel spots deemed important from a security standpoint. He was so engrossed in what was in front of him, he didn't even notice Ariel charge by, but would witness her silhouette on a monitor as she exited out the back.

It didn't take long to sprint through the cold snowy night to her car not far from the employee entrance. The ground was covered in a soft blanket of clean white snow. So far, a couple of inches of the fluffy white stuff rested in mounds on the hood, windshield, wiper blades, and door handles. She fished out her warm knee-high boots with the fleece lining from the floor behind the driver's seat. She never locked her car doors unless she was transporting something of real value.

The bright security lights in the parking lot illuminated snowflakes as they floated and swirled out of the depths of the black night sky. She was temporarily mesmerized by the white crystals spiraling through the air. As her gaze traveled back toward the direction of the hotel, one of the lighted rectangle shaped windows on the lower level caught her eye. There was an outline of a man's upper body, shoulders and face pressed against the window pane peering down scrutinizing her. The second he realized her gaze landed on him, he retracted with a quick motion. Ariel immediately realized how cold it was outside; she shivered and clutched her boots to her chest and raced toward the door.

---

10 – The Blizzard and the Confrontation

She was huffing and puffing from her short sprint. Chuck turned toward the big, glass-paneled wall of the office as he saw her fly through the wide plastic strips that hung a few inches just inside the door and served to partially block the cold air flow from the outside. He stepped out into the hall.

"Good grief, whatcha doin' out there Ariel?" he inquired with interest.

"I wanted to get my snow boots before it was too late. Have you heard about the blizzard on the way? It'll be hitting hard in another hour or so, but it's not bad yet," Ariel panted.

"Yeah, I heard, was listenin' to the radio in the office. A few of the smarter people are startin' to skeedaddle out of here," Chuck drawled.

Ariel went on, her chest heaving. "There was a man staring out the second story window at me. He gave me the creeps."

"Are ya sure he wasn't just checking on the snow situation?" Chuck volunteered.

"I don't know, but it sure felt like he was watching me and he jerked away when he thought I saw him. Maybe it was just my imagination. Hey, I've got to get back to the kitchen. My team probably wonders where I disappeared to. See you later, Chuck."

Seriously, what else can I take this evening? Ariel wondered. Between the rage she felt spotting Jake and his new flame, the high she experienced meeting two members of Corkscrew, and the fear that zipped through her from seeing the man in the window, she decided she couldn't take much more tonight. The only thing that she could control at the moment was to get back to work and finish out her shift.

The hall was quiet aside from a couple of servers on their way between the kitchen and one room destination or another. She slowly passed the doorway where Sean, Ed, the band guys, and others had congregated a bit earlier and it was now clear except for Ed, the lone assigned guard of the back door behind the makeshift stage. A strum from the bass guitar and a couple of quick beats from the drum —boom, boom— wafted out into the hallway indicating the band was preparing to kick off their first song. She acknowledged Ed with "Hello again" as she slowed and glanced through the slightly open doors. The crowd's excitement was growing and the room looked full. The lights had dimmed and she was unable to lock in Jake's table through the movement on stage. She kept moving.

After giving her boots a toss into the employee coat closet, she breezed through the kitchen doors, back to the clatter, noise, and bright lights. The radio in the background served as an ongoing reminder of the deteriorating weather situation. Ariel merged with her friends who were engaged in final clean-up and shut down. The Ontario and Erie rooms were silent now, the tables naked—stripped of tablecloths and napkins—and void of guests who had either slipped in to experience the band or headed for the safety of their homes before the storm arrived. Willow and Maple were in a similar state of emptiness.

Although the walls were fairly soundproof, the pulsating beat of the drums and the wailing of guitars along with muffled singing voices sifted through the cracks and crevices so that the service staff could enjoy the entertainment to some degree—audio but no visual. Ariel and her friends gathered around bare tables to fold clean napkins, sort hot silverware fresh out of the dishwasher, fill salt and pepper shakers, and in general, prepare things for the next day of service. Others returned the party paraphernalia and decorations to the storage rooms in the back hall.

Jessica, Ariel's closest friend of the banquet crew, sat next to her and they chatted and joked with others at the table as they worked. Ariel confided to Jessica about the situation with Jake that had her stewing, bubbled about meeting the two band members, and shared the eerie experience of seeing the odd man in the window. They swapped stories with each other about the parties they had serviced. Jessica recounted an incident in Willow that caused a bit of a ruckus when one of the servers tripped and splashed hot coffee on a lady. Mr. Blackstone had to come to the rescue and offered to pay for her dry cleaning. Although the lady appreciated that, she warned that the hotel might also receive a doctor bill for the burn on her thigh.

Michigan/Magnolia was the remaining nerve center in the ballroom area. The Paradigm club in the northeast corner of the hotel was also still an energy hot spot—the dance floor jammed, booths and tables all crammed with a younger crowd. Many of them weren't even aware of the famous hometown band in the ballroom and for the most part they had tuned out the weather situation, oblivious to anything but their immediate social surroundings.

A good forty-five minutes had passed and things were finally shaping up in the kitchen. The rooms were back to normal and had passed inspection by supervisors. Mr.

Blackstone was flashing his short thumb in the air giving the signal for people to check out. Ariel and Jessica were grateful as they got the thumb from him. They were exhausted and a little punch-drunk and just watching him zip around the place made them giggle. It was approaching seven and a half hours that they had been on their feet performing strenuous labor.

"All right, I want to change clothes and see if SECR will let us peek in on the band. I'm jealous that you already got to meet them; at least I want to see them on stage!" Jessica said excitedly.

"Well, I've only got one thing on my mind before I go and that is to confront Jake." Together they tossed their aprons into the laundry bin on their way out of the kitchen and into the back hall. Next to the employee coat closet were the employee restrooms, which housed lockers to store their clothing. They would quickly change out of their banquet uniforms once they clocked out.

Other than Ed, whom they had passed, pacing in the back hallway and guarding the door for the band, Sean, Chuck, and Randy were missing in action, most likely scattered around the hotel keeping an eye on things. At the moment the Security Office was vacant.

A couple of waiters bundled in big heavy coats in their black work shoes had just punched the time clock and were heading for the door. "Hey, let's peek outside to see what's going on," Jessica urged. The girls tagged behind the guys to check out the situation. As one of them pushed the back employee door open, a whoosh of white stuff swirled in on them with a strong blast of icy air. "Holy crap, looks like the blizzard is here," one of the guys shouted. The two guys surged out with heads bent low, forging into the blinding storm and were quickly swallowed by the swirling tornado of stinging snow and ice crystals.

"Oh, my God," Jessica shrieked. She and Ariel jumped back and looked at each other in surprise, their mouths agape in amazement. "Can you believe this?" I don't remember a winter storm like this ever!" Ariel exclaimed. Less than a minute later, the two bundled-up storm troopers returned at the door, gasping and brushing snow off their thickly padded shoulders, shaking it out of their tousled hair and stomping their feet to rid themselves of the attack. "We ain't goin' nowhere tonight," one of them proclaimed. "Yep, there's no frickin' way," declared the other.

By this time, other late-shift employees had punched their time cards and were preparing for departure, but quickly learned of their fate as they watched the spectacle at the back door and realized they were going nowhere. Some on the early shift had escaped in the nick of time and hopefully made it to their destinations. Similarly, at the three public hotel exits, people were learning the storm had closed in quickly and that had they left even just a half hour ago, they might have made it out, but by now the snow was piling up too deep and the wind was too strong. It wouldn't be safe, smart, or even feasible to leave shelter let alone drive at this point. The TV screens flashed alerts of the intense blizzard hitting the metro area. Strong winds, white-out conditions, and snow accumulations made travel impossible.

For partiers and travelers who had pre-arranged a hotel stay, life was good. But for others who had simply arrived to enjoy a special night out, or for employees who came to work, they quickly realized they were hostages of a situation beyond their control. They would be bunking the night here, room or no room.

There was a sense that all chaos could cut loose and SECR would have their hands full. The revelry from the ballroom had grown stronger. Jessica, who was determined to get a glimpse of the band, tugged Ariel's arm. "Let's go!" She drew

Ariel along with her toward the noise; the drums thumping, guitar waling, and the strong vocals amidst the cheering and clapping. They entered through the side door labeled Magnolia. Just inside, the hired uniformed police officer was listening as a concerned Chuck in his less authoritative navy suit hashed over the latest news of the blizzard plight. Jessica and Ariel slipped past them and shuffled through the merrymakers in a zigzag movement toward the stage and near the perimeter of tables surrounding the dance floor.

A normal post-work shift dictated that employees were not allowed to patronize any private party, the bar, lounge, or club per hotel policy. Tonight was an anomaly—the rules had all gone out the window. Ariel scanned the crowded dance floor and the far side of the room for Jake and company. Her eyes locked down hard as she caught sight of him nuzzling in close to ponytail woman, their heads together, and his arm on her shoulder apparently enjoying their physical closeness. She gave Jess a sharp elbow and pointed across the room. "That's him!" she mouthed into the noise.

Now was her chance to put him to the test. She fished her cell phone out from her Coach bag and sent a text "hey whts up havnt tlkd to u 4evr whr ru—Ari." Ariel held her stern gaze. He never went anywhere without his phone, and with the noise level, he would surely have it set to vibrate. The seconds ticked . . . nothing. Suddenly, he straightened and slid his hand into an inside pocket at the front of his suit jacket. His eyes squinted at the lit up screen. He stood, brushed the tips of his fingers across the woman's smooth back under her suspended, swinging lock of dark thick mane, and whispered into her ear as he excused himself.

Ariel watched as he wove through the crowd away from their table, head down, apparently working on the keypad of his cell phone. Her phone lit up. "Jst gt home b4 storm whr ru." Her face reddened. Was he that stupid? Just because he hadn't seen her during the Brickman party, surely he knew she was in the hotel and that she knew what he was up to. Never mind that she had set him up with her text. What a loser! Her fingers swiftly keyed a response "wtching Corkscrew mt me at the waterfall." His reply came, "whtr u tlking abt." She zinged back "I c u." She left Jessica mesmerized by the band and indicated she'd be right back. Her eyes remained locked on her target. His eyes lifted as he warily scanned the crowd and edged toward the door. She was on a trajectory to intercept him.

Their collision course occurred just inside the door and when they met, their eyes locked, faces firm. They edged on out into the hallway and didn't make it to the waterfall in the atrium. Ariel sucked in a big breath to try to maintain composure before delivering her wrath. "Just made it home ahead of the storm, huh?" Ariel's words raked him like a razor. She didn't care what the confrontation might bring. She was pissed. He looked down at his shiny black loafers, slid his hands into his pants pockets, and then brought his eyes up slowly to meet hers.

Before he could speak, she continued in a demanding tone. "Why are you flaunting yourself around *my* hotel with this woman on your arm, and who is she anyway?" Ariel gestured, her arms sweeping widely as she spoke.

Jake hesitated and delivered a slow deliberate response. "She is just a friend I know and she invited me to join her family's dinner party."

"Oh yeah, she looks like a real casual acquaintance. I've seen the two of you enjoying yourselves tonight," Ariel shot back.

Jake continued to defend himself as a victim of the situation. "I only agreed to join her at the last minute as a favor. She's just a friend."

Ariel's breath caught and she stiffened as she saw the dark skinned beauty sweep through the door into the hallway where they stood off to the side. The creature moved toward Jake as she threw a sideways glance Ariel's direction. "Oh, there you are, sweetie. I was going to visit the ladies room. Was your phone message urgent?" she chirped. The color rushed out of Jake's face but in his usual style, he quickly gained composure and in a very casual demeanor introduced the two women. "Ariel meet Denise Brickman; Denise meet Ariel Sterling."

Uncomfortable was an understatement for the way Ariel felt. She had been lied to and there she stood in the company of a woman who was dazzling from head to toe, polished and confident, knowing heads turned when she walked into any room. Not only was she beautiful, but she was tied to the wealthy Brickman family, owners of Brickman Lighting.

The knot in Ariel's stomach tightened and her nails dug deep into the palm of her hand as she clenched a fist. Before she could speak, Denise in her smooth, confident style, chirped how nice it was to meet her, gave Jake a quick peck on the cheek and glided off down the hall. Ariel shook her finger at Jake. "You are such a liar and I am so done with you. Done, done, done. Finished, over—do you hear me?" She raged in a spiteful tone. He reached out to grab her arm, but before he could place his hand on her, she reeled and raced back through the doorway to find Jessica. The lead singer was just announcing they'd take a short break as Ariel, fuming, reached Jessica's side for support. Jessica immediately could tell the encounter had not gone well. "Are you okay?" Ariel bit her lip and nodded.

---

11 – Snowed In

The check-in area looked like shark-infested waters when a piece of meat is dropped. Folks surged and pounced upon the front desk as the realization struck that they were stranded and needed to make room arrangements quickly before their luck ran dry and the rooms were sold out.

Normally two or three clerks could handle routine check-ins quite efficiently. At this hour, only Malcolm and Troy, the Front Desk Manager, remained. The dynamic duo looked the part in their deep mauve jackets with nametags and together, they expertly and professionally managed the mob. Driven by demand, room prices pushed to the high end of the scale just shy of being deemed a price gouge. The hotel rooms were not only filling due to those caught off guard, but earlier, travelers had found their way to the Capitol Plaza off I-35 and I-80 as the brunt of the storm dictated they exit due to the interstates shutting down.

At the time they had booked their elaborate holiday party back in October, Brickman Lighting Company had reserved a block of suites for family members and their guests for an overnight stay option. Some of the other ballroom groups had made similar provisions ahead of time as well. What a wise decision that turned out to be. These fortunate ones were unconcerned by the raging storm outside, or by the furious squall in the front lobby of people vying for a room for the night.

Some frustrated people, in lieu of parting with an unbudgeted expense, decided to claim a plush loveseat or chair in the open lounge area as their makeshift bed for the night. Slowly, but surely, the room vacancy dwindled.

To accommodate the staff, the manager on duty blocked four rooms on the south second floor. With employee discounts and the bill split among several people, it was an affordable stay and many were excited about the perk. On regular nights, the end rooms on the southwest corner, second level were always the last to be released to guests, unless absolutely necessitated, as noise from the laundry and engineering workshop could filter through and be a factor. However, tonight no one, employees or guests, were in a position to complain as long as they had a place to sleep.

Given the current hotel atmosphere, including the energized crowd in the ballroom and the boisterous young adults in the dance club, coupled with the elevated adrenaline that the unexpected blizzard produced, it was quite possible it would be a late night for many. While the band was on break, Jessica and Ariel rounded up other friends with which to share a room. They gathered in 203 to stake claim of a bed or pull-out couch. Next to them were rooms reserved for the guy servers and kitchen crew, SECR, the two front desk guys, managers and any employee who wanted to share quarters for the night. Ariel was glad they were on a lower level. A top floor would give her hives.

On all levels, the room doors faced to the inner atrium and from any location outside a room, you could see across the wide expanse of the hotel to the other side with only a four-foot-high stretch of wall around the perimeter separating the drop to the floor below. She stood out in the hall waiting for Jessica and the others to finish primping so they could head back downstairs and top off their night with the hometown band. "Come on, guys, hurry up," Ariel called toward the room through the slightly open door. Just as she was ready to push the door open, the hotel turned solid black. Seems the storm had won out over the power lines—no electricity! Inside, the girls screamed and Ariel jumped and pushed through the dark doorway. One of the girls was groping for her handbag to find a lighter.

The chief engineer, trusty Slade Sobronski, knew just where to find a flashlight, even in the dark. He was a confident and capable man, ready for any emergency and knew how to keep his hotel running in tip-top shape. He felt at home in the engineering room. Sliding his hand along the rough wooden surface of the large carpenter table in the center of the main work area, he found his way to the back office in the pitch black. He reached his desk and felt for the handle on the big bottom drawer. Like a blind man with superior senses, he quickly located the much-needed light source. He flicked the power button on his heavy duty flashlight and swept the beam of light toward the back doors of the main work area that led to the boiler room.

The boiler room housed the powerful engine sources for the hotel. It was filled with monstrous mechanical boilers, gigantic water filter systems and tanks, gadgets that maintained water pressure, heating and cooling mechanisms, and machinery of all designs guaranteed to keep the hotel humming. Slade swiftly worked his way to the large backup generators that were rarely used, but were available in an emergency such as this. He flipped the big switches and with a motor-revving sound, the energy surged through the massive machines and sparked through the electrical veins that fed power to the main parts of the hotel.

After the brief panic, all the primary areas of the hotel were once again humming and restored to full service. The girls, relieved to have the lights restored, were determined to continue their once-in-a-lifetime opportunity. They headed for the door and down to the back ballroom.

Ariel kept a vigilant watch to be sure she didn't run into Jake. It was funny how she had wanted to break off their relationship, but seeing him with someone hurt, and the fact that he was flaunting it right in front of her made her want to get even somehow. Deep down, he was just a player, a liar, and a smooth talker. He would never change and she knew it. She best get over him for good.

The band entertained their hometown crowd and did not disappoint. They ended their set with a sweet melancholy number that just about made Ariel cry. She fought to hold back the salty moisture that rimmed her eyes. Every cell in her body screamed exhaustion, yet the elation she felt for the opportunity to be in the presence of such great musicians helped stave off her weariness. Emptiness and anger gnawed through her bones. There was that mixed-up emotional feeling running through her once again.

It was pushing one o'clock as she and her friends rode the glass elevator to the second floor. Before retiring to their room, Ariel decided to walk down the open hall and lean over the ledge to scan the open atrium and get a good angle of the glass elevators just in case she could see Jake and get his whereabouts. She didn't know why. She wished she didn't care but she couldn't help it. She got lost in people-watching for awhile.

Looking down, she could see scores of bodies stretched out on the sofas and limp figures curled in chairs across the way in the lounge, and people milling around looking out the front doors trying to get a grasp on the storm. An extra-loud group, one floor up on the opposite open hall, was trying to access their room but couldn't seem to make the key work. She spotted young, clean-cut Sean and lanky Randy in a fast clip heading across the atrium toward the back, their navy coat tails flying. She called down and waved at them as they passed under the second floor balcony. She decided that hotels were interesting places—people from near and far mixing and mingling.

The elevators continued to haul people up from the ground level and deposit them at their designated floors. All of a sudden, there was Jake and his crew in the elevator going up. Thank goodness by the time she saw them they were past the second floor. What would she have done had they got off and saw her standing there? She froze, sucking in air, hoping they didn't see her. Most people looked out the glass at the view to get the maximum effect of the ride as the elevator whisked them upward. They, however, didn't seem to care about anything except each other—all talking, all laughing.

Ariel made a mental note that they stopped and exited four down from the top—sixth floor. She kept her eye on them as they rounded the corner and stopped just a couple of doors down. From that angle, all she could see were the tops of their heads and shoulders until a couple in their group stood close to the edge and peered down to the floor below to take in the scenery. She pulled back under the overhang of the floor above, closer to the rooms, so she wouldn't be spotted. As she backed up and bumped a door, she suddenly remembered the face in the window. Although she couldn't be certain, this had to be the approximate location of the room where she had spotted the strange man in the window earlier. *Oh, my gosh.* Startled, she headed back to the safety of her friends in 203 as the possibility of another power outage flashed in her mind.

As the night wore on, the raging storm howled and whined. Snow snarled, swirled, and drifted higher and higher around the sturdy, well-built lodging structure, unfazed by the brutal winds. In the dark wee morning hours, it was finally peaceful inside the Capitol Plaza. A quiet calm had settled over the place as people, tired from socializing and partying, drifted off into deep slumber, or simply passed out.

In the pale swatch of light that filtered gently from one corner lamp in the front room and cast dim shadows around the walls of 628, a brave intruder with gloved hands stealthily stroked the dark luxurious strands of hair and gazed down on the sleeping beauty. Near the grip of the sparkling band that clasped her hair into a tight bundle, the scissors operator worked with precision—snip, snip, snip. The only noise was the soft grating sound of the scissors blades mixed with quiet breathing. Quickly, the woman's prized possession was cut away and placed in a large, plastic zip-lock bag. In a flash, the perpetrator slipped out the door with the stolen treasure and ducked down the back staircase.

- - -

12 – A Bizarre Mystery

Not long after many people found sleep, a fresh morning dawned. The sun crept up along the eastern horizon illuminating the pale blue sky with dazzling brilliant light reflections as its rays bounced off thick piles of soft, fluffy white powder and diamond-like crystals as far as the eye could see. The wind had calmed and the air was crisp and cold.

Early birds who enjoyed a full night's sleep started to wake and rub the sleep from their eyes. Going straight to the windows, they pulled back the curtains to see what greeted them. It was an arctic wonderland. As fast as the storm had arrived, it had blown through over night. Snow plows had already begun the arduous task of clearing the record snowfall from major roadways. Maintenance staff fired up the snow blowers and worked with fervor to clear the walkways around the hotel to allow anxious folks a chance to reach their cars and find freedom.

Ariel and her sleep mates, oblivious to the arrival of a new day, slept in long after the sun rose. Although one-by-one they began to rouse, they chose not to relinquish their warm beds and spent some time reminiscing about their good fortune the night before.

With the curtains drawn tight and feeling the effects of their late night escapade, the occupants in room 628 also had no trouble sleeping in long after the sun arose. Jake, groggy and slightly disoriented, was the first to discover that Denise's beautiful long locks and diamond hair clasp were missing. "What in the hell happened here?" His voice cracked with fear and disbelief when he caught sight of her head poking out from the covers with a whacked-up hair job.

Who could have done such a thing? Was it a deranged psychopath with a hair fetish, an overly fanatical supporter of locks of love, a prank gone too far, or did someone know that the sparkling pony tail clasp was sprinkled with real diamonds?

Denise snapped fully awake at Jake's outburst. There he stood over her, staring down, blue eyes wide, and a shocked, ashen look on his face. "Your . . . your hair," he stuttered. She touched her head slowly at first then more frantic, fingers splayed, running them through the short feathered remnants that sprouted from her scalp. She sat straight up staring across the room into the mirror. Visualizing the damage, she shrieked and fainted to the pillow. The other couple awoke to the chaos to see firsthand what the commotion was all about. Jake pondered the possibilities and decided it had to be an act of revenge. *Where was Ariel?* he wondered. Without saying a word he stormed out the door on a mission to the front desk to have them help locate whom he deemed responsible for this atrocious act.

Ariel was on her cell phone touching base with Rachel to see how her roommate had weathered the storm when the Front Desk Manager called room 203. Jessica answered. "Hey, it's Troy; is Ariel there? Please have her come to the front desk immediately. There is an agitated man here demanding to see her."

Ariel stiffened as she laid eyes on Jake standing there in

baggy sweat pants and sweatshirt with a concerned look on his face and daggers in his navy eyes, wondering what he could possibly want with her. "What's wrong? Is everything okay?" she cautiously questioned in a soft tone.

"I have a feeling you know damn good-and-well what is wrong," he accused.

Her tone raised a notch. "What in the world are you talking about?"

About that time, Ed and Randy appeared as summoned by Troy. Troy, in his feminine manner, motioned them all off to the side, out of earshot of others checking out of the hotel. He took charge in as manly a voice as he could muster. "There's been an incident in one of the Brickman suites, room 628." He gestured toward Jake. "According to this gentleman, his girlfriend's pony tail was lopped off and a diamond hair clasp was stolen during the night while they slept."

Ariel's jaw dropped and she looked with round eyes at Jake. "Oh, my gosh!" She was shocked at what she had just heard. "And you think I had something to do with that? Are you out of your mad mind?" She shook her head in disbelief at the story she had just heard and the fact that Jake thought she had anything to do with such a travesty.

After quizzing Jake further and taking notes, albeit there wasn't much he could offer, as he hadn't seen or heard anything, Ed and Randy were off to question the victim. Before they could step away, however, Jake reinforced with them his suspicion that Ariel had a vengeful hand in the incident. Ariel just rolled her eyes and shook her head. Ed and Randy looked at Jake like he was from another planet.

"That doesn't at all fit the profile of the Ariel I know," said Ed with confidence, "but I'll make a note of it." Ed took his job in security seriously, but enjoyed dreaming of bigger and better things. He was forever proclaiming proudly that one

The Concierge

day he would work for the FBI.

"We better get to the scene of the crime and check on Denise," suggested less competent and sometimes aloof Randy. The pair of navy suits strode off toward the elevators and left Jake and Ariel to continue their sparring.

"I can assure you I had nothing to do with that awful situation," Ariel promised Jake. "I was with my friends on the second floor and we were in the room around one o'clock and up talking probably until 2:00 a.m. Since I was one of the first ones asleep, I have a solid alibi."

"Whatever you say, Ariel," Jake scoffed and took off to console his poor dear, now short-haired girlfriend.

The policeman who had left the premises earlier that morning was called upon to return so an official police report could be filed. Ed and Randy had no real evidence, no one saw or heard anything and the last computerized time stamp of the key card entry was 1:09 a.m. when the foursome had all come up to the room together. Aside from holding the door ajar with the metal door prop as they slipped in and out for ice and a trip to the front desk for a forgotten toothbrush, they hadn't left the room and didn't remember using the key after their initial entry. No one in room 628 could claim with 100 percent certainty that the door had been shut when they retired, although Jake knew it was closed when he raced off to the front desk earlier. The real kicker was that it was entirely possible someone had entered and hidden in the front closet while the door was cracked open with the metal flip lock. With the suite style arrangement, a living room area in front and larger common area in the back flanked by two bedrooms, each with their own bathroom, a perpetrator could have slipped in unnoticed and hid while the victim and her friends were preoccupied in the back.

The front desk, SECR, and the West Des Moines police

were all stumped. Guests on the sixth floor in the vicinity of room #628 had been questioned and no one noticed or heard anything suspicious. There were no fingerprints or clues left behind. Despite Jake's best effort to pin the guilt on Ariel, her alibi held tight as her friends verified she was with them and that she was one of the first to fall asleep. At the present time, it was an unsolved mystery.

---

13 – Concierge in Training

Before Ariel realized it, December was history. After the big New Year's Eve extravaganza, the nightly parties dried up, and the need for extra servers was over until next season. She was a bit relieved as it had been a grueling several weeks of hard work, yet it was sad to leave the hotel and turn in her burgundy banquet uniform. She signed her termination papers and picked up what she thought was her final paycheck.

As she exited the H.R. office, she was instantly greeted by the head concierge, seated behind the big mahogany desk. Never really having been acquainted with her prior to this encounter, since her focus had been in banquets at the back of the house, Ariel knew her only in passing. She was actually quite friendly.

"Say, you wouldn't happen to know anyone that might be looking for a part-time job would you? One of my gals just put in her notice and I need to fill a position for some nights and weekends."

"Uh, no . . . not really," Ariel stretched out the words slowly as she was thinking.

"My name is Dina, by the way," she said with a smile that

revealed really white teeth rimmed by plum colored lips.

Ariel introduced herself. "So what does the job require?" she asked.

"Well, you know, it is really a lot of fun and relatively easy. You just take good care of the guests that stay here and assist other hotel departments as needed. And the best part is, you meet a lot of interesting business men, or, ah, people that come through here." She winked, puckered her mouth to the side and clicked her tongue on the inside of her cheek, as she tapped her manicured white tipped nails against the polished desk top.

"Yeah, I can imagine that you would," Ariel concurred. "Well, I can let you know if someone comes to mind that —"

Dina cut her off, mid-sentence. "What about you? You'd be great. You're already familiar with the hotel and know a lot of the staff—I know you'd love it," she enthusiastically chimed in a convincing tone.

Dina drew a deep breath and went on to proudly explain the history of the concierge.

"While concierge services have evolved over the years and are more diverse than ever, they are all about providing personalized service to people in need. The word concierge originated in the mid 1600s and is a derivative of the word *conservus* meaning fellow slave. Concierge services, as you may know, are especially common in Europe and often it is a male with formal training that fills the position." Pausing just long enough to fill her lungs with air, she proceeded to share her knowledge. "At the Capitol Plaza here in the Midwest, though, it just makes sense to utilize fresh-faced college grads and professional young women as it suggests the promise that all guests will be coddled and served with respect to meet their every whim while adding a bit of charm into the mix."

"That's quite interesting," Ariel responded in a warm, easy

going manner. Dina had surprised her with her in-depth knowledge and spiel.

Dina drummed her fingernails, reached up to push a wisp of blond hair from her eyes and then crossed her arms under her full breasts. "So what do you think?" Before Ariel could answer, Dina went on to add, "You give off the impression that you are a down-home, hospitable, strong work ethics, and high standards kind of gal."

"Why thank you very much," Ariel modestly replied.

Dina shared what the general manager, her boss, always said. "There's nothing like a pretty woman to add a sense of flair and hospitality to the hotel environment. It's a great business strategy. But you know what I always tell him?" Dina winked again. "It's just as much of a benefit to us women, especially if you are single and like to socialize." She laughed a hearty laugh and shook her head. "You know, I really love this job."

Ariel smiled and confirmed that she, too, was single and enjoyed the social aspects of life. "Actually, I have a full-time day job so a couple of nights a week and weekends would suit my schedule."

Before Ariel could say another word, Dina stood to shake Ariel's hand. "So you'll take the job?"

Ariel nodded. "Yes, I think this will be a good fit for me."

"Wonderful," Dina flashed her pearly whites. "That will be absolutely perfect. I re-welcome you to the Capitol Plaza Hotel. Can you be here Wednesday at 5:30 and we'll start training? Just a couple of nights should do it and you'll be on your own by the weekend."

Before Ariel grasped what had transpired, she had swapped her burgundy uniform of the hard working banquet staff to the mauve attire of the more leisurely and sophisticated concierge position. She was off to tell Rachel her surprising and exciting news. It had felt good to tell Dina she was single. Jake had been out of the picture since the wicked hair incident and she was getting used to the idea that he had faded out of her life. She often pondered what kind of a psycho pulled the hair caper. It made her edgy to think that some crazy person was in the hotel that night and that he had not been caught.

Thoughts of her upcoming new job at the hotel had Ariel excited and a little nervous. Her first night in the mauve uniform behind the big desk was spent training with Dina who reviewed the hotel policy with Ariel, provided an overview of the operations and familiarized her with the computer and phone system. "As you probably guessed, this computer stores all kinds of information pertinent to running this hotel. Most important for our job is having access to the guest room database including the names and personal data of those checked into each room at any given time." She swiped at her blond bangs to brush them away from her eyes and continued. The top two floors are the ones designated to receive the concierge services and one of the first things you do when a guest arrives and gets settled in is to greet them with a call. See here, room #902 and #1017 flashing red—the front desk activates this at the time of check in providing our signal to contact that room for their courtesy call."

Ariel looked on as Dina in her perky voice, proudly continued with a description of the system, clicking and *mousing* her way to files and folders that were accessible to their department. "The Internet access comes in real handy to tap into the around-town happenings so you'll be well informed for the countless requests about where to go and what to do. Also we have our interoffice e-mail exchange so all the departments can stay in touch." Ariel nodded understandingly.

"Now let me show you how this is done." Dina toggled back to the room list and clicked on #902 flashing in red. Up came information regarding Ross Barbaria:

Business guest—Yes

Company—Skylar Health Products

Address—245 Straw Lane, Glendale, CA

Last Stay—December 19

Wake-up calls—6 a.m.

Interests—pool, sauna, and gym in the morning. Frequent guest; often dines out with business partners and holds seminars at the hotel.

Miscellaneous—tall, dark, and handsome. Dina giggled. "See, here is a place for free-form entry. I entered my own opinion there."

"I guess you'd have to be a bit careful what is written there, right?" Ariel questioned. Dina waved her hand to downplay the inquiry. "Nah, the front desk people are the only ones that see this and they don't care. I only insert positive comments—never anything derogatory," she defended herself. "The nice thing is by entering facts or quirky information about our frequent guests, it helps us provide exceptional service, because we always know their personal preferences. It makes them feel really special." Ariel smiled and nodded with interest at Dina's proclaimed insight into the service industry.

"Here, let me demonstrate a welcome call." Dina reached for the phone and her white-tipped forefinger dialed room 902. She pursed her lips in anticipation of the connection. Three rings later, tall, dark and handsome answered. "Good evening, Mr. Barbaria; it's Dina calling to welcome you back to the Capitol Plaza and make sure you're settled in. Might there be anything I can assist you with at this time?" She paused.

"Sure thing, I'll take care of that for 7:00—party of four and I'll send up the wine right away. Also, I've got you set for your usual 6 a.m. wake-up call tomorrow, is that correct?" Another pause, "Okay, please let me know if there's anything else you need." She placed the phone in the receiver, looked at Ariel, and explained his request for two bottles of Cabernet.

"Will you please deliver and open the wine for him while I make his dinner reservations?" Not really asking, rather instructing, Dina sent Ariel off to find Bud, or as everyone liked to call him, Bud-lite, for the wine. Ariel came to the realization that she would spend a lot of time on the top floors, which made her tense, but decided that just maybe she would become desensitized of her fear of heights eventually. She tracked down Bud-lite and gathered the wine. Now with two bottles tightly clutched in the crook of her arm, four wine glasses hanging through her fingers by the stems in one hand, towel over her arm, and a wine opener in her pocket, she took the back service elevator up to ninth floor.

Dina was quite right, assessed Ariel, when Mr. Ross Barbaria opened the door upon her tapping. He was indeed a very handsome man, about 6 foot 2 inches with short dark hair and dark eyes fringed by dark eyelashes. He was well-built, well-groomed, and sported casual business attire. He was also very professional and greeted Ariel with warmth within seconds of her tap on the door. "Hello, my name is Ariel. Here is the wine you ordered, sir. May I open it for you?" She gently set the glasses on the table and turned the wine labels toward him for his approval.

"No, I'll take care of it," he said in a confident voice as he pressed a bill into her hand and reached for the bottles she presented. She placed the wine opener and towel next to the glasses.

"Thanks and please let us know if you need anything further." She exited the room and glanced at the tip in her hand. *Wow, I love this job! Dina was right again.*

Ariel didn't feel quite deserving of the tip on her first night, so offered it to Dina since she had set up the delivery and scheduled Mr. Barbaria's reservation. "Oh, keep it, honey, you earned it," Dina said, waving it off. "That's one of the perks of this fabulous job," she smiled showing her white teeth.

"That was really generous!" Ariel gushed.

"Trust me, it's peanuts to him."

"So how long has he been staying here?" Ariel inquired.

"Well, I'd say he's been around off and on for, oh, the last six to nine months. He sells health supplies and equipment. I help him sometimes with his business needs, you know, copying and organizing his meeting materials, mailing packages, and so forth."

Ariel nodded. "So, there are a lot of business people that stay here?"

"Oh, definitely, especially during the week, but on weekends you see more families and people just passing through on vacation and travels," Dina explained.

"Sounds like it can get pretty busy."

"It sure can. In fact, while you were delivering the wine, I contacted rooms and made Mr. Barbaria's reservation at the restaurant plus answered some questions for people who stopped by. If you ever get too busy and need help, don't be afraid to contact someone to assist, whether Room Service, Security, or a manager, whoever might be appropriate and they will come to the rescue if you are in a real jam," Dina reassured Ariel.

"That's good to know." Ariel nodded with relief.

Dina reached into the top desk drawer and pulled out a key ring that dangled two sparkly red and white dice and a lone key. "The next thing I want to do is show you the concierge closet." Dina opened the door near the big desk and exposed its contents: lower shelves filled with boxes of complimentary toothbrushes, small tubes of toothpaste, combs, plastic razors, little bars of soap, and bottles of lotion for guests who forgot or needed extra. The middle shelf held irons and a plastic tub with odds and ends. The upper shelf held a sewing kit, a calligraphy set, and a basket of art supplies. Reams of paper were stacked neatly on the floor under the lower shelf. It was very well organized.

"Obviously, this is where you'll find supplies that guests might need and you will always offer to deliver if they call, but also people just stop by for things. It's understood that the top floors get the special perks and concierge service, but we also help any hotel guest who might need a little assistance."

"So what is the strangest request you've ever received?" Ariel wanted to know.

"Hmmm, well I've been asked to sew buttons on shirts and pants—not so strange, and um, recently I had a woman demand a specific kind of white tea bags. Oh, and get this. There is one man who stays frequently and expects there to be a jar of green and blue peanut M&Ms in his room, which I have yet to understand what that is about. But in the name of service, I do keep them in stock and there is a special jar here in the closet to fill when he visits. He also usually requests a platter of olives, cherry peppers, cheese —specifically Muenster and Brie—wheat crackers and some Granny Smith apple slices. The kitchen has all that, but I give them plenty of notice when he checks in." Dina shook her head and smiled. "He is one peculiar fella." The information is noted on his profile record. Sometime just for fun, you can peruse the frequent guest list to see the various notes on people."

"For sure, I'll check that out when I get a chance. It sounds rather interesting."

The evening progressed. People stopped to inquire about recommended restaurants around town, copies and faxes were handled for business needs, and an assortment of requests had been juggled. All in all, it was a smooth, productive affair. Ariel absorbed her pleasant surroundings, happy she had agreed to the position. She looked forward to working with the front desk employees, the security guys, and others whom she had come to know. Howard, the older bellman who was on duty the day she first came to the hotel, had stopped by to say hello. He always had a smile and was quite the conversationalist. His genuine kindness provided a dose of grandfatherly support that was comforting.

By the end of the night, under Dina's tutelage, Ariel had a good grasp of what the job entailed. Another night together and she would be ready to go it alone. "So what do you think after your first night?" Dina fished for Ariel's approval sensing that she, like herself, received the same sense of fulfillment that this job offered.

"It was absolutely wonderful—so much better than working in banquets where the work is physical. Even though it can be busy, it didn't seem as taxing. I really enjoyed myself. Thanks for suggesting that I give it a try!"

"Also," added Dina, "the sense of freedom is nice, because we have the run of the place. We can go wherever needed. Tonight was fairly typical, but now and then, someone or something comes along that is new or different and adds a twist. "Oh, before we wrap up for the night, another thing you just have to see is the Presidential Suite. It is over the top and sometime you might get asked to show it to someone interested in renting it. Let's get a key card from Troy."

The pair of women in mauve proceeded to the front desk to chat with Troy and get a card.

"Hey, how's my main man Troy?" Dina placed her

manicured hands atop Troy's long bony fingers, which he placed out on the granite desk top as they approached. "You know Ariel, don't you?" she questioned as she cocked her head Ariel's way.

"Yes, we've met," Troy and Ariel said smiling at each other in recognition.

Plain and simple, Troy was gay: tan, lean, angular features, bony wrists, designer hair, short and highlighted, sculpted lips, a dimple in the chin and that voice—soft yet peppy. He was beautiful. You couldn't help but adore him. "Will you please get me a key card for the Presidential Suite?" Dina implored. "I want to show Ariel how amazing it is."

"Sure thing, Dina doll, anything for you." He handed her the card. "Here you go and you two have fun." He responded in a playful, enthusiastic manner. Then he added, "Ariel, so glad you're on board with us in the front of the house. It's a lot of fun around here. I look forward to working with you."

"Thanks, I'm looking forward to it, and we can get a chance to know each other better. See you later."

Dina and Ariel rode the elevator to the tenth floor. Ariel steered clear of the railing at the top and favored the internal wall as they headed for the Presidential Suite. The little light turned green as Dina slid the key card into the slot and the door opened to reveal an expansive, sleek, exquisitely decorated penthouse in rich colors with an abundance of amenities. The windows allowed a surprising view of downtown, the shapes of familiar and major buildings visible and silhouetted in lights and color in the distance.

"Oh, wow, this is incredible!"

"Yeah, I especially like the décor; it was recently redone."

The living area could accommodate a large party comfortably with multiple chaise lounges, ottomans, and coffee tables sectioned into intimate settings. The kitchen area inclusive of a large modern stove, refrigerator, dishwasher, and deep sink, was streamlined and surrounded by an L-shaped cherry wood bar topped in white creamy marble above which were suspended chrome lights. Six shiny silver bar stools hugged the L-shaped area. Ornately cut glass was set into the dark wood cabinets that showcased the kitchen. Ariel slowly scanned her surroundings to absorb the beauty.

Past the main living and kitchen areas was the master bedroom, which featured a four-poster king-size canopy bed. Softly draped gauze-like fabric flowed down from the beams that linked the top corner posts. Egyptian cotton sheets were turned down over the edge of the thick off-white down comforter and rich chocolate brown shams and pillows of all shapes and sizes were layered at the headboard. A brown and off-white patterned bed skirt skimmed the plush carpet. "Wouldn't that make a nice love nest?" Dina said dreamily. "Room service, champagne, breakfast in bed, a handsome man—what a little slice of heaven that would be right here," she giggled.

"I suppose this is booked a lot for honeymoons?"

"Yes, often times for that and then there are some folks who just plain have money to spend. Actually, there is a well-known businessman, who owns a successful manufacturing company and a couple of night clubs here in the Des Moines metro. You've probably heard of Oscar Kaufman?"

"The name does sound familiar. I'm sure I've read about him in the paper or heard his name mentioned somewhere."

"Well, he books this place every couple of months. It seems rather secretive but he sure likes to entertain his employees and/or friends and throws quite a party—even imports girls from California to liven things up. He has his own corporate jet so is on the go here and there. I think the last time he booked this was New Year's Eve and also he was here before Christmas. He'll probably be back in another month or so."

Dina motioned Ariel into the master bath and flipped the light switch. "Holy guacamole, this is to die for." A huge elevated Jacuzzi tub centered the spacious bath under soft lights. Large fluffy towels garnished a rack nearby. Off to the side through glass doors, a large walk-in double shower with massaging nozzles was visible. All-in-all, the Presidential Suite was impressive.

While the women continued to explore and enjoy their lavish surroundings, a not so enjoyable scene was unfolding in the room directly below. The Do Not Disturb sign swung slightly as the occupant in 901 placed the communication piece on the outer door knob. The business woman was looking forward to a quiet evening. She turned the lock lever until it clicked and flipped back the metal hook to secure the door against any intruder, a prudent habit. Unfortunately, it made absolutely no difference whatsoever.

---

14 – A Bubble Bath

Outside the door of 901 stood the lean, muscled, intelligent, smooth, and meticulous assassin. He listened briefly as the earpiece he wore amplified the sounds inside. He was pleased to hear the subtle drone of the senseless blah-blah-blah on the TV. It was a bonus to hear water running to mask the slight noise as the key entry was tripped. He smiled at the metal flip fastener that was intended to keep out prowlers. To him, it may as well have been a paper clip. He glanced over his shoulder and quickly scanned the floors—no one in sight. He appeared just like any guest with a cart in tow carrying a large suitcase and a bag. Anyone spotting him wouldn't give him a second thought.

The water was running full force and clouds of misty steam hovered above the tub as the woman slipped out of her clothing in anticipation of a relaxing soak in the frothy white bubbles that hinted at the smell of cherry blossoms. As she settled into the sudsy hot water and tilted her head back to rest on the towel fashioned into a pillow, she was sure she heard an unexplained noise in the other room. Immediately, her survival instincts surged. She sucked in a breath and froze to listen for further sounds. It was quiet, except for the TV background noise. *Seriously, I need to get a grip,* she thought.

The soothing bath began to relax her mind and her body. The silky water lapped at her breasts, the foamy bubbles rising like bread dough. Her mind drifted and gauzy thoughts floated through her cerebrum.

Meanwhile in the other room, light footsteps glided, and swift, slithering hands organized her belongings. The bed sheets were pulled down and mussed to appear as though the bed had been slept in. When he was satisfied that everything was in order, he stepped to the door of the bath area and rolled up his sleeves. Through the slightly open door, he could see the woman's reflection in the mirror. Her auburn hair was pulled back in a head band. He paused for awhile, admiring the scenery and grew excited imagining her reaction when she learned that she had company.

Shortly after, he stepped through the door into the bath area and stood over her. Her reaction was exactly as he had anticipated. She gasped and her body wilted in recognition of the vulnerable position in which she found herself. Before she could squeak out a sound, a piece of duct tape was plastered across her mouth. He turned off the water. "You know why I'm here. You got too nosy and I have my orders. I might as well have some fun while I'm working," he whispered in a gravelly voice.

He didn't wield a knife, a gun, or any weapon. Her eyes pleaded as she shook her head back and forth. She put her hands up for protection as she cowered lower under the bubbles. "After I'm done with you, there will be no trace. You will simply vanish into thin air—a real magician's trick." The smirk on his face expressed amusement at her predicament. A throaty laugh conveyed his superiority. The man in charge slipped two nylon cords out of his pocket and placed one between his teeth. With precision and speed, he tightly bound her hands with the other. His hands plunged under the water to locate her feet. She kicked and splashed, but was quickly overpowered. In the same precise motion, he had her ankles bound.

"Now, there's no real reason to get in a rush. I'm going to let you marinate in your bath and admire the view. It looks like a few items here need to be gathered up." He bent to pick up her clothes that had been recently shed and cleared her personal items from the area around the sink.

"Also, I have a lock to replace," he said with a smug grin. "By the time the water turns tepid, I'll be ready to load you and your possessions and we'll be on our way." He gently brushed the hair out of her eyes and stroked her face. He then peeled back the tape to reveal the corner of her mouth and pushed a pill through the small opening before quickly pressing the tape shut again. "Sweet dreams, sweetheart." He was amused at his own creativity. How powerful and in control he felt.

Part II

15 – Ariel on Her Own

Her first solo night as concierge had Ariel's heart beating like a drum. Just past the Eighth Street exit, traffic picked up speed, and she surged west toward the hotel. The last two nights of training had been fun and educational. She hoped she was ready. Her mind shuffled through the events of the last six weeks like clips from a movie. Images of Jake, his bankruptcy news, the announcement that he'd be leaving town, ballroom parties, the snowstorm, Corkscrew, the mysterious ponytail incident, Troy, Dina, and other new acquaintances she had made flashed by in her mind.

Ariel tried to imagine all that was yet to transpire. As the exit ramp approached, she fully refocused and reached for the gearshift to throttle down for a safe exit off the freeway. Just a few minutes and she would reach the Capitol Plaza Hotel.

With the clock ticking and three minutes to spare, Ariel raced down the back hallway with her mauve suit in tow. She needed to quickly change and be at the desk on time. Her pace was unmistakable; her heels clicked with purpose. She was a bit anxious thinking that Dina wouldn't be there for support. Dina would be going off duty as soon as Ariel arrived to take over. *Hopefully I won't encounter anything too complicated or out of the ordinary my first night alone,* she thought optimistically.

Dina, in her carefree style, promised that Friday night would be a breeze since the bulk of the business travelers were gone until Monday morning and they constituted the volume of the work handled by the concierge. There would be families and other travelers making inquiries but she would do just fine, she had reassured Ariel as she prepared to leave. "Here's a basket that needs to be delivered before the guest checks in at 7:00 p.m.," she said, as she swept her hand toward a beautiful, cellophane-wrapped wicker basket of wine, cheese, crackers, and fruit, with #1015 noted on a card. "Also, I left you a note for another delivery that I received just a few minutes before you arrived." She pointed to a pink sticky note on the computer. "Okay, I think that's it! Any questions before I go? I've got to get ready for my date tonight."

Dina pulled her coat out of the closet. She was chomping at the bit to get going.

"I'll be fine; you go have fun." Ariel swiped her hands in the air to shoo Dina on her way.

"See ya later, alligator!" Dina called over her shoulder as she took off past the elevators toward the back, prancing like a race horse. Little did anyone know that Dina clocked out, accessed her car for an overnight bag, and did a U-turn straight back to the hotel side door. She sneaked to the back employee elevator, ducked inside, and headed for the fifth floor to join her date. It wasn't the Presidential Suite, but she was pleased as punch anyway.

With beaming confidence, Ariel slipped behind the grand desk and admired her surroundings. She checked the computer screen for any new occupancy on the upper levels— nothing flashing at the moment. She glanced at the sticky note and saw that room 920 was in need of a few personal items. Ariel opened the closet and fished out a plastic wrapped toothbrush, toothpaste, and a razor and slipped them into her pocket. She made a visit to the front desk to get a key card from her buddy Troy. "Hey there, Troy, I've got a basket to deliver; will you help me out and assign a key card for #1015?"

"Sure thing. Anything for you, my dear. Say, when are you taking your break?" Troy piped up in his soft, peppy voice. "It would be fun to have a dining partner."

"Well, to tell you the truth, since I just got here, I hadn't thought about it," laughed Ariel, "but," she paused, "if things are slow enough I'll take my half hour around 7:00—and you?"

"How about the same?" he touched his right hand to his heart and put the other hand on his hip. "I would love to chat and fill you in on a little hotel gossip." His green eyes glittered and he parted his sculpted lips in a warm smile.

"That sounds good to me. Now hand me that card so I can get my work done." She pulled the card from his tan, manicured fingers.

"I'll stop by your desk for you," he called after her as she turned away. She gave him the okay signal.

It was easy to stay busy. She directed guests to ballrooms and answered questions. She sent e-mails to the kitchen for room service requests. She made phone calls to those on the top concierge floors to welcome them. Before she knew it, there stood her tan, lean co-worker in front of her desk, ready for their break. "Just let me make a quick call and I'll be ready in a sec."

Ariel turned to dial Engineering. "Hi, Slade. It's Ariel at the concierge desk. The guests in room 420 have voiced a complaint about their heater. They are freezing and not very happy about it. Please have someone check it out pronto. Okay, thanks, bye."

"Just let me lock the closet and we'll be off." She dropped the sparkly red and white dice key chain into her pocket. They headed in haste through the atrium and past the pre-convention area. As they emerged through the back north hallway, both caught sight of a man neither had seen before. Tall, blond, and well built, he wore a well tailored suit jacket, starched white shirt, and colorful tie. Pressed slacks and shiny black loafers completed his attire. He was authoritatively communicating orders to a group dressed in burgundy at the entrance of Ontario. Ariel and Troy looked at each other with arched brows and took a good look as they skirted the engaged group.

"Whoa, who was that?" Ariel questioned with a hint of desire in her voice as they strode out of earshot.

"Boy, I sure would like to know," exclaimed Troy as he fluttered his hands near his face. "I think he replaced Mr. Blackstone. He was gone as of last week."

"Really, I didn't know he was leaving. What a nice guy. I sure liked him. He was a good manager and supported his staff so well," Ariel ruminated.

"Well, I'll tell you what. I bet you will like Mr. Stud Muffin back there even better!" Troy turned to take another peek before they veered off through the back kitchen doors.

The employee break room just off the kitchen was buzzing with conversation. The TV positioned in the upper far corner of the room was tuned to CSI Miami and as usual, a gruesome discovery was unfolding. Troy and Ariel exchanged hellos to fellow workers and checked out the chafing pans to see what options awaited them. They each loaded a plate with salad and a baked potato and found a table. "So, do you really think the tall blond guy took over for Mr. Blackstone?" Ariel leaned forward in her chair, eyes wide and questioning.

"Yep, I'd say there is a new sheriff in town. Out with the old and in with the new," Troy stated matter-of-factly. "I'll get the scoop on him, don't you worry." He shook his finger as he spoke.

A smile spread across Ariel's face as she watched his determination. "I'm sure you will, detective."

"Wouldn't he make a great catch?" Troy shot her a quizzical look.

"How can you say that? I don't even know him, and trust me, even if it were an option, I have no desire to get involved in a new relationship. I need a break." With her elbow positioned on the table, she brought her hand to her forehead and massaged her temples with a finger and thumb.

Troy smiled a big wide grin and patted his long fingers just under the collar of his mauve jacket. "What do you mean, doll? I was thinking of myself." Ariel laughed and shook her head. "Nope, sorry, he's not your type. I could tell."

"He may not be now, but wait 'til I'm done with him, honey," he jested.

"Oh how funny! He's probably married with three or four kids and a real family man."

They continued to joke and enjoy small talk in between bites of salad and potato. "So Troy, how long have you been working here?"

"Ever since it opened," he replied proudly. "But I'm also taking classes in cosmetology, which I absolutely love. Someday I want to move to New York and run a top hair salon. That's my dream job, anyway." His eyes displayed a look of hopeful desire.

"Oh, how awesome. I bet you will. One of these days, I'll

pick up a Cosmo magazine and in the fine print under a gorgeous model it will reference 'Hair by Troy.' I'll be able to say: I know him!" She offered an encouraging smile.

He sighed and fluttered his lashes over his green eyes. "Yes, maybe some day."

"Speaking of hair, what do you think happened to that Brickman girl whose ponytail was cut off?" Ariel questioned with furrowed brows.

"I have no idea," Troy shook his head slowly, "but that morning she left she had the hood of her coat pulled up over her head. I bet she was just sick about what happened and scared, too. Can you imagine waking up to find out someone had done that to you in your sleep?"

"Well, for all I know it was Jake, my ex-boyfriend, who pulled that caper. He has some major issues."

"Are you serious? I wondered what kind of relationship you two had when he asked me to call you down to the desk that morning."

"We dated for about eight months but things didn't work out. He went for the shock factor when he showed up that night with her. I had no idea until I saw them together. He's supposed to be moving to California soon, which reminds me, I need to pick up some of my kitchen gadgets and other personal things before he leaves town. I need to touch base with him, which I'm not too thrilled about."

"You know, I can't be sure but it seems I've seen him in the hotel before." Troy stroked his jaw in thought, caressing his finger over the dimple in his chin.

"Maybe you have seen him. He was involved in some of the subcontracting phases of this hotel as it was being built. Knowing him, he probably stops in now and then just to admire his work."

"Really, he must do well for himself if he's in that business?"

"Not necessarily, it's a long story that I'll have to tell you sometime."

Troy tapped at his overly large, shiny watch, which hugged his bony wrist. "I'd sure like to hear it, but for now I guess we'd better get back to the front."

"Gosh, time flies when you're having fun! Thanks for inviting me to join you tonight. We'll do it again." Ariel genuinely enjoyed the company.

The phone was ringing when Ariel returned to the desk. It was Shawn. The youngest of the SECR foursome, he was usually energetic but this time conveyed an extra spark of enthusiasm in his voice. "Hey, just had a call from a woman in 312. She is stuck in her dress, and says she can't get the zipper down. She sounded pretty frustrated and out of breath. I told her I'd be right up to handle it, but she sounded a little disgusted and demanded a woman, so I'm turning it over to you."

"Oh, my goodness, are you kidding me? You said 312? Okay, I'm off and running." Ariel dropped the phone into the cradle and headed off to the call of duty.

The middle-aged woman opened the door slightly to Ariel's announcement that she had come to assist. There she was, red faced and short of breath. "Come in, come in," she motioned. The zipper in her dress was indeed stuck firm as the delicate fabric had drawn into the zipper track as she had repeatedly attempted in an increasing panic to free herself. "Oh, thank God you're here. I've been working on this awhile." A scent of perfume mixed with body odor wafted in the air. "Just give it a rip if you have to! At this point I don't care." Ariel worked calmly for a bit and then did just that. She grabbed the fabric at the back opening of the dress on either side of the zipper and gave it a strong tug to pull apart the entangled fabric. R-r-rip—the woman was free at last and thankful to be liberated from the grips of the garment from hell. Although the beautiful dress was ruined, she was truly grateful.

Ariel considered the zipper incident a comical example of the endless possibilities that the concierge job offered. Like the box of chocolates referenced by Forrest Gump, you never knew what you were going to get. Before concluding thoughts of chocolates and possibilities, Ariel did a double-take as she glanced toward the front lobby. A strange feeling came over her as she realized it was not a human checking in at the front desk, although one of them was. The non-human was taller than his gentlemen partner, and was furry and brown, standing seven feet tall on hind legs, wearing a pink tutu. Fortunately, a leash was strapped around its neck and a muzzle encapsulated its big powerful jaws. The bear appeared poised and ready for check-in. Ariel hadn't heard the circus was in town, or perhaps it was just a man and his companion needing a place to sleep for the night. Wow, who knew what was next!

Other than the zipper ordeal and the latest bear sighting, the night yielded a normal flow of inquiries and deliveries. She loved the variety that hotel life offered. Where else could you find such amusing diversity while earning a paycheck? She looked forward to catching up with Rachel and Tori when she clocked out in another half hour so they could exchange details of their Friday night adventures.

Before she knew it, it was ten o'clock. Ariel pulled her coat out of the concierge closet and dialed Rachel as she headed toward the back.

"Hey, Rach, where are you?" Ariel inquired as her roommate answered her cell phone.

"Tori and I are just leaving Jimmy's. What's up?" Ariel could hear laughter and noise in the background.

"You're just now leaving?" her voice rose in question.

"Yeah, there were so many people here that we knew, and we didn't realize how long we'd been here!"

"I'm checking out now—let's meet at The Cove. Some of the hotel crew headed over there and it will be fun to hang out with them."

"So how was the first night solo?"

"It went well . . . was interesting. I'll fill you in. Talk to you in a few minutes."

---

16 – The Cove

The Cove exuded a pleasant oxymoronic vibe—it was a calm environment, just as the name suggested, yet there was an exhilarating sense of energy in the air—which created the perfect balance and sense of well-being. Not many venues achieved the ideal equilibrium. It was decorated in shades of turquoise, sapphire, pale green, and silver with soft lights. The opaque floor along one wall opposite the bar was raised and soft, colored lights glowed and swirled underneath. The raised area supported several groupings of low tables surrounded by firm leather seating. The platform area was prime pickings and was usually filled.

Ariel found a spot in the less coveted area and sat facing the door so she could witness Rachel and Tori's arrival. She waved when she spotted them entering the door off the main entry near the restrooms. Ariel had already placed an order of appetizers. "Hungry?" she asked as they removed their coats and sat down.

"Of course, you know me," Tori responded and rubbed her hands together.

"Food should be here any minute." They settled in and took in the crowd to see if they might recognize anyone. The place was well occupied, but not uncomfortably packed.

"Some of the hotel staff is over there," Ariel pointed toward the back end of the bar. "We'll have to go say hi to them later. I see Ed—he's one of our security guys—and it looks like he's with some of the banquet and kitchen shift.

Tori scanned the group. "Are any of them single?" she piped up in a hopeful tone.

"Yes, I'm sure some of them are," Ariel said with optimism. "I'll introduce you to everyone after we eat. You know, I told Troy to stop by, but he said, quote, 'The East Village is calling my name tonight'." Ariel mimicked Troy's mannerism by placing her hand over her heart as she conveyed her friend's quote. "I really want you to meet him sometime. He is so much fun. But certainly, he's more comfortable in his own neck of the woods, so we'd probably have to travel across town to hang with him."

"That could be quite a fun adventure. Let's plan on it." Rachel smiled with a gleam in her eye.

A waiter appeared with a platter of nachos piled high and a steaming dish of artichoke spinach dip and bread along with plates. He promised to return with their drinks of choice. While enjoying their food and drinks, they swapped stories of the evening. Ariel shared her valiant rescue effort to free the woman imprisoned in her own dress and of the beastly guest in the pink tutu. The stories had them all chuckling. Rachel and Tori asked questions about the hotel and updated Ariel on the scene at Jimmy's and the latest who's who. After finishing her plate of food, Ariel wiped her mouth with a napkin. "Excuse me a minute, while I run to the lady's room. I'll take you back to the gang when I get back." She headed toward the restrooms near the main entrance.

The powder room at The Cove had a unique feature for women to enjoy. It sported a one-way mirror which allowed a view over the entire floor from a level above. It made for great people watching. The men's room, on the other hand, did not offer that amenity. Ariel took advantage of the view alongside a few other gals. She saw that Rachel and Tori had attracted a couple of male friends. As she scanned the bar, her eyes found none other than Mr. Ross Barbaria with a martini in one hand and cell phone in the other. Why is he still in town on a Friday night? Usually the business folks clear out at the end of the week. Actually, now that she thought about it, Dina had mentioned he sometimes stayed in town over the weekends for extended business. She hadn't noticed him at the hotel that night—probably was out on the town all evening.

Mr. Tall, Dark, and Handsome mechanically worked his thumbs on the keypad of his cell phone. He turned sideways on his bar stool and Ariel could see his profile. His lips began moving as he held the phone to his ear and stretched his neck to look down the end of the bar toward the Plaza crowd. Ariel shifted her gaze to see whom he might be connecting with. Ed, too, was talking into his phone as he stepped away from the group. He looked down Mr. Barbaria's way, but otherwise didn't acknowledge him. Ariel squinted and glanced back and forth at each of them to determine if they were actually conversing with each other and decided it was no coincidence when they simultaneously put their phones away. Ed edged back toward his hotel buddies. Mr. Barbaria polished off his martini, grabbed his coat jacket off the back of his chair, and headed for the door. Within minutes, Ed was saying his goodbyes and then bolted for the door.

Hmm, how strange is that? Ariel paused for a second in thought before relinquishing her post at the mirrored window. She reunited with her friends below who were carrying on a lively conversation with some folks at the next table. "Come on, let's go say hi to the Plaza gang." They said goodbye to those around them and made their way to the end of the bar. Ariel was greeted by her hotel friends, and she introduced them to her roommate, Rachel, and friend, Tori. "Say, wasn't Ed here just a minute ago?" Ariel asked.

"Yeah, he said he had to get going. You just missed him," one of the servers explained. Ariel provided introductions and Rachel and Tori blended in with the hotel company. Tori whispered to Rachel. "That Ed guy who left, he was the one I had hoped to meet."

"Really? Yeah, I guess he is kind of cute and get this, he is in the FBI training program."

"Oh that sounds rather intriguing. I'd like to ask him about it sometime!" Tori couldn't conceal that she was impressed and hoped to learn more about Ed.

By the time The Cove was shutting down and patrons were clearing from tables and the bar, Ariel had temporarily forgotten the Ross/Ed incident. The girls had made some new friends and had enjoyed their social outing. In their opinion, it was a successful Friday night out on the town. They concluded that for those who embrace the opportunities, there were an abundance of venues, a variety of people, and enough creativity on any given weekend to carve out any number of exciting new scenarios for themselves. They left The Cove laughing and talking, and headed for home in the cold winter night.

At 1:00 a.m. sharp, a white cargo van slowly navigated into position at the loading dock of the Capitol Plaza Hotel. The driver was punctual. He flipped a cigarette butt out the window and sparks danced on the gravel below. His eyes traveled to the rear-view mirror, and he provided complete focus on the two men he trusted with his delivery. He watched their subtle hand movements as they maneuvered him into position against the retaining wall of the dock. Other than the red brake lights of the van, it was relatively dark. The motion-sensor lights of the dock had been disabled and the closest overhead parking lot light was too far away to provide much illumination.

The two waiting men quickly went to work unloading eight two-foot by three-foot white boxes stamped Capitol Plaza Hotel—Security onto a cart, which was quickly whisked to the back storage area and dropped into a secret, specially built storage room under the brick floor. There were no words exchanged between the driver and the two men who extracted the boxes. The van quickly departed. The delivery had taken less than five minutes. "This whole operation has worked out better than we predicted," gloated one. "Yep, life is good, man. Can you believe it?" remarked the other. They punched each other on the arm and reveled in their secret, successful venture.

---

17 – Jake Departs for L.A.

I t was mid-January on Saturday morning when Ariel met Jake as he packed his belongings including a baby grand piano, a collection of expensive art work, furniture, clothes, and a beloved dog to head for anonymity in sunny California. Ariel and Jake had not spoken since the morning at the hotel when he confronted her over the hair fiasco, but because she wanted to reclaim some personal odds and ends, she decided it was now or never.

As she pulled up on the side of the street, Jake was in his comfortable mode of operation, barking orders to his friend struggling under the burden of a heavy box and to his mother gingerly negotiating the steps off the front porch. Her scuffed, flat shoes cautiously searched for the next level down, an ornate hand-carved mirror gripped tightly in her hands. Heaven forbid she slip and damage one of his prized possessions. The sight of her reflection—tight lips, clenched jaw, and concentrated focus—angled into view as she maneuvered down the concrete steps. Ariel realized in that instant just how much she cared for her son, despite any kind of trouble he may be in or what derogatory comments he may have ever said to her. She was a mother with a golden heart, silver hair, and a soft voice. She was a dutiful woman. Many times it seemed she was walking on eggshells, but loving it. As Ariel continued to observe the scene, the realization hit her that another chapter was truly closing on her life. A scrambled feeling of melancholy and relief washed over her.

As Ariel walked up the sidewalk, Jake bellowed out a pleasant hello. Despite his authoritative, commanding orders, he was actually in a cheerful state of mind. It was apparently exciting for him to think of leaving the cold behind and re-situating himself in the land of sunshine, far away from his troubles. Icicles were drip, drip, dripping off the roof of the porch and chunks of wet ice had built up beneath the overhang. The air was crisp, the sky was bright, and the park on the backside of the property was patch worked in worn-out snow. Trails and tracks crisscrossed the rolling hillside. A sturdy row of evergreens provided a soft backdrop against the overly bright landscape. It was actually a beautiful day for January.

Fable, the fluffy dog that Ariel had come to love, bounded out to greet her as she arrived. She bent down to give him a hug as he jumped up to lick her face. A lump collected in her throat, and salt stung her eyes. Thinking of never seeing her furry friend again was harder than she imagined. Jake, on the other hand, would be easier to live without.

"Your things are in a box on the porch. I've got all my stuff loaded and I'll be out of here in less than an hour," Jake marveled. Ariel said a quick hello to Jake's mom and hoisted her box off the porch floor. A glimpse through the window confirmed that the inside was bare and he really would be moving on.

Just as she turned to maneuver down the steps, Jake was there in front of her pulling the box out of her hands. "Here, the least I can do is give you a hand." He effortlessly bounded down the steps toward her car, and she followed. Balancing the box in one hand and opening the back car door with the other, he placed her few belongings in the back seat.

They stood facing each other, an odd silence between them. Finally, Ariel managed to say something. "Well, I wish you luck in L.A. and I hope you get everything sorted out. We've had some great times together." Jake looked deeply into her eyes and slowly shook his head in agreement. She went on to tell him about the concierge job that she landed after the banquet season ended. "I really am enjoying the hotel, and the concierge position is going to be perfect for me," she said.

Something about his deep penetrating look seemed mysterious and incongruent, which made Ariel shiver despite the sunshine. His gaze seemed to contain volumes of contradictory emotions, and it wasn't clear what was really churning through his mind. "Hey, it's not like we'll never see each other again," he suddenly exclaimed.

"That's right, Jake. I'm sure you'll be back to visit your family sometime, and maybe our paths will cross. You know where to find me. Take care of yourself."

"You too, darlin," his voice trailed off as she slipped behind the wheel. She would be late for work at the hotel if she didn't get going.

As she pulled away, she watched the sight in the rear-view mirror trail off. She wound through the back streets of Des Moines heading west toward the freeway, deep in thought.

---

18 – The Latest Hotel Incident

At the hotel, Troy and Malcolm were busy checking-in one of the most dreaded convention groups—the Axelrod Revolution. It was a group of tough, leather-clad women who were demanding and clueless about hotel etiquette. The phones were ringing and the rough hoard at the front wasn't patient or understanding. *Why in the world do the sales people book these radical groups,* Troy thought. *They're nothing but a pain in the ass for everyone starting with the front desk at check-in and ending with the front desk at check-out.* Dina was probably hiding out. Troy checked his watch. She'd soon be out of here and Ariel might have to deal with the brunt of this group's chaos, he figured.

Ariel arrived and was settling in behind the big desk. It would be a few more days before she felt completely comfortable, but at least she had her first solo night out of the way. She glanced toward the mob of women at the front. Troy and Malcolm looked a little frazzled. Should she be nervous? Fortunately, as the women got their room assignments, they trailed by her desk with suitcases in tow and didn't give her a sideways glance. They were dressed in jeans and black leather. They clearly tortured the English language as they exchanged loud banter between themselves.

After the stormy wave of women passed, it was a rather calm and quiet Saturday afternoon aside from guests trickling in at sporadic intervals. Ariel worked at the computer, stocked the closet, and organized her desk drawer. As she sat observing the open atrium, flashes of the seemingly secret exchange between Mr. Barbaria and Ed the previous night resurfaced in her mind. Something just didn't compute.

Ariel was an intuitive person by nature. As a youngster, she was an avid reader of the Nancy Drew series, loved mysteries, and more recently, was into true crime novels. The human psyche fascinated her—people's actions and words sometimes diverged, but Ariel believed that at the core, the human species was characterized by a pure and wholesome spirit. Occasionally outside negative influences tugged at a person's good intentions to temporarily sidetrack their benevolent rationale, but overall they remained trustworthy and kind. On the flip side, a very small percent of the population were classified as true psychopathic deviants. Locked in a state of evil manipulation, veiled by periodic false positive endeavors, they were true chameleons awash in the art of deception and capable of things beyond imagination.

With a bachelor of arts degree in psychology, she had the intention of completing post-graduate work to practice clinical psychology, but schooling had been put on the back burner, postponing opportunities in her field of passion. For now, she felt the hotel was the perfect place to be, and the latest hotel happenings had definitely piqued her interest despite a bit of fear about the unknown.

As she sat at the computer typing an e-mail for the kitchen regarding a request for a room delivery she was organizing, her thoughts were suddenly interrupted. "Reece Rhetlock" a soft, peppy male voice delivered unto her.

"What?" she turned to see Troy standing there grinning from ear to ear.

"You know, Mr. Blackstone's replacement. His name is Reece; he was transferred here from Austin, Texas, and is recently divorced."

Ariel covered her ears. "Remember I don't care about meeting anyone new or hearing about single men. The last thing I need is to get tangled up with anyone, especially if they've been through a recent divorce."

"I just thought you'd be interested to know the latest and greatest," Troy said as he cocked his head to the side for emphasis.

"Nice to know, thanks for the newsflash; now I have to get this done." Ariel turned back to the computer and continued typing.

"How about joining me for break later?" Troy questioned with a hopeful tone.

"Sure, why not, around 5:30 sounds good if I'm not too busy."

"Okay, doll, it's a date." Troy did a little dance shuffle as he edged backwards toward the front desk to resume his post. Ariel just shook her head and laughed at his antics.

Early afternoon had been pleasantly slow, and it seemed it would continue that way for awhile, so Ariel decided to take the opportunity to observe other departments in action and roam through the hotel. She swung by the main hotel entrance to exchange small talk with her grandfatherly co-worker, Howard. He was happy to banter and have some light-hearted company for a bit. After bidding him farewell, she was off to the back kitchen to confirm the order she had submitted for later that evening.

She chatted with the kitchen and wait staff with whom she had previously worked in banquet services. They were happy to multi-task, lacing lively conversation with their prep-work.

Ariel could honestly say she didn't miss that laborious and stressful job even though the energy level was high and the company was great fun. She diverted from the kitchen into the back hallway and continued her leisurely tour. Past the Convention Services office she cruised, and with a furtive glance, she saw Reece Rhetlock doing paperwork, his head bent low. A strong energy emanated from his presence even through the glass window. He didn't see her glide past and apparently didn't sense her eyes lock onto his profile.

Further down the hallway, Randy came into view sitting in the Security Office. *He is an interesting dude,* thought Ariel. His indolent nature seemed at odds with the other security staff, and he was never overly engaged in his work. It usually looked like he was just killing time. Ariel smiled and waved at him as she rounded the corner. He habitually lifted a forefinger and was otherwise expressionless aside from offering a lazy, crooked smile.

Just as she was ready to pass through the doors to the south side hallway, Ariel was nearly bowled over by Slade Sobronski who burst through the doors in a panic, gray uniform wrinkled, sweat stains visible under his arm pits. "Damn it, Larry," he barked into his cell phone. "We have a code brown. Grab the plunger and mop and bust a move over to the front men's restroom; it's a beast of a mess." The Phantom Shitter had struck again.

Ariel could hear Larry through Slade's cell groan in agony. "Why me?"

"Cause it's your lucky day," quipped Slade as he hit the red disconnect button on his phone.

Ariel grimaced and shook her head. "Fun stuff," she said to him with a chuckle.

"Crazy assholes put this plumbing to the test. I swear there is something other than a human using the toilets around here." With a look of disgust, he strode off toward Security to share the latest with Randy. Security was a good stop-off for hotel story exchanges.

Off the south hallway, not too far from the Security Office and Housekeeping, were private doors that led to the Engineering Room. This was Slade and Larry's domain. They excelled at keeping the hotel running in prime shape and they were proud of it. The only two in gray uniform, they actually looked like they could be related with their dishwater brown hair and the same muscular build with visible signs under their fingernails that they worked with their hands. Ariel thought gray was a fitting color based on the type of work they did. They both dealt in manual labor but were also sophisticated in maintenance technology.

As she entered the Atrium area, Ariel was startled to see a uniformed police officer at the front desk talking with Troy and Malcolm. *Hmm, probably just one of the regulars stopping in for a friendly visit,* she thought. She eyed the front desk with curiosity, but stopped at the concierge desk to check messages and provide a presence for visitors since she had been away for a few minutes. It was hard not to study the trio in what appeared to be serious conversation. Troy's brow was knit in a furrow, and she knew his facial expressions well enough by now to feel concerned. Malcolm, too, was somber and answering questions asked by the police officer.

Soon, Troy and Malcolm were coming out of the office behind the front desk and ushered the officer toward the elevators just past her desk. As they walked by, Troy shot her a hardened look with eyes narrowed and shook his head as if in disbelief. Ariel returned an inquisitive look trying to understand what was going on. She knew Troy would fill her in later, but this didn't seem good. She wondered why Hotel Security wasn't involved, but this apparently required a more sophisticated investigation. Barely had she finished her thoughts when up strode Randy toward the group as they stepped onto the elevator. Randy was probably the least competent security guard they had on the premises, so she was pretty sure he wouldn't add much value, but at the very least he was following protocol.

As Ariel was trying to wrap her head around the latest possible hotel incident, she looked up to find a hotel guest stopping by in need of some information. She quickly composed herself to offer assistance. The last thing that anyone in the hotel needed to know was that there was something involving police work going on under their roof. It was a good policy to keep police investigations on the down-low. Panic in the hotel needed to be avoided at all costs.

As the guest thanked Ariel for her information and turned to leave, who should appear but Ross Barbaria. He was composed, sharply dressed, and requesting her assistance. He held a box in his arms. She recalled Dina mentioning that she frequently helped Ross and was more than glad to! He was a successful businessman, and he needed her help with mailings for his health supply company. Mr. Barbaria nodded his head, smiled, and said, "Good afternoon."

"Well, hello, Mr. Barbaria, what can I do for you today? I'd be more than happy to help," Ariel responded in her warm, friendly manner.

He set a very large box on the desk and said he would return with one more of the same. It was filled with smaller packages. On top was a sheet with a list of names and addresses to where he wanted his items shipped. "Will you please just type, print, and affix the labels and be sure they are shipped first class, today?" This past week he had held a couple of seminars in the hotel, so he explained the need to ship some small supplies and brochures that had been requested by the attendees. "Do you think you can have this ready in an hour? I'll check back to review the list and labels. I promise I'll make it worth your time."

"That's what I'm here for. I'll make sure everything is ready when you return." Ariel got busy at the computer. She was going to have to work in overdrive to prepare the sixty-some mailing labels in an hour. It was interesting to see the addresses, many going to sites in the Chicago area, East Coast, Atlanta, Texas, and Florida.

Promptly at 3:15 p.m., Ross returned to Ariel's desk to check the progress of the assignment he'd given to the concierge on which he depended. Thankfully, she was down to the last three labels for the last three packages, and she quickly finished. He perused the list of names now flagged with the checkmarks Ariel had made while affixing labels to ensure she hadn't missed any. He was satisfied with the results as he rechecked the list against the mailing labels. The last mail pickup at the hotel was at 4:00 p.m. They had made their deadline. He smiled and laid a fifty dollar bill on the desk. Ariel was a bit shocked but thrilled.

Ariel had been so busy with the project Mr. Barbaria had given her that she was behind on some check-in calls. She also needed to make some deliveries to rooms she had promised guests as they stopped by. Sticky notes stuck to her computer served to remind her. She hustled to the front desk for key cards. Troy was busy with new check-ins, but Malcolm had a second to get her the cards to the rooms she needed. She and Troy had planned to meet for break at 5:30 if they could get away. Hopefully, there would be a chance for them to spend time over a quick bite, and she could learn why in the hell the police had been at the hotel earlier.

- - -

19 – Paranoia

Fortunately, 5:30 offered an opportunity for a quick run to the break room. Troy flew out of the office door, and Ariel moved out from behind the desk when she saw him. He grabbed her arm, almost for support as much as to get her to hurry along. He briefly and quickly explained that the police were searching for a missing woman. She checked in Wednesday night and was set to depart Friday morning.

"Are you kidding me?" Ariel responded, eyes round with disbelief.

"No, I'm not kidding you, I swear. I'll tell you the full details in a minute, although maybe we should find a spot other than the break room so the other employees don't hear about it. We need to keep this quiet as long as possible. No need to alarm everyone, but it will probably be out in the media soon enough."

The break room was beginning to get busy. The two friends grabbed plates and filled them with food from the chafing pans and slipped into a corner of one of the quiet unoccupied ballrooms. "Did you say the woman had checked in Wednesday night? That's the night I started training," realized Ariel. "What room was she in?"

"It was the ninth floor—901—right below the Presidential Suite. It's not clear when exactly she disappeared, but Malcolm took a call yesterday and confirmed our records, which showed she had checked out Friday. He didn't think much about it since the receipt, which is customarily slipped under the door for fast and convenient checkout, was gone, as were her belongings. She had not used the hotel shuttle, but rather had arrived by taxi. One would only assume she departed with her things the same way. It was her family from California who called because they expected her to be home late Friday."

Ariel was riveted on Troy's delivery, watching, eyes wide, taking in the latest hotel mystery. She leaned in, elbows bent and on the table with her thumbnails resting between her teeth. Troy shook his head and declared that something must have happened to her on her travel across town after she had left the hotel, or at one of the airports, or even after she reached her final destination in California.

"So what did room 901 look like when you guys took the police up?"

Troy recapped what he learned earlier. "Totally normal, but of course the maids had cleaned it. The officer interviewed the maid who serviced the room, and she told him from what she could recall, it was fairly clean—no trash, the bed had been slept in. The woman obviously hadn't left in a hurry, and there were no telltale signs that anything had happened in that room. The officer took notes, looked around, and that was it. He said he was off to interview the taxi company."

"Thank God there wasn't a body!" Ariel shuddered to think about the possibilities. "You know, Troy, I have to confess that all of a sudden, this hotel makes me nervous. There have been some strange happenings around here just since I started. Has it always been so weird? Even the day I came for my interview, when I went into the women's restroom near the elevators, I felt such a strange sensation like someone was watching. I don't use that bathroom unless I see other women going in. I don't like being in there alone."

"Well, no, the police have been here twice in the last two months, but to be honest, I don't recall anything before this."

"I sure hope I don't get paranoid. I have enough trouble on the top floors with heights. I don't need to become afraid of my own shadow, too."

"Gosh, we better eat and get back up front," Ariel prodded them along as she pointed toward Troy's wrist at the big watch face. The long hand was crawling toward 6:00 p.m. Breaks always went fast especially when there was news to discuss. They quickly finished, dropped their plates off in the kitchen, and hustled to the front to finish their evening shift.

Ariel remained busy with guests, e-mails, and typing. Deliveries to rooms were especially nerve-racking. As she dropped off requested items, she half expected an ogre to open the door, but every time there was a smiling, friendly face of a gracious traveler who thanked her for her services. She couldn't help but wonder what happened to the gal in 901. Where was she?

By 10:30 p.m., Ariel was tidying up the desk and organizing the closet, ready to get home and tell Rachel of the latest. So far, nothing had been reported on the news about a disappearance. Rachel's cell phone went straight to voicemail when she first tried, but thankfully after a repeated attempt, Rachel answered. "Hey, where are you?" Noisy conversation and music could be heard in the background.

"I'm downtown on Court Avenue with Steve and some of his friends. Are you done with work?"

"Yeah, I'll be out of here in another fifteen minutes or so. I was hoping you'd be home. I'm really tired but need to talk."

"Are you okay?" Rachel's voice expressed concerned. Ariel could barely hear her above the phone background noise.

"I'm fine. I'll see you when you get home—I'll be up."

Ariel was glad it was her week for the garage, and as she pulled into the driveway on Plum Tree Lane, she watched carefully in the rear-view mirror to be sure she hadn't been followed. There was a warm, soft glow in the front window to greet her. She and Rachel always kept a lamp on at night when they left their duplex. Once inside the hall entry, Ariel locked the door behind her. Only after flipping on light switches everywhere and checking the back patio door and front door to ensure they were secure, did she finally relax. *It would be nice to have a dog,* she thought wishfully. She got out of her work suit, put on pajamas, and removed her makeup. She made a bowl of popcorn, turned on the TV, and settled into the comfy couch.

Finally the faint grinding sound of the garage door being raised caught Ariel's ear. Rachel had arrived home. They both carried remotes and used the garage entry regardless of whose turn it was to park in the garage. Rachel was pounding at the door to the hallway that was normally never locked. Ariel jumped up to let her friend in. "Gee, do you have enough lights on?" she quipped as she came in pulling off her coat. "I could see our place all the way down the street, lit up like a Christmas tree!"

"Oh, hi, I'm so glad you're home," Ariel tried to sound nonchalant. "How was your evening with Steve?"

"It was good. What in the world is going on?" Rachel demanded to know.

Ariel explained what she had gathered from Troy earlier that evening. "I am starting to get edgy with the stuff going on at the hotel."

"Well, I can't say I blame you. Some bizarre things have

happened, but aren't there a lot of great people who work there?"

"Sure, but the thing is, you can never be certain of whom to trust. How do I know if someone at the hotel is involved in something shady, or if people staying there are up to no good? At any given time, there could be a deranged psychopath lurking around. You have to admit, the things that have happened since I started working there are beyond bizarre. You know, I guess I trust Troy more than anyone right now. I'm glad we've become good friends. We share a lot. But heck, for all I know, he could be hiding something."

"Oh, Ariel, that woman will surely turn up. There's probably just been a misunderstanding, and she is with friends or family and just skipped out on work." Rachel responded with her usual positive outlook. She picked up the popcorn bowl, stirred it around, selected prime kernels and then popped them into her mouth. Ariel watched her friend pick at the white fluffy stuff. She let out a big yawn. They continued talking while Rachel shut off the lights that were blazing both inside and out. Finally, they were both ready to turn in for the night.

Shortly after 1:00 a.m., Ariel's head hit the pillow, and her exhausted body was grateful. Yet slumber did not find her until almost an hour later. Eventually, sleep did overcome her, but it did not bring peace and tranquility; rather, tormenting and foggy images swirled in her head. She was at the hotel, strangely filled with trees and thick underbrush—a dark forest. The waterfall was pouring out of the top floor that looked like a wall of rocks, pounding water down around her feet. There was a slight clearing around the pool of water, and a large tree loomed above her, but rather than branches, distorted haunting faces ebbed and flowed in and out of focus among the leaves. Jake was mocking her. Shawn and Ed in their blue security uniforms were laughing as though they shared some kind of joke that was on her. Handsome Ross Barbaria's expression seemed to hold a guarded secret. Mr. Blackstone's face and thick neck bobbed out from behind branches, and he looked disheveled and frazzled, waving his hands about him. Slade and Larry, the guys in gray, were ducking behind the limbs and leaves trying to remain hidden while working with some type of tool on a covert operation. Troy was at Ariel's side, but he was small—only about four feet tall, and he had a tiny voice. He was pulling her away from the tree of faces saying, "Come on. Come on, before they get you." A lock of dark hair sparkling with diamonds dangled from his back pocket. It reminded her of a lucky rabbit's foot.

Ariel's cotton nightgown was twisted around her body. She had been turning and twirling, around and around, like a rotisserie chicken, hot on the grill. She was covered in sweat and suddenly as the tree branch faces began to bend toward her, she awoke with a startled gasp. She pulled herself upright and tried to calm her heavy breathing. Oh, thank God it was only a dream. She straightened her nightgown and reached for the water glass on her night stand. As her breathing calmed and the familiar surroundings of her dark room came into focus, she forced her mind to return to the details of the dream before they faded away and were lost. How bizarre. Ironically, she could see how the dream might represent deep-seated feelings of the people she had come to know, and of Jake, who she felt like she should know, but didn't. Paranoia was setting in. Who could she really trust anymore?

- - -

20 – Reece

As her routine race from downtown to the hotel and the transformation from business woman to concierge became more comfortable, Ariel decided a pattern was emerging. She noticed on more than one occasion as she hurried down the back hall to change her clothes for the evening, there was Reece Rhetlock emerging from his office as she neared. He always had a smile and nice hello for her. He would head down the hall toward the Security Office and by the time she had changed and passed by the time clock to check in, he was finishing up a conversation with one of the security guys and again offering a comment. "Have a nice evening," he'd say, or "enjoy yourself," some pleasantry to let her know he was there. He had a presence about him that was confident, friendly and sincere.

During visits to the employee break room, Ariel observed the genuine easygoing manner he had with employees. She could tell they respected him. One night after a banquet, there were a few leftover meals. Reece offered her one, and she accepted. The food was definitely a notch up from the basic food served in the break room. Ariel took him up on the offer and thought it was a nice gesture. Other than small talk, there was little interaction, and Ariel deemed Reece a nice acquaintance.

Eventually, Reece would find reasons to swing by the concierge desk and offer small talk or tell a joke. If Troy happened to notice, he would look Ariel's way and give her an ornery signal of some sort that made her want to strangle him. Sometimes it was a gesture of his forefinger toward Reece and his thumb back at himself while he mouthed the words 'he's mine.' He would then grin broadly. She knew he was teasing and she would just roll her eyes and shake her head.

Finally, after a couple of such antics, enough was enough, and she decided to get even. One evening, as Reece stopped briefly by her desk, Ariel saw Troy's wide smile and gestures out of the corner of her eyes. "Reece, you know Troy, the Front Desk Manager, don't you? Did you know he has a thing for you? He's watching you now."

Reece turned his head and broad shoulders toward the desk and Ariel could see a red flush break through Troy's tan as he realized what Ariel must have said. Reece just responded with a hearty laugh. "I can't say he's my type."

"No, I didn't think so. I'll have to break the bad news to him." Ariel laughed along.

"Say, I was wondering if you would mind typing this handwritten memo for me. It's to my staff, and I have to admit, I'm not much of a typist—more of a hunt-and-peck kind of guy on the keyboard."

Ariel looked at the scrawled words on the sheet of paper. She squinted as she tried to make out the writing. "I'm afraid you're not much for handwriting either." She read through the note and needed help deciphering a few of the words. As she pointed at the ones with which she needed his assistance, Reece stepped around the desk and leaned in to provide input. Heck, even he stumbled over some of the words he had written. As he leaned closer to her, Ariel smelled a wonderful, clean, manly aroma. His cologne smelled fresh with a hint of the ocean breeze. Her mind conjured up an image of him on a white sandy beach in colorful swim trunks with a tan and muscled upper body, with the sun, wind, and surf all around. Suddenly, he spoke and jarred her out of her thoughts. "I think it would be best if I just read it to you as you type."

"That sounds like a good idea."

Reece stood behind Ariel, enjoying the bouquet of her fragrant hair and the sweet perfume that drifted into his nostrils. His strong voice delivered the message as her fingers flew over the keyboard.

"Wow, that didn't take long—a team effort. You are really good at typing. This would have taken me awhile." Ariel was pleased to have assisted him, and Reece was glad he had asked. He touched her softly on the shoulder. "Thanks a lot, I really appreciate it." He stepped out from behind the desk and the fresh smell of cologne wafted in the air as he moved away. Upon rounding the desk, he hesitated and lingered.

He gazed at her and then casually asked, "Do you ever go to The Cove after work?"

"Sure, I've been there a few times, but usually only on the weekends since I have to get up early during the week. It's a great spot. And you?"

"Yeah, in the four weeks since I arrived, I've stopped in after work quite a bit. I don't know anyone in this town except people here at the hotel, so it's another place I feel welcome. I'm sure not used to this winter weather. Compared to Texas, it's like the arctic."

"You're lucky you missed the blizzard we had in December. People were literally stranded in the hotel over night," Ariel recollected and shared highlights of that infamous night for him.

"Are you serious? I've never experienced a blizzard." He was intrigued. "That sounds like a crazy ordeal but it seems like a fun place to have been trapped for awhile, especially with good company." He arched an eyebrow and smiled. "So, what about stopping by The Cove for a bit tonight?"

Ariel pondered the offer and decided it wouldn't hurt to stop and chat with everyone. "Okay, I'll stop for just a bit but I can't stay late tonight."

He smiled. "I'll see you there, then, a little after ten."

It had been a quiet evening in the banquet area that Thursday night. The end of January saw nowhere near the volumes of the previous month of December, although the weekend nights were beginning to pick up again. Reece checked back with his banquet staff to ensure they were shifting gears to close out the evening and get rooms set for the following morning. He was looking forward to time with Ariel after work tonight.

Shortly after 10 p.m., Ariel entered The Cove and shook off the chill from the cold January night. She removed her black gloves and rubbed her hands. Glancing down the bar, she immediately spotted a group of co-workers who had taken over the back section of the establishment. Reece was circled by some of his banquet staff and all eyes were fixated on him as he was finishing a humorous story. Laughter ensued. Sean and Ed were sitting at another high top table close by, the elbows of their navy jackets almost touching, with drinks in hand. Slade, the chief engineer, was beside them hoisting a beer to his thirsty lips. Bud-lite and some of the kitchen staff had also recently arrived and were settling in around the Plaza assemblage. Ariel approached the group and greeted them with a warm hello.

When Reece realized she was there, his eyes locked in on hers, and he quickly stepped to assist her with her coat and welcome her to the group. "Hey, thanks for stopping by. Do you want a drink?" he inquired.

"Hot chocolate sounds good tonight."

"Done," he said as he flagged down the bartender. In no time flat, she had a warm, steaming mug of hot chocolate with whipped cream on top between her hands. Individual conversations started up, and Ariel turned to face Reece. His colorful tie was loosened and his once starched white shirt showed signs of wrinkle from the wear and tear of the workday, but he still looked sharp, and he still smelled like the ocean breeze. His sport jacket, which was the extent of his winter coat, hung on the back of his chair.

Reece engaged Ariel in light conversation. *Gosh, he was easy to talk to,* thought Ariel. He asked pleasant questions and listened intently as she shared little pieces of innocent information about herself. Ariel was a guarded person and didn't believe in revealing too much information too soon to someone new. Her philosophy matched that of whoever said, "Establishing friendships is like peeling down the layers of an artichoke; it takes time to get to the core."

As Ariel asked questions of him, he willingly and openly responded to her not-too-invasive inquisition. "So how did you decide to leave the warmth of Austin for this cold and snowy destination?"

"Well, I worked for a hotel down there that is under the same parent company as the Capitol Plaza, and this was a good opportunity that opened up for me. I like to explore new places and had never been to Iowa."

"So what do you think so far? Do you like the Plaza, and are you glad you gave it a try?"

"So far, it's been great, but I have to say, I underestimated how much snow there would be."

"Yeah, it's been an unusually cold and snowy winter this year. We just need to wrap up January and get through February. Even in March, we typically get hit with one big snowstorm, and sometimes there are ice storms in the spring, but I like the seasons. We get the variety in the Midwest. They say in Iowa that if you don't like the weather one day, not to worry, cause it will change."

"You know, I like the people here. They are really friendly and helpful. Austin is a friendly city, too, and has lots of entertainment options and is a great music venue. I'm looking forward to exploring Des Moines when I get a chance, if only I didn't work so much!"

"You do work long hours," Ariel agreed, and sipped on the warm hot chocolate as she gazed into Reece's kind blue eyes. "Well, this town has lots of great districts and establishments for eating and shopping. One thing you'll have to experience for sure this summer is the State Fair. It has been described as the Eighth Wonder of the World. You can experience every kind of food imaginable on a stick and there is entertainment galore, not to mention the best people-watching anywhere."

"Hmm, that sounds quite interesting. 'Eighth Wonder of the World,' huh, I'll have to see about that!" He smiled and changed subjects. "Are you from Des Moines?"

"No, I grew up on a farm in Southeast Iowa and landed here after college."

"Really, I would have pegged you as a city girl, but that is pretty neat that you grew up on a farm."

"Yep, I can drive a tractor and round up cattle on a horse like a true cowgirl. I have great childhood memories, but enjoy the city life now." Reece nodded in appreciation of her surprisingly diverse abilities.

Time passed quickly sitting there with Reece and other familiar faces. Although she knew everyone around the tables, they were mainly work acquaintances rather than close friends. Jessica, whom she had grown close with during the banquet season, had departed once the season ended. It would have been nice to have her there, too.

Conversation came easy for a group of people who shared a commonality, and so they fondly swapped hotel stories and shared jokes. It was comforting to forget the past bizarre events in the midst of laughter and the warm ambience that surrounded them.

Although her intentions were to stop for a few minutes to say hello, Ariel was shocked to see it was approaching eleven. "I've got to get going. It's late for me," she announced to the table suddenly, but more to Reece than anyone. She stood, and he followed suit. He retrieved her coat from a nearby chair and held it so she could slip into the sleeves. "Thanks for suggesting I stop by and thanks for the hot chocolate. It was nice hanging out with everyone. I'll see you tomorrow night." She waved toward the table and turned to go. Reece couldn't help but trail her out of eyesight.

On the drive home, Ariel considered how fortunate it was to have new friends in her life. She felt relaxed and comfortable, quite the opposite of last Saturday when she was overly emotional and paranoia had completely overcome her. Everyone tonight had such an innocuous appearance about them and the hotel was truly a nice place to work. *Hmm, I wonder if Reece has anything to do with my mood,* she conjectured. After Jake, she was convinced that dating was not for her, and she really believed it. Her heart had been trampled too many times until finally, it felt like a meat cleaver had hammered on it. Nothing ever worked out, and even though she had an open mind and had dated a diverse range of men, it was not meant to be. Everything happens for a reason, she reminded herself. She vowed to not get involved with anyone although there would always be room for new friendships, and that was the category in which she placed Reece—a new friend.

---

21 – Reece and Ariel

The following night after work began as a mirror image to the previous evening, aside from commencing an hour later. There at The Cove, surrounded by the Plaza crew, sat Reece and Ariel side by side consumed by each other's conversation and enjoying a blossoming friendship. Tonight Ariel could care less what time it was. Tomorrow was Saturday!

In Ariel's opinion, Reece was a brilliant mix of a man. He was a great conversationalist and very social. She could see others warmed to him easily. He had the strong, rugged, manly qualities that made her feel safe, yet there was tenderness in his heart that allowed her to feel safe in a non-physical way. They shared a similar sense of humor and easily conversed about many topics. It was comfortable to be in his presence and easy to remain in the moment. The past didn't matter. The future didn't matter. She sipped on her red wine and felt at peace.

Little by little, their group dissipated. Before they realized it, their friends had all headed for different destinations, and it was just the two of them remaining at the table that previously was surrounded with energy and lively dialogue. The Cove was still in full swing so they stayed awhile longer.

They carried on their flirtatious conversation and leaned in closer to one another, tuning out the world around them. Reece's hand brushed Ariel's thigh. It was electric. Ariel enjoyed the sensation then drew away, bringing the surroundings into her focus once again. It was beginning to thin out around closing time.

"Gee, everyone is about gone from here." Despite the sensual rush from a few seconds ago, Ariel stifled a yawn. She was sure Reece didn't think she was bored. He was astute enough to recognize she probably wasn't used to these late night hours and suggested they call it an evening. She agreed that she'd had a very full day and was ready to wind down.

"Thanks for the company," she said.

"The pleasure was all mine," returned Reece as he gazed at her soft brown eyes. "You working tomorrow?" he inquired.

"Yep, I'll be in at three, my usual time on Saturday. And you?"

"I'll be there ready to go at seven in the morning. I like to get there before any of my staff and go over upcoming events for the day. There is never a shortage of things to do, and business is starting to pick up now that we got through the first few weeks of January. Ariel gasped, "Oh goodness, by the time you get to bed, you'll only get a few hours of sleep. I'm sorry I kept you out late."

"No worry on my part," he said with sincerity. "I enjoyed tonight. Hey, what would you think if we actually plan some time together?" He pulled on his loosened tie and inhaled a deep breath anticipating her response.

"Well . . ." Ariel drew out the word. "What do you have in mind?"

"I . . . I don't know exactly. I mean, meeting here is nice, but it might be fun to try a new place."

"I'll tell you what," she suggested. "Why don't you join me and my roommate at our duplex tomorrow night when you get done at the hotel?" Rachel would enjoy the company unless she already has other plans; either way, how about my place?"

"Okay, thanks, that sounds like a deal," Reece responded with enthusiasm. He helped her with her coat, and they headed for the cold snowy night.

At her car, they parted ways. Reece had already started his car with his remote starter—the air was set to warm to beat the nasty cold. How different than in Texas where the switch was always set to cool to beat the sweltering heat. He slid into the driver's seat and watched to make sure she got going without any trouble. He should have let her wait in his car until hers warmed, but she was dressed for the cold with her coat, gloves, and wool scarf. He instinctively felt she was an independent woman who liked taking care of herself.

During the short drive home, Ariel's thoughts swirled with happy reflections of the evening and then tentative doubts. *Should she have invited him to her place? She'd better be sure that Rachel was there tomorrow night!* She actually couldn't wait for tomorrow night to arrive. *Oh dear, what is happening? Next week, I'll play it low key and take a break from Reece*, she decided. *But he was different than other guys and men she'd dated, wasn't he, or was he*? What a mess her mind was in.

- - -

22 – An Important Guest Arrives

On Saturdays, Ariel had no need to run down the back hallway to change. She arrived in uniform, ready to roll. That meant no bumping into Reece near his office upon arrival. As usual, she entered through the back employee doorway to clock in by Security, and she couldn't help but look down the long hall to see if he was there somewhere. Gosh, he had practically put in a full day already by the time she got there.

At the concierge desk, Dina was drumming white tipped fingernails of her left hand on the desk and fiddling with her necklace that nuzzled close to her cleavage with her right hand, waiting for Ariel to appear. They exchanged hellos, and Dina wasted no time in filling her in on the events for the evening, explaining that Oscar Kaufman would be checking in to the Presidential Suite any time now. "You remember me telling you about him, right? He is an important man. Meet with him right away to find out what all he needs—both immediate and for the length of his stay. Be sure to coordinate and prepare the kitchen staff, and don't let anything fall through the cracks. It's very, very important to make sure he is well taken care of," she instructed with seriousness in her voice that Ariel hadn't recalled hearing before.

"I promise I'll see that his every need is met with precision and timeliness," Ariel confirmed.

"Okay, good, then I'm outta here." She quickly packed up and was on her way as usual. Dina liked working the early shift to keep her weekend nights free and fortunately for Ariel, she enjoyed the later shift.

As she got busy behind the desk, she kept an eye out for Mr. Kaufman to show. She had never met him before, but had an image in her mind—probably middle-aged, tall and thin, well-groomed with neatly trimmed hair. She had instructed Troy and Malcolm to give her a signal when he arrived. It wasn't long before she saw Malcolm flag her with a forefinger, inconspicuous to the new guest at the front. Troy was professionally greeting and checking in a man totally unlike what Ariel had envisioned. The only thing she had pegged was that he was tall, but rather than thin, he was beefy and looked about ten years younger than she imagined. He wore black cowboy boots and a black western-style trench coat. The tufts of hair peeking out from under his black cowboy hat were white as snow. Around his pouty lips a white handlebar mustache hung, and a small goatee rested on his chin. Good grief, he looked like a western Santa Claus. In his hand was a leather briefcase, and behind him stood a bellman with a cart full of luggage. The bellman might as well have been an elf, and the cart of luggage a sleigh full of toys. Ariel smiled at the sight.

At the same time that Oscar Kaufman was getting settled in at the Capitol Plaza, his private corporate jet was rolling out of the hangar at the airport in Burbank, California, where the temperature was a balmy 72 degrees, and the sky was full of sunshine. The two pilots were checking their flight path and preparing for their departure to snowy Des Moines, Iowa, temperature 28 degrees. The flight would take about four hours and then another thirty minutes to get to the Capitol

Plaza for the Kaufman party and business meeting in the penthouse that night.

Oscar's five passengers were laden with sacks of goodies along with their luggage for their relaxing and enjoyable sky expedition. The pilots politely assisted them with their belongings and got them settled. The plane itself was stocked with champagne, beer, soda, snacks, and expensive chocolates, so they had plenty of decadent refreshments from which to choose during their flight. One man and four young women settled into the plush leather seats and prepared for take-off to meet Oscar in Des Moines. In no time at all, the computer monitor visible in the main cabin showed they were crossing the Nevada border heading east at the speed of 420 miles per hour. Flying in a private plane was the ultimate luxury.

Mr. Kaufman exchanged pleasantries with Troy and Malcolm as he checked in for his stay in the Presidential Suite. He had just finished speaking with his pilots who affirmed they were ready for take-off and would be arriving at the hotel around 7:00 p.m. central time. He had four hours to log on to his computer and do a bit of work and then take a nice quiet nap before his business partners and party girls arrived.

Ariel rose as Mr. Kaufman approached her desk. He politely removed his hat. She greeted and welcomed him. "Would you like me to get your room service order squared away for tonight, or shall I check with you a bit later after you're settled?"

"Now would be fine." He instructed the bellman to go ahead and deliver his luggage to his room and handed him a bill of a rather large denomination. Ariel printed a room service sheet from the computer and offered him to take a seat while she listened intently as he placed his order. The bar was stocked with the basics. Food needed to be arranged. He decided upon an assortment of appetizers, soup, salad greens, shrimp, and lobster for the main entrée, the dessert variety tray and four bottles of chilled expensive champagne.

"We'll have your appetizers and soups ready around eight," Ariel confirmed.

"That sounds perfect. I'm sure my guests will enjoy everything." He winked and thanked her as he pushed his burly body up out of the chair and replaced his hat.

As Ariel sat working at the computer behind her desk later that evening, she heard Howard's grandfatherly voice. She looked up as he rolled by, his cart piled high with Louis Vuitton luggage. Four stunningly beautiful girls, three blonds and a brunette flanked his sides.

"Hey, Howard, what's up?" Ariel called. He had a grin like the Cheshire Cat. The girls were so not from the Midwest. Despite the cold, two of them exposed their bare, long tan legs, which stretched out from short skirts and balanced keenly on expensive high-heeled shoes. The other two wore tight fitting slacks that showed tan ankles, and they also sported expensive heels. Their skin, hair, and makeup were flawless. Though they wore jackets and sweaters, it was evident that they had each met the hand of a skilled plastic surgeon whose gift ensured they were blessed with what nature had not provided.

It was hard not to stare as Howard and the girls who could easily have been models or girls from Hugh Hefner's treasure trove passed by. Howard was stealing furtive glances and attempting small talk with the beauties. They stepped into the elevator and glided heavenward.

While the elevator zipped them to the tenth floor, Ariel darted to the front desk to get the scoop from Troy. She assumed they were here to join Oscar Kaufman.

"Aren't they adorable?" Troy stated in a matter-of-fact rather than questionable tone.

"Well, they sure gave Howard a heart surge. He'll be reeling for the rest of the evening. In fact, I better go check on him to see if he needs a bag to breathe into so he doesn't hyperventilate," Ariel joked. After about fifteen minutes, Howard came swooshing down the elevator with an empty cart, still smiling.

"Gee, Howard, did you enjoy your company?" Ariel teased.

He shook his head, let out a soft whistle, and said, "Wow, you don't see that every day. You know though, Ariel, those girls don't have anything on you. You are just a more wholesome version."

"Oh, Howard, you are making me blush, but that is sweet of you to say." She gave him a pat on the back.

---

23 – Party in the Presidential Suite

Settled into the Presidential Suite, the business partners relished in their good fortune as they sat around the ornate wooden table, the plush rug underneath comforting their feet, the drinks in front of them soothing their tension, and the conversation bolstering their egos. All was going smooth and as planned. The foursome was tight-knit, and the fact that they had known each other since high school served to strengthen their bond of loyalty. Outside of their clandestine business, they rarely interacted or socialized with each other, but they kept the communication lines open and vowed to continue making money—lots of money.

"Hey, the only snag is that my ex-girlfriend is the damn concierge on duty tonight, and I have to be extra careful," voiced an irritated Jake.

"But I've got your back, buddy," piped up Ed with an air of self-confidence. "I was able to whisk you up the employee elevator, so she didn't see a thing."

Ross leaned forward and slapped both hands on the table with a puzzled look on his face. "What the hell did you just say? That gal—what's her name—Ariel, she's your ex-girl friend? What are the odds?" He threw his head back in husky laughter.

Oscar was equally surprised. He stroked his white mustache. "I met her today, a nice helpful young gal." He took a sip of his drink, careful not to dip his mustache in the glass. "Okay, okay, now, I don't see any reason to get worked up over this, but Jake now that you no longer live in this town, you better damn well have a good excuse ready for being in the hotel if she ever sees you. As usual, we will keep our classified business on the down-low except when in complete privacy. In fact, when and if we are seen chumming around together, it is as friends only. No discussion in public. As we know, it wouldn't be prudent. I think from now on, for these business purposes, we'll pick another location—somewhere exotic and warm. Hell, we can afford to go just about anywhere now." Oscar continued to pontificate. "Let's continue to be vigilant and cautious. God, we would all go down the toilet faster than a loose stool if our operations are exposed. It's imperative that we maintain good judgment to keep things tight."

What had started as a confident and cocky discussion was now cast with a shadow of reality. The fact that they were deeply involved in illegal activities was nothing to sneeze at. Their last recourse when and if anything went wrong was to rely on their hit man *Triple S* to work his magic. He had already pulled off one dirty job, because the woman learned too much and was a liability. They took no chances and didn't fool around getting rid of potential whistle-blowers.

Ross reassured Oscar and the other two how clean and precise they had been and would continue to be. "Our standard operating procedures are tight, and things are running like a well-oiled machine. Everything will be fine. In fact, I propose we discuss plans to open another hotel branch."

"Hey, let's not get too greedy," countered Ed. "That's when things can start to unravel. You know, in another year or so I'll be working for the FBI, and I'll really have some power—real power that could come in handy."

"That'll be the day," Jake said in a sour tone. "Besides, your place is here inside this hotel, running security operations."

Ed shot back. "Well for now that's true, but trust me, not forever."

Oscar slid his chair from the table and rose. "I'm with Ed. We don't want to open another operation at this time. It's too fast." Oscar edged toward the bar to make another drink. "Jake, what's your opinion?"

"Uh, I guess I have to agree with you two. Let's stay the course and put any talk of new operations on hold."

"So it sounds like I'm out-voted," Ross spoke with a bit of defeat in his voice, "but I trust you guys."

"Anyone else for a refill while I'm up?" offered Oscar. Three empty glasses were hoisted into the air. Drinks were replenished, and a toast was made. "Here's to us—to entrepreneurship and success." Glasses clinked, and smug smiles were exchanged.

"Guys, it won't be long before our dinners are delivered. Let's lighten things up for now and get ready for room service," suggested Oscar. "The only requirement is that you three take a hike to the back room when our food arrives. We don't dare let little miss concierge see you here. She might wonder what the connections are with the four of us."

While the men conversed around the table in the main living area about serious business, the California girls lounged on the sectional sofa in the master bedroom, knowing they were not privy to topics of discussion. It did not concern them, but once the meeting was over, there would be plenty of time to socialize.

Lora Lee Colter

The phone rang. Oscar answered. "Room service will be here in about twenty minutes," he announced. The girls were welcomed to the front room, and there was chatter and laughter over the music that played in the background. They lounged and milled about, drawing the drapes open to look out the window at the downtown skyline seven miles away. It was a rather quaint site for the girls who were used to the glitzy lights of L.A.

Before long, there was a tap, tap at the door. Oscar made a slashing motion across his neck with his fingers and mouthed "get the hell outta here" to the three men who he felt should not be visible for this arrival. There was no need to open up questions for the curious concierge. Ed, Jake, and Ross scrambled toward the back hall. Ed and Ross continued on to the bedroom, and Jake took a turn into the bathroom.

The room service cart full of appetizers and soups was parked outside the Presidential Suite. Ariel was there to coordinate the delivery and assisted the waiter by handing in the appetizer plates and soup bowls, so he could place them around the table. Oscar stood near the table facing the two at work.

From her position at the entrance to the suite, Ariel first noticed the twinkling lights of downtown in the distance through the large glass window. In another instant, she realized there was an additional reflection that angled into view from the back bathroom. It was like an illusion. First, pretty twinkling lights then—impossible! Ariel was sure she saw a soft outline of Jake, or was it his ghost?

She stared and felt her blood thin. She was sure the color had drained from her face. It was him. He stood facing the bathroom mirror with the door ajar as though he was listening to the conversations beyond. Ariel tried to catch her breath and finish the delivery. She looked at Oscar and managed to speak. "We'll let you enjoy your starter dishes and will be back with the salads and main entrees in about a half hour." She glanced over at the girls who were preparing to come to the table. One neared the drapes and pulled the filmy panel across the window to soften the glare. Another one dimmed the lamp lights.

Ariel looked again toward where Jake had appeared and the image was gone. She felt light headed, but managed to ask Mr. Kaufman if there were any further needs they could fulfill at the moment. She felt too silly asking him about the man in his bathroom as the idea seemed preposterous. Plus, she sure didn't want to confront Jake here and create an unusual scene. Oscar thanked them and followed them to the door.

"We'll be back soon." Ariel turned and grasped the handle of the cart to give herself some support and prevent her knees from buckling.

Returning with the salads and main entrees, Ariel was anxiously, yet covertly, looking for Jake, but there was no sighting. There were the girls and Mr. Kaufman, but oddly there was no sign of anyone else despite eight salads and eight dinner plates to deliver. Ariel did her best to create light conversation while secretly glancing to the back.

Something very fishy was going on here. She was bound and determined to figure out just what it was. Troy! He could help her sort this out.

Stepping off the elevator on the ground floor, Ariel practically ran to the front desk. Breathless, she planted her hands on the hard countertop surface and leaned in to search for Troy. Where was he? "Troy, are you back there?" she hissed in a loud whisper.

He poked his pretty head from around the corner of the back room. "What's up, Sunshine?"

"I need to know who all is checked in with Mr. Kaufman in the Presidential Suite."

"Sorry, he only lists himself as the occupant, but we know he's got the four girls staying there, too. Beyond that, I have no clue."

"Well, I have to find out! Give me a key to the room kitty-corner to the Presidential Suite," she demanded. "Is anyone in it?"

"Girl, what are you going to do?" He fidgeted and hesitated for a second. Then, his fingers tapped on the computer keyboard to check for vacancy in the room Ariel had requested. "It's open!" His voice was laced with excitement as he felt drawn into Ariel's scheme.

"Great, I'm going to set up a spy operation to see if I can catch anyone coming or going. I swear my ex-boyfriend is in that room with Mr. Kaufman, and I want to know why." She explained to Troy what she had seen. Troy was captivated and more than happy to join forces with detective Nancy Drew. He handed over the key card. "Keep an eye on my desk and call me on my cell if someone needs me," Ariel instructed. She raced off, leaving Troy with a puzzled expression across his fine facial features.

As the glass compartment gently stopped at the tenth floor, Ariel scanned the perimeter and confirmed that all was quiet. She stepped cautiously out of the elevator and hugged the wall away from the balcony as she scurried past the Presidential Suite and on to the room that would serve as her lookout post. The key card slipped neatly into the slot and she slipped discretely inside. From the room, she called room service to make sure they were on their way with the dessert tray soon, and then she positioned herself to see through the crack in the door, which was in line with the Presidential Suite. After several minutes sitting in the dark and the quiet, Ariel decided detective work was boring as she realized she could potentially wait for hours and see absolutely nothing. She blew her bangs out of her eyes with a puff of air. Maybe she was crazy.

It wasn't long before the cart rolled into view carrying desserts, the last of Mr. Kaufman's order. Ariel pressed her face closer to the crack in the door. Maybe if she wasn't with room service, the mystery guests would come forward. Yeah, what are the chances of that? She could hear voices exchanged—it was Mr. Kaufman, thanking the kid for desserts. Her ears strained to hear, but that was the extent of the conversation. The door closed, and the room service cart was being wheeled away. Damn.

The light from her cell phone lit up in the dark shadows as she pressed the button—it was 9:03. She called the front desk. "Troy, it's me. I'm going to park myself here awhile to keep watch—so far nothing! Cover my desk, but let me know if you need me." She pressed the phone off. In the darkened room, she suddenly felt vulnerable, thinking of the woman who had vanished and of Denise Brickman who had lost her beautiful long lock of hair. Neither would have had reason to suspect any danger in such a beautiful and tranquil hotel setting, yet they were targets of foul play. Although she didn't want to live in fear, the truth was, she didn't want to be naïve to the possibility that a seemingly innocuous front, such as the hotel, could hide all kinds of nefarious activity right under everyone's noses.

Oh! Ariel's stomach tightened and her heartbeat kicked up a notch as she saw two clean-cut men in their late twenties or early thirties approaching the door to Mr. Kaufman's conclave. They knocked and were immediately ushered inside. Within another ten minutes, a single man strolled by her cracked door. She flinched. Caught off guard, she tightened the crack in the door. The well-dressed, middle-aged man headed to the Presidential Suite. He must be a guest here at the hotel since he didn't come up the elevator! Soon a man and woman dressed in festive attire were knocking at the party den.

The real party had begun. *I guess this means people will be coming, but not going for awhile,* thought Ariel. I can't hang out here any longer tonight; better get back to my desk and do my job. It would be time to wrap up for the evening before long. She felt some sense of defeat that she hadn't learned more, but thankfully remembered that Reece was coming to her place after work. She could sure use a strong, soothing presence and forget about this nonsense for tonight. "Tomorrow's my day off, and I can resume my stake-out! Great idea, detective," Ariel muttered to herself.

- - -

24 – Déjà Vu and Discoveries

There was a knock at the door on Plum Tree Lane. Ariel jumped. He was here! Reece had wrapped up his work almost forty minutes later than she had finished. He labored such long hours and never complained. Ariel glanced around the place. Everything was orderly. She checked her reflection in the mirror near the front door. Her uniform had been replaced by comfortable jeans and a warm sweater. Peeking out the side window as she flipped on the front light, she met his gaze and couldn't help break out in a broad smile. He looked cold standing there in his lightweight jacket, dress shirt, and slacks, tie loosened. He carried a bag in one hand and what appeared to be a book in the other.

She flung the door open wide and greeted him inside. "Come in and get warm." She shivered as a blast of January chill swirled into the front room.

He offered the bag to her. "Treats for you and me," he smiled.

"Oh, how sweet of you." Ariel smiled back.

He held up the large book, which turned out to be a photo album. "I had this in my car and thought you might enjoy seeing some of my earlier life history."

Lora Lee Colter

"Would I ever!" exclaimed Ariel. "That would be enlightening. So just how far back does this history go?"

"Well, I've got pictures of me and my family when I was growing up, my Air Force buddies and me, pictures of Europe, plus there is also a special picture of someone I'd like to show you."

"I can't wait to see them. What a great idea to help me get to know you better. First, let's get settled, and you can show and tell me everything."

Ariel carried the bag to the kitchen. Reece followed to assist. He pulled a bottle of red wine from the bag, while she sliced cheeses and opened a can of mixed nuts and crackers he had brought. She turned to look at him. "You are so thoughtful." They returned to the couch with their late evening snack. Ariel offered Reece a section of the blanket she threw over her lap. He scooted a bit closer, which she enjoyed, and they leaned in for the picture reveal and stories that went along with them. In the front pages were Reece's high school picture and photos of him goofing around a swimming pool with his brother and two sisters, hair wet and slicked back, face crinkled in a smile for the camera. There were more pictures of him with his family at a barbeque and at holidays and vacations. As they strolled through Reece's memory lane, Ariel suddenly felt a funny wave of déjà vu. She reached over and touched him so close beside her and just looked at him for a few seconds.

"What's wrong?" he asked with a hint of concern on his face.

"I . . . I'm . . . not sure, but it's okay. It's all good. I'm just really enjoying that you are sharing this with me."

They flipped to the section of the Air Force photos and boy, did Reece have some crazy, funny stories to tell along with the details of places he had traveled—to Switzerland,

Germany, and Italy. Ariel asked lots of questions about his start in the Air Force, and they discovered with amazement that their paths had crossed years earlier as Ariel was college bound and on the road trip to the University of Northern Iowa, passed a National Guard convoy heading to Camp Ripley in Southern Minnesota. Reece had been driving one of the Army Service trucks. Ariel had the opportunity to scan the faces of the men in uniform as she cruised past. Apparently, Reece's face had been seared into the dark recesses of her memory bank until it was triggered to the surface via review of his photos and listening to stories of his time in the service.

"Oh wow, that is amazing that we actually have seen each other before, if just for a few seconds." It was at that point she shared her déjà vu feelings that she felt earlier. There was just something indescribable about Reece Rhetlock's presence that Ariel hadn't ever experienced before.

Continuing through more pages and more stories, Ariel listened intently. Toward the last page, Reece stopped and turned to face her. "There is something I haven't told you yet." He paused.

"What is it?" Ariel wanted to know. She looked concerned.

"Oh, I didn't mean to scare you. It's nothing bad." He hesitated. "I . . . I have a daughter. It broke my heart to leave her when I came here. Of course, I talk to her almost daily and will go back to see her when I get a chance."

Ariel listened quietly, sensing his heartbreak. "How old is she?" Ariel asked softly.

"She's five—in kindergarten."

"Oh, how difficult that must be." His gaze drifted off in silent thought. "I'm sorry that you had to leave her, Reece." She laid her hand gently on the back of his strong, sinewy fingers.

He turned to show he appreciated her sensitivity. Slowly he turned the page. "Here's my baby."

Ariel was drawn into the little girl in the photo; her bright blue eyes sparkled, fringed by long lashes. Her grin was shy and cute. "Reece, she is adorable, and I see the resemblance of you in her eyes."

"Are you saying I'm adorable?" he joked.

"Maybe I am."

"I'd really like to see these again." Ariel pulled the album to her lap and bowed her head low for maximum visibility. She took pleasure in poring over the memories that were captured forever in the pages. She enjoyed the family vacation pictures: Niagara Falls, with a freeze-frame of his captivated family, watching the water explode high into the air behind them; she could imagine the deafening sound of the powerful energy roaring over the cliff; the bright sunshine illuminating smiling faces in front of the San Diego Zoo sign; South Dakota, taken when Reece was a teen at Mount Rushmore. It showed him posing with his mother and sister behind, which grandly stood one of the most famous stone monuments in America. Ariel gasped. Barely visible, yet unmistakable in the background, in the far lower corner of the worn photo, revealed a side profile of young Ariel with her little brother gazing at the four presidents carved in granite. "Reece!" Ariel practically shouted as she grabbed his arm. "Look, look there's me and my brother, Aaron!"

"What? No way! Let me see that."

He lowered his head to the page to inspect the photo. "Is that really you?"

"Yes, without a doubt. We took a trip there when I was that age, and yes that is really me!"

What a shocking coincidence that Ariel's family, too, had

visited Mount Rushmore that very same summer. "Oh my gosh," squealed Ariel at the discovery. "Unbelievable! What are the odds that we've crossed paths twice in our past?"

Reece, too, was flabbergasted at the thought. Suddenly, several layers of the artichoke were peeled away at this, their latest reunion and discovery.

"Do you believe in destiny?" Ariel wanted to know.

"I believe in you," Reece responded as he leaned in to brush her lips with a kiss as he softly touched her cheek. Ariel was surprised at what a comfortable gesture it was.

They exchanged stories and talked with ease, unaware and uncaring of the passage of time. It wasn't until they heard the sound of the garage door opening that Ariel realized how late it was getting.

Ariel was excited to see Rachel and introduce her to Reece. "It's really nice to meet you," said Rachel as she reached out to shake Reece's hand. "I've heard some good things about you," she said as she glanced at Ariel.

"Likewise," he said with sincerity.

They shared with her the astonishing discoveries of their past. Rachel was in awe as they recounted their story. She helped herself to some of the snacks spread out on the table, and they sat and chatted awhile before Rachel announced she was ready for some shut eye.

"I need to get going, too," Reece responded as he rose from the couch. "It was so nice to meet you, Rachel; seems like you two have a lot in common." They both nodded and smiled.

"Hope to see you again, soon," Rachel told Reece as she headed up the stairs. Ariel picked up the photo album and handed it to Reece. "Thanks for capturing and sharing your incredible memories. This was truly a fabulous evening." She

Lora Lee Colter

walked Reece to the door. They embraced and closed their evening with a long good-night kiss. Ariel was on cloud nine, or perhaps cloud ninety-nine.

---

25 – Spy Operation

Sunday morning came all too soon after a late night. Ariel had set her alarm with plans to resume her spy watch before the occupants in the Presidential Suite departed. Of course, she thought it quite possible they had left the night before, but she wanted to cover all the bases and couldn't take any chances of missing out on who was in that room with Mr. Kaufman—and then to figure out what they were up to!

Ariel stretched and got out of bed. She showered and dressed, then called the hotel. She asked for Troy. In a few seconds, he answered in a smooth, even voice. "This is Troy."

"Hey there, it's Ariel. I didn't get a chance to tell you what happened last night on my stakeout."

"What did happen?" he wanted to know.

"Well, unfortunately nothing. It was a disappointment. That's why I need you to hold that same room today. I'm coming in on my day off to do some detective work. By the way, check to see if there are any notes in the database about Kaufman's habits, like what time does he usually check out? Does he arrive and leave at the same time? Who else could be staying with him in that room?"

While Troy was punching the computer keys, Ariel changed gears with marked enthusiasm. "By the way, I'll have to tell you about my date with Reece! You won't believe it. I'll see you in a bit."

Life at the moment played like an emotional roller coaster. Ariel was riding the highs of the strong attraction she felt for Reece, mixed with the wild and dangerous turns of foreboding mystery that seemed to envelop the hotel. Despite the recent questionable activities that had happened at the Plaza, Ariel still relished her job and the hotel environment.

Thank goodness Reece had arrived at the hotel. He was a comforting breath of fresh air, and they found ways to meet and talk during work. So much for the cooling down period on which she had coached herself a few weeks ago; emotions were staying warm and getting hotter all the time. At times, all the feelings she felt for Reece overrode and pushed away the other worries and troubling thoughts she had encountered the last couple of months.

Troy made comments on the amount of time she spent with the new hot man in her life, but was supportive of her newfound relationship. The two of them remained close friends and joined each other for breaks when possible, as they always had much to share. Right now, she was counting on Troy to cover her back as she continued her spy mission.

"I cannot believe you are here on your day off," Troy stared and shook his head as Ariel appeared out of uniform at the front desk.

"Well, neither can I, but there is a job to do. Did you gather any more information on Oscar Kaufman?" Ariel wanted to know.

"Yes, as a matter of fact, I did. He's scheduled to leave around 11:00 this morning according to room service. I checked with them; they're delivering breakfast now, so you should have awhile before you need to take your post."

"Why don't you come on back, hang out, and tell me what happened with Reece last night."

"Oh, Troy, you're not going to believe this!" She recounted the incredulous discovery the previous night as they pored over Reece's pictures.

"Wow, it sounds like fate that you two got together."

"Yeah, it is pretty incredible. He is a super nice guy, and I like spending time with him. We have always had an easy time talking and now more than ever, we have so much to talk about."

Troy smiled. "I'm glad you're happy." Malcolm covered the front desk as the two conversed.

"I better not waste too much more time. I want to catch Jake leaving if he hasn't already."

"So, Ariel, honestly, what are you going to ask him? So what if he's friends with Oscar and just happens to be partying with him? They are both Des Moines businessmen, and it wouldn't be that surprising that they know each other."

"Correction, he *was* a Des Moines businessman. Remember, he went bankrupt and suddenly left town for L.A. And even if he's back, why did he have to sneak in? We know he didn't come through the front entrance."

"Good question, Sherlock. So confront him and demand an explanation if you want, but personally, I'd leave it alone." Troy crossed his arms and stood firm with a no-nonsense look on his face.

Finally, after much persistence, Troy gave in and provided Ariel with a key card so she could see for herself who left the suite. As Ariel's eyes peeped through the crack in the door across the way, a bellman had arrived to load up luggage.

After a heavy knock at the door, the bellman disappeared inside and soon, out came Oscar and the four girls. The bellman towed the luggage cart toward the elevator with Oscar and the girls on his heels. No sooner had the door swung shut, but what it edged slightly open again. Jake's head poked out, and he furtively glanced both ways. Ariel flinched when she saw him and tightened the crack in the door through which she peered. He waited until the bellman, Oscar, and the girls entered the elevator and dropped out of sight before he slinked out the door. He looked around again, comfortable that no one was visible, and then darted out, continued past the elevators, and down the hall toward the back staircase. He had no luggage in tow which meant it was with the others. Ariel quickly went into action as he fled out of sight and raced to the service elevator to reach the first floor.

She hurried to the south side to wait and watch. After a few minutes, sure enough, around rolled a big black SUV with Oscar Kaufman at the wheel and in jumped Jake as quick as a rabbit. What the hell. He got away.

At the front desk, Troy watched as Ariel walked slowly toward him, her usually high square shoulders were drooping and a distraught look was spread across her face. *Oh dear, what had happened?* Troy wondered. He soon found out.

"It really was him that I saw in the reflection last night. He is sneaking around like a fox in a hen house. He's hiding something," she stated. "I don't know how, but I intend to find out what that no-good bastard is up to."

---

26 – Exploring the Boiler Room

It was going to be a busy Saturday. It was Valentine's Day, and the hotel promotion of the romantic heart-to-heart package reeled in couples by the droves. Ariel had been instructed to arrive earlier than her usual time. When she arrived, Dina was surrounded by bottles of champagne, souvenir champagne glasses, roses whose stems were stuck in small plastic tubes of water, mini heart-shaped boxes of chocolates, and baskets. She was curling red ribbon and checking a print-out of the rooms that would receive the Valentine's Day special. The two women got busy assembling the baskets and tying the bright, curly ribbon to the basket handles. They chatted and laughed, keeping the conversation light as they focused on their work. Soon, they were loading the festive baskets onto carts for room deliveries.

Once that major task was complete, Ariel checked the computer for messages and saw an e-mail from the front desk marked urgent. Please arrange for a masseuse in room 1010 later tonight. This is for a semi-celebrity male who has requested room service and spa treatment—will arrive around 10:00 p.m. The kitchen was copied with a list of food to prepare. "Hey, Dina, we need a masseuse tonight." Ariel looked to Dina for direction.

"Oh dear!" Dina expressed a sense of concern and pursed her plum-colored lips.

"What is it?"

"Georgette called in sick earlier today. Personally, I think she had her own hot Valentine party planned and said screw the hotel."

"So what are we going to do? This is for some male celebrity type who is arriving at 10:00 p.m. Don't we have a back-up?" Ariel expressed a sense of hopefulness.

Although the hotel didn't have full spa amenities 24-7, they offered individual masseuse services upon request. Such requests were not that common, so the odds of needing their hotel masseuse the day she was out was Murphy's Law at work. Of course, Valentine's Day in general would be a prime time for spa requests so Ariel would be surprised if there were no back-up. No sooner had she finished her thought, than Dina piped up. "Unfortunately, no, we don't have a back-up." Dina giggled. "However, if I wasn't busy tonight, I'd handle the job myself."

Ariel placed her thumb and forefinger to her temples and massaged as she glanced at the computer screen for the time. Dina had already stayed a half hour after her normal quitting time. She would be taking off any minute and leave Ariel to figure it out. Sure enough, Dina announced that she better get going, although she did offer a suggestion.

"Check the Internet. There has to be someone in this town who would be happy to take care of a celebrity."

"I, ah, don't believe he is too much of a celebrity—remember I said semi—that probably means either old and washed up or some one-hit wonder. Anyway, I will get *crack-a-lackin'* to find someone to take care of this mystery man."

Dina was nodding her head with a close lipped smile and a

furrow in her brow that suggested a hint of empathy.

"Okay, let me know how it goes," she said as she edged away from the desk. The phone was ringing.

"Concierge services," Ariel answered politely. She raised her hand toward Dina and wiggled her fingers goodbye as Dina did the same.

Couples were beginning to check in at the front desk. It was going to be a busy night, and Ariel put on her creative thinking cap to handle the celebrity request. First of all, she needed to have the massage table transported to the guest room. She dialed Security and Sean answered. "Hey, Sean, I need your help to get our massage table to room 1010. Will you get that taken care of for me?"

"Sure thing," responded Sean eagerly.

"Thanks, buddy." Ariel's mind was reeling, and she started a Google search to locate a masseuse or masseur on short notice. All of a sudden, she remembered something. What about Sun Sook, the maid whom Ariel heard had just received her license? Ariel scrambled to dial Housekeeping to track down Sun, her fingers crossed. Luck was in the house as Sun agreed she could do the job after Ariel promised it would be worth her while.

"Oh, yes, I be very happy to work after shift and take care of massage, miz Ariel," Sun enthusiastically agreed in her broken English.

Thank goodness for hard-working people. Ariel inwardly admired Sun's eagerness and thanked her profusely. Rumor was, she was the best maid the Capitol Plaza had ever seen. She could shank toilets and shine a bathroom to spotless perfection in no time flat, pull sheets, remake a bed, and stock linens and toiletries like a super hero. She out-performed the other maids two-to-one with her speed and thoroughness. Her supervisor was always impressed.

Sun's best-kept secret to success lay in the fact that she relied on a little white guy to help her with her tasks. Dex was the light of her life, although he kept her up at night and encouraged her to eat more than she liked. When life got demanding, he was always with her pumping away and keeping her chipper. Dex was a blessing and a curse, and she knew she was treading on thin ice with his company. Dex was short for Dexamethasone, also known as steroids. Sun understood the lure of this nasty little devil. With the right woman, one who truly needed his power, and if authorized by a doctor to share his company, it was a match made in heaven, but for Sun, the companionship was not at all healthy. She knew it wasn't safe or a good idea, and the minute she sprouted facial hair, or if she gained too much weight, she promised herself she was finished for good. For now, though, she would roll with twenty milligrams of Dex a day and be the super maid, the super mom, the super hero.

As Ariel hung up the phone with Sun, the second line rang and Sean was on the other end explaining how he couldn't find the massage table in the storage room. "I think it needed a leg tightened, and it may be in Engineering," he said.

"Okay, then I'll track down Slade or Larry for help."

"Slade is off-site for awhile, but Larry should be around," offered Sean. She switched lines to dial Engineering. No answer. Ariel's impatience kicked in, and she decided to go locate the table herself.

The door to Engineering was shut tight so Ariel turned the door knob and called out. "Hello, is anyone here?" Her words were met with silence. She stepped through the door and gazed around the large windowless room, which was lit by overhead fluorescent lighting. A carpenter's fantasy land, she thought. The walls were covered with panels of hooks that held every tool and gadget imaginable from hand saws to neat rows of wrenches and hammers plus a section of pull out drawers that housed nails, screws, nuts, and bolts. It reminded her of her father's workshop when she was growing up.

The entire room was extremely well organized and hinted of a light, pleasant smell of grease and Old Spice. In the middle of the room was a long wooden work table that could accommodate repair projects. A small office was in the back to the right, and in the back to the left were huge double doors that led to the boiler room. Ariel scanned the perimeter of the room, however didn't see the massage table for which she searched. Hopefully, it had been fixed and stored in the back.

She pushed open one of the large doors to the boiler room. In the dim light loomed the monstrous outlines of the mechanical generators, boilers, and the water cooling tower, which created chugging, clanking sounds and noises of air blowing. She found some light switches and flipped one that threw on a bright light in the immediate section of where she stood. Her eyes scanned the area in search of the missing massage table that she so desperately needed to find. There was a large storage closet and cabinets along one wall. Adjacent to that were cardboard boxes with various thingamajigs, apparently parts for the big mechanical machines. According to the labels, there were blow down valves, burner belts and pulleys, drive cables, valve wheel keys and micro switches. In an opposite corner were tables and chairs with broken legs, extra hotel furniture and accessories, and some kitchen equipment.

Ariel rummaged around growing more frantic to find what she needed for room 1010. Out of desperation, she decided to check the closet. Although it had a padlock, it wasn't locked and the small, silver key dangled in the lock mechanism. She lifted the padlock from the hardware and opened the door. The closet was about six feet deep by four feet wide with a bare bulb exposed on the ceiling from which a string hung. A tug of the cord illuminated a bright light in the small space.

Lora Lee Colter

Directly to her right and just lower than eye level on a shelf was a strange snakeskin case that caught her eye. She temporarily forgot what she was searching for; the unusual, briefcase-like box seemed so odd and out of place, she was drawn to it like a magnet, and curiosity got the best of her. She half-expected it to be locked, but she pressed the silver button, and the flip mechanism popped open. She jumped.

Slowly, Ariel lifted the lid and gasped as the air was sucked from her lungs. Her body stiffened in shock, and she blinked in disbelief and tried to swallow. *This is surreal. Is it just a bad dream?* She wondered.

---

27 – A Horrible Secret Revealed

On display in the snakeskin box were four individually sealed, clear bags of various shades of hair locks—a light blond braid, a swatch of platinum blond, a baggie full of tousled curly reddish auburn hair and the long, luxurious, dark pony tail with the glittering hair piece. These four were visible on top, but it appeared that there were a few other bags below. Ariel was shaking uncontrollably now and abruptly realized what a precarious position in which she found herself. She reached out to touch the bag that contained the pony tail—the pony tail that Denise Brickman had so proudly displayed.

Suddenly, out of nowhere a deep familiar voice boomed across the room. "Did you find what you were looking for?" She slowly turned to see Slade striding toward her in long even steps. "What the hell do you think you're doing?" he demanded.

"I . . . I'm looking for the massage table." Her voice was shaky. Slade stepped up and put his face close to hers.

"Well it's *not* in this closet and I see you've been into something that doesn't belong to you." As he pressed into her, she could smell the stench of chewing tobacco and could almost feel the prickly stubble on his face. His grey-green eyes narrowed. His face was flushed with rage. "If you talk to *anyone* about this, I will dispose of you, like that." He snapped his fingers. "Do you understand?" Ariel bit her lip and nodded. "I said. Do you fucking understand me?"

"Yes, Slade, I do. I will not say a word—it's already forgotten. I promise."

"You better believe it, 'cause if I find out otherwise, you will conveniently have an accidental death, or you will just disappear. Either way, it will not be pretty. I guarantee you that." Before he backed away, he reached out and stroked her hair. "Just remember, your pretty hair could become an addition to my collection if you fail to obey my instructions." He smiled and his jaw hardened.

Strangely, as if a switch was flipped, Slade's voice promptly changed to a strict business tone. "By the way, the massage table is right around this corner. It is sound and sturdy. I fixed it myself," he boasted. His lips curled up in an evil grin as he hoisted the collapsible table up with his strong arms. "Where does this need to go?" he inquired.

"Room 1010, and . . . and thank you." Ariel managed to say. Her heart was thumping hard, and she couldn't wait to return to the public area. *Slade could change his mind and easily snuff me out right here and now*, she thought. She worked her way toward the doors to exit the boiler room and through the engineering area as Slade followed. She held the doors for him to be polite, but the minute he was out of sight she practically ran to her desk.

She flopped down in her chair, swallowed hard, and attempted to wrap her head around this nightmare of a situation. She looked down to see that her hands were visibly shaking. *Oh, dear Lord, what have I got myself into? How am I ever going to get through the rest of the day?* she wondered.

Pull yourself together and act normal. Tell no one. Tell no one, she repeated over and over in her mind. *You are a strong person and can survive this nightmare. This discovery is one huge piece to the hotel puzzle, and finally, I know the creep who pulled off the Denise Brickman hair caper!* Quite possibly, she abruptly realized, the missing woman's hair might also be in that box? *I've got to figure this out!*

In the engineering office, Slade, too, sat at his desk deep in agonizing thought. He had immediately returned to his office hideaway after setting up the massage table for room 1010. He popped two pills for his headache and mentally lectured himself for his stupidity. *How could I be such a fucking careless idiot and let myself get sidetracked from locking that closet?* He was extremely angry with himself. *If that little bitch tells anyone about my secret I'm in deep shit. I'll definitely have to keep my eye on her.*

As a killer for hire, Slade would be punished to the nth degree if his boss found out he took memorabilia from a victim for his own personal pleasure. That was a risk that would never be tolerated given he was supposed to be a professional hit man. His passion for hair had started a couple of years ago when he dated a cute petite blond who eventually pissed him off. His thoughts drifted. They had broken up after a flashy argument, and he felt entitled to take her blond braid with him as a souvenir. She had been asleep, and although she knew he did it, she couldn't prove a thing. Slade chuckled at the thought. And that, he guessed, was what sparked his insatiable hair fetish.

---

28 – Dwelling on Things

Ariel had avoided her co-workers as best as she could after the discovery of the snakeskin box and threat from Slade. She was so shook up, she didn't think she could act normal and didn't want to be questioned. Thankfully, the hotel was busy enough that she and Troy hadn't had a chance for a concurrent break, and she and Reece only spoke on the phone from office to office. She let Reece know that she was exhausted and was going to head straight home after work. He promised he would call her later that night. She managed to get through the rest of the day by popping a couple of pain relief capsules, taking care of the guests, and working on the computer.

The minute she clocked out and stepped out the back door, Ariel scanned the parking lot and made a beeline for her car. She glanced in the back seat before she slid behind the wheel. *Is this what life would be like now,* she wondered, *always worried that someone would jump out from dark corners and grab her, or that her car would explode as she started the engine?*

Rachel's cell phone rang as Ariel tried to reach her roommate and check her whereabouts. She and Steve were out on the town for a Valentine's Day rendezvous, and she didn't pick up. While Ariel wanted Rachel to be there for her when she got home, she also didn't really want to do much talking. She needed time to think and collect her thoughts in private. Her rear-view mirror showed no signs that she was being followed as she left the parking lot and headed for home.

The soft glow of the lamp in the front window was visible as she pulled into the driveway and opened the garage. Safely inside, Ariel turned on several lights and checked all the outside entry doors to ensure they were locked. Although she wanted to lock the door from the hall to the garage, she didn't want to be obsessive and tip off Rachel that she was paranoid again. Plus, she wanted her to be able to get in when she got home. Once she confirmed that all the doors were locked, she then worried that someone might already be there. She listened carefully for any sounds. She again thought how nice it would be to have a dog. *It would be a real reassurance,* she thought.

Knowing that Reece would be calling later was a comfort. She prepared a hot bubble bath, poured a glass of wine, lit some candles, and placed her cell phone on the edge of the tub. Settling into the soothing warm bath, she began to relax. The more she relaxed, the more she decided she could handle the situation. She wished she could tell someone about what she had seen—Troy, Reece, Rachel, the police, someone—but it was just way too risky. For now, the ugly secret was hers alone to carry.

Ariel deeply contemplated the situation, letting her mind rewind to the night of the snowstorm, the night the pony tail disappeared. She could only imagine the euphoria Slade must have felt upon laying his eyes on that luxurious lock of hair—what a prize!

Had she seen Slade that night? Yes, for sure he had been hanging out with the security guys at one point and she remembered seeing him in the south hallway near the engineering room during the time the band played. He could have easily spotted Denise with everyone going in and out of the ballroom where Corkscrew performed, which was not far from the engineering area. The hotel rules were very lax once the snowstorm had hit. Hotel employees were enjoying perks that were normally off limits, freely entering the ballrooms and lounges at will.

Ariel tried to envision Slade sneaking into the suite occupied by four people, snipping the pony tail, and sneaking off down the back stairs. She imagined it was a couple of hours after the excitement wore down and everyone was completely passed out when he did his dirty work. On the one hand, it was a relief to know who pulled that caper. How ironic that the victim was with Jake. Jake—what a snake. He was full of shit and shenanigans. Oh gosh, what would happen if she informed Jake that she knew who scalped his date? And speaking of Jake, exactly why was he with Oscar Kaufman in secret, and who else was with them?

As her mind mulled over recent events, the cell phone on the edge of the tub began singing its familiar ring tone. Ariel glanced at the digits that lit up. It was Reece's incoming cell number. She took a deep breath and answered. "Hey there."

"Hi, gorgeous." He hadn't called her that before, but she liked the sound of it. "What's up?" He wanted to know.

"Well, I'm enjoying a nice bath and sipping on some wine before bed."

"Oh, wish I were there." She could hear the grin in his voice. "Hey, since we worked so hard today and didn't get to share Valentine's Day, I think we should celebrate as soon as we can. How about Monday? I've got it off and am hoping you do, too." He sounded hopeful.

"Actually, I do have Monday night off. How lucky am I?

What did you have in mind?"

"Let's just make it a surprise. I'll pick you up at your place around 6:30 p.m."

"That sounds really great. I'll plan to leave work downtown early so I have plenty of time to get ready. So are you going to give me any hints?" she implored.

"Just think romantic, and that should cover it. I am looking forward to a special evening with you."

"Okay, me **too**. I have tomorrow off from the hotel, but you work, right?"

"Yes, bright **and** early as usual," he confirmed.

"So I guess I won't see you until our special date. I can't wait."

"See you then." The phone clicked off.

Beaming with shear joy, she wrapped her arms around her shoulders and gave herself a hug. She felt like the luckiest woman alive—lucky, but tired. She finished her bath, towel dried, and slipped into her nightgown. Thoughts of fear and concern were currently replaced with jubilation. She crawled into bed and slipped into peaceful slumber with visions of Reece and her together on a romantic rendezvous.

---

29 – Valentine Rendezvous

Ariel cut out early on Monday at her job downtown and scurried across the skywalk, barely noticing the distance between her and the floor below as she thought about her upcoming date. The routine was all too familiar. Down the elevator, past the flower shop and the Sapphire Club, to the bank of elevators that would carry her to the parking ramp. She checked her watch—4:30. By the time she got home at 5:00, she'd have an hour and a half to get ready for her date with Reece. She was so excited and wanted to be sure she looked her very best. She took extra time with her hair, makeup, and nails and picked out a slim fitting, black skirt and a cute, sexy blouse and grabbed a sweater.

It was very close to date time. As Ariel peeked out her bedroom window, she saw a white stretch limo coasting toward their duplex on Plum Tree Lane. She shook her head, smiled, and softly said, "Reece."

Before she could reach the front door, the doorbell rang. She hurried to open the door, and there he stood. With his strong jaw, generous smile, big blue eyes, and a winning character, he was one of the most handsome men she had ever known. He made her heart race. She felt giddy all over.

They reached out to greet each other, and then he took her hand and led her toward the limo where the driver waited with an open, inviting door.

Inside on the seat were a dozen red roses wrapped in tissue paper. Some champagne was chilling on ice. The limo pulled away as Reece and Ariel settled into the leather surroundings. Holding hands, they eased into conversation as Van Morrison's smooth, strong voice serenaded them in the background. All was right with the world.

"May I?" Reece pulled the champagne from the ice bucket and popped the cork. Without missing a beat, he reached down and pulled off Ariel's high heel and poured champagne into her shoe and drank from it. Ariel laughed until her sides ached. He then took two glasses and poured one for each of them, so they could have a proper toast. "Here's to newfound friendship—to us." They gently touched their glasses together in a soft clink.

"To us," she proudly proclaimed.

"Are you hungry?" Reece reached for a cooler that held some chocolate-covered strawberries, crisp, seasoned jicama, cheese, and crackers. "We'll be stopping in a bit for a real meal, but I didn't want you to starve or get too light headed from the champagne," he said.

"Yes, how perfect. Thank you for a really amazing outing."

After cruising around town, their ride returned to the west side and pulled into The Dish, a trendy restaurant and bar. "Oh, I've met people here for drinks before. This is an awesome place—a really good choice," Ariel said excitedly.

"I got this recommendation from some co-workers at the hotel since I'm not yet familiar with all the places around town. I hear they serve tapas."

"What? Topless?"

"No, silly, tapas. That means small plate dishes featuring flavors from around the world."

"Oh, I guess I hadn't heard it called that before—that's interesting."

"Come on, let's go check it out." He grabbed her hand as the chauffeur opened the door to let them out.

"Mm, I'm up for that. It sounds great."

They were escorted to one of the nice, big, outfacing booths toward the back. Even for a Monday evening, the place was busy; apparently others had the same idea of having their belated Valentine's Day dates. The two agreed to sample from the American, Latin, Mediterranean, and Asian cuisines, and they ordered Boursin Mushrooms, Tuna Tataki, Lettuce Wraps, Tequila Lime Shrimp, and Grilled Sea Scallops. "Also, we'll take a bottle of the Prosecco. We need some tiny bubbles to celebrate," Reece instructed the waiter.

Ariel couldn't get over Reece and how nice he was to treat her to an expensive night out on the town. She was enjoying herself and once again lost in his world. Although they got an early start on the evening, it wouldn't surprise her that it would turn into a late night. While waiting for the waiter to return with the Prosecco, Ariel excused herself to go to the ladies room.

She made her way to the back, between tables full of diners and lovers enjoying themselves, past the kitchen and the wine rack wall. As she approached the restrooms near the back entrance, she stopped dead in her tracks as just outside the glass door, there in the shadowy streetlights was none other than slimy Slade Sobronski looking sinister and disgusting, arms folded, staring at her. He directed two fingers to his eyes and then pointed at her. She quickly ducked into the women's restroom and immediately encountered a mirror. The color had drained from her face. She was shaking.

It was a warning from Slade and a reinforcement of what he had said that she better not tell anyone. *How awful,* she thought. *Had he followed them all the way from her place, or had he just heard through the hotel grapevine that she and Reece would be here tonight?*

Once again, it was going to take all she could muster to pull herself together and act normal. Her life was never going to be the same. She did some deep-breathing exercises to regain her composure and prayed that Slade was gone. It was just a matter of time before Reece would come checking on her if she didn't return to their table.

She tentatively stepped out of the restroom and peeked to the back exit door. He was not there, although she couldn't be certain that he wasn't out of sight in the shadows. She hustled back to the booth and safety of Reece. "Are you feeling okay?" Reece asked with genuine concern. "You look a bit pale."

"I think I just need some food, and I'll be fine," she lied. Slowly, but surely, as she took in their surroundings and enjoyed their delicious food samples and conversation, Ariel began to feel better. Reece was good at helping her forget anything but him. She soaked up his positive energy. She took in his presence. In the wardrobe category, he received an *A+* for style. In Ariel's opinion, he nailed three very crucial items that always caught her attention: hair, shoes, and fingernails. His hair was shaved on the sides and around his ears and a little longer on top, his nails were short and well-manicured and his shoes were top-notch leather, polished and stylish. Beyond that, his personality engulfed her like a wildfire.

"How do you like the food? Here, try one of these." He guided a succulent sea scallop toward her mouth, and she leaned in to accept his offering.

"Oh, that is so tasty. It's hard to choose a favorite. I love it all." She licked her lips. The bubbles fizzed and popped in their champagne glasses. The effervescent liquid tickled her nostrils as Ariel took a long, slow sip. Soon her mind was swathed in a sea of giddy calmness.

They languished in the service and atmosphere, and in each other's company. Although they were full from their main course, they couldn't resist a sweet dessert to share. The chocolate and pink, mini-heart cakes were to die for!

At last they were satiated. Not another bite could either of them endure. They wrapped up their dinner at The Dish. The limo driver was waiting. As they stepped out of the restaurant, Ariel's senses piqued and her fear returned. She covertly scanned the parking lot for signs of Slade. Was that someone in the shadows or just an illusion? No, it was her mind playing tricks. She didn't see him. There was a chill in the February air, and she pulled her sweater tightly around her.

Once inside the comfortable, warm luxury of the limo, she snuggled into Reece's chest, and he curled his arm around her. She soaked up his wonderful manly smell. She closed her eyes and felt safe. "You're amazing," she said. "And thank you."

"Not half as amazing as you are. And you are welcome," he replied. "Will you be my Valentine?"

"I would love to be your Valentine, tonight and every night." Her lips pursed together softly. She touched her fingertips to her pucker and blew him a quiet kiss.

Blue eyes, brown eyes, reflecting in each other's soul, they traveled to an unearthly place—a place of magic and possibilities. Ariel was nestled comfortably on Reece's lap, their fingers were threaded together, palms touching, and faces close. They shared in each other's secret world, a strange new sensation, one of exciting freshness and yet laced with a sense of comfort and familiarity. The limo driver glanced in the rear-view mirror. Reece reached over and gently pressed the button to seal the panel between the front and back. They kissed, talked, laughed, and relished their time together.

The driver dropped them off back at her duplex. Again, Ariel looked for signs that they had been followed—nothing. Reece came in, even though it was getting late and knowing they both had to be at work early in the morning, it was so difficult for them to say goodbye. The evening had flown by way too quickly. Eventually, they released their embrace at the door and Reece departed, but turned back to look at her standing in the doorway. She waved, and as he turned away, she scanned the streets and neighborhood for signs of anyone hiding in the darkly shadowed night. She quickly shut and locked the door as Reece ducked into the waiting car. She peeked through the window to watch the beautiful white limousine gently roll out of sight into the night. Shiny stars were winking down from an inky black sky. It was the best night she could ever remember and one she knew she would never forget.

- - -

30 – Puzzle Pieces

The Capitol Plaza Hotel was a mini-community consisting of many functional areas: Sales, Security, Food Service and Banquet Operations, Front Desk and Bellman Services, Engineering, Housekeeping, HR, Accounting, and Concierge Services. By now, Ariel knew most of the staff well and had cultivated a variety of friendships. With the large number of hotel employees plus the many guests traversing through the hotel, it was easy to meet new people. Ariel, the social butterfly, embraced the opportunity, although lately, she was more guarded than ever.

Not surprisingly, visible romances blossomed, and it was interesting to see who might turn up together. Ariel accepted the fact that she had become part of the hotel romance statistics as she and Reece were undeniably a couple by now. As many relationships developed, the hotel was like the Love Boat on land.

Too, there were the not-so-visible romances that took place around the hotel. Currently, there were suspicions of a clandestine romance occurring between Sienna, the Director of Sales, a well-coiffed and well-manicured, thirty-something and Chester, the shoeshine man, a buff, handsome twenty-something. One of the security guys jokingly suggested he noticed shoe polish on Sienna's knee caps—perhaps just another cougar on the prowl. This was a tale that was kept alive via the rumor mill that churned with vigor in and around the Security Office, which served as the primary communication channel hot spot.

The physical ambiance of the hotel was pleasant and offered a soothing environment. The pockets of energy that resonated as people filtered through the lobby or stopped at the front desk were uplifting. Ariel noticed most visitors thrived on their hotel experience, enjoying the comforts and perks of allowing others to cater to their needs and tend to details.

Periodically, the weariness of business travelers who missed their families was detected. Smiles were reciprocated, yet the faces were slack and the eyes hollow. Ariel felt sorry for them and wished she could take away their loneliness, but the best she could do was make them feel welcome. That was her job and her duty to all guests of the Plaza—to offer a warm and welcome experience.

Some of her favorite moments were when a friend or acquaintance would unexpectedly appear at her desk. And it was always a welcome surprise to see family members, such as her Aunt Jane and Uncle Dwain, in town for a meeting or shopping, stopping by to say hello or even better, informing her they would be staying at the hotel. On one such visit, they were there to book a ballroom for an upcoming anniversary celebration. She was very happy for them, but underneath wished she could disclose the secret veil of danger that hovered over the place.

Ever since she learned of the dreadful secret that lurked in the closet of the boiler room, her job had become more challenging. She tried to avoid at all costs the despicable Slade Sobronski. So far, she had upheld her end of the bargain to keep the awful secret. Although she wanted him exposed more than anything, she was truly terrified of him and didn't doubt that he would follow through if she told anyone. Her mind churned constantly, thinking about what to do, and she believed this was just the tip of the iceberg.

There had to be a connection to Slade and the woman who disappeared, but why, and where was she? There were also other mysterious things going on around here. What did Ed and Ross Barbaria have in common? They snuck out together, yet separately from The Cove the other night a few weeks ago. And why was Jake here with Oscar Kaufman just after leaving for California? Maybe the two were acquainted through construction business ventures. Although with Jake declaring bankruptcy, it didn't seem appropriate that they were celebrating something. Who else was with them in the Presidential Suite?

Despite the fast-paced evening, for which she was grateful, her mind wandered when not immediately focused on providing assistance or working on a project. When she got an opportunity, she decided to do a Google search. Just as she typed in Slade Sobronski, she heard Troy's voice. "Hey, let's do a break? Will you join me?"

"Ah, sure, why not? We haven't hung out in a while, and I've got things to talk about." She turned to block him from potentially seeing what she had keyed in to the computer.

"Well, let's go then," he encouraged. She pushed her chair back, rounded the desk, and together they strode toward the back.

As they settled in with plates of food in the break area, Ariel didn't waste any time quietly asking Troy about the woman who had stayed in room 901.

"So I've still been wondering about the woman who disappeared. Don't you think it's bizarre that she has never been found and that there are no leads?" she whispered.

Ariel heard Slade's words echo in her mind. *If you talk to anyone about this, I will dispose of you like that,* as he had snapped his fingers. "I'd like to check our database to gather any information on her."

"Well, the police did all that when they questioned me and Malcolm. She was here to assist Ross Barbaria with his health products, and it was the day after his seminar at the hotel that it was discovered that she disappeared."

"Why didn't you tell me that before?" Ariel hissed in an irritated tone. "I didn't know she was associated with Mr. Barbaria. The article in the paper just mentioned she was in town for a seminar. I saw her picture in the paper—of course in black and white. What color was her hair?"

"Why?"

"I'm just curious to know more about her. She was a pretty woman," Ariel said.

"Well, you know me. I'm so into hair that I do recall. Honey, I notice it all—the good, the bad, and the ugly. She actually had reddish auburn hair with a natural curl. It was very well conditioned, but I believe not her natural color," stated Troy with confidence.

Ariel drew in a breath. *My God, the hair in the baggie had to be hers.* She bit on her lip and looked away. *I am dying to tell Troy, but I just can't. He might freak out and ruin everything.*

"Are you all right?" Troy questioned with concern in his voice.

She squirmed in her chair. "Uh, yeah, I'm okay. It's scary. I wonder why she was taken."

"What do you mean taken? It seems like something must have happened to her after she left here. All signs appeared that she checked out and left in a taxi."

"Right, but I think something terrible happened. I can't explain it. If she disappeared, then don't you think she was taken by force?" Ariel wondered aloud. All she could really think of was the auburn red hair in the snakeskin box. "When we get back to the front, let's check to see when Ross Barbaria has his next seminar scheduled. I wonder if he will hire a new assistant to replace the one who inexplicably disappeared into thin air."

Together they checked the database at the front desk. "He's got a seminar scheduled for two days next week in Willow. Seems he's holding more and more of these meetings. I guess his product is really taking off."

"You know what? I'm going to take some time off from my day job next week to check some things out around here," Ariel suddenly decided.

"Gee, are you crazy, girl? Do you really want to hang out here on your days off?"

"Well, I think there are some things worth looking into. That's for sure."

Troy arched an eyebrow and shook his head. "So what are you going to do?"

"I'm not really sure yet, but I'm going to see if Dina wants a day break. I'd like to see what it is like to work a week day rather than nights and weekends."

Ariel returned to her desk and awoke the sleeping computer screen. Up popped Slade Sobronski's name she had typed to Google. She cringed to think she had left that name exposed on her monitor, even though it was not likely anyone else would sit at her desk. She added the word crimes to narrow the search. She hit enter and glanced to be sure no one was coming. As she browsed through the various sites that contained combinations of the three words she entered, she located a California newspaper site of a report that appeared to have validity.

A Slade Sobronski was implicated on charges of breaking and entering and assault and battery a few years ago in an L.A. suburb. A woman had identified him in a lineup, and he was sentenced to jail time. *Sounds like a match*, Ariel thought as a shiver shook her spine. *Seriously, how is it that these kinds of things slip through the hiring process—is there no sense of caution when it comes to screening and selection for hotel positions here?* she wondered.

---

31 – Hotel Happenings

Her decision had been made. She contacted Dina to offer her two days off during the upcoming week, which coordinated with Mr. Barbaria's next health seminar. Dina was actually in grateful agreement for some time off since she needed time to run weekly errands and thought that was a nice gesture. Ariel put her request in for two days off from her day job for the upcoming week. There were things to investigate!

She was beginning to connect some dots. So far, she was pretty certain that Slade was involved in foul play with the auburn-haired missing woman. The missing woman had assisted Ross Barbaria with his business, and Ross and Ed from Security had some sort of secret association. The fact that Denise Brickman was linked to Jake and that Slade had her ponytail in his snake-skin box collection, seemed like no coincidence. Also, shortly after leaving for L.A., Jake was back in town and in cahoots with Oscar Kaufman and those party girls along with two mysterious, unidentified people that had joined him for his dinner party. Some strange connections were sure taking shape and it wasn't a Raggedy Ann and Andy situation—more like a *Criminal Minds* episode unfolding.

The atmosphere during the day was a bit different than

weekends and evenings. Weekdays were all about the business travelers and the entrepreneurs and business folks holding their seminars and meetings. The ballrooms were all in use. Reece and his crew had been busy with room preparations to ensure the seating arrangements and settings were as requested and that all the audio/visual equipment was in place.

Mr. Barbaria was organizing the Willow room with displays of his health products consisting of vitamins, nutritional supplements, and energy drinks, along with brochures and pamphlets of information. He was preparing to conduct his usual back-to-back, 45-minute presentation to willing recipients, excited to learn how they could improve their health and get in on ground floor selling opportunities of Skylar's newest health craze creations. Ed and Randy each rolled in a cart stacked with boxes labeled with the company's logo. These boxes contained more of the products for backup.

Ariel said hi to the security guys as she popped in to see if she could assist Ross with his preparation or materials. He was surprised to see her rather than Dina. "Hi, I just wanted to offer any support here if you need it. I know Reece and his crew took care of the room set up, and the kitchen provided you with drinks and snacks, so it looks like you are in good shape here, but if you need anything, please let me know. Also, if you don't mind, I'd love to listen in a bit. I'm interested in knowing more about your products."

"Ah, sure that would be fine. I don't think I need anything now. We will have the shipping ready for tomorrow from today's seminar orders, so if you are here you can help," Ross responded in his smooth, polished style. "Dina usually does this, but of course, you helped me one Saturday so you know what needs to be done."

"Well Dina is off tomorrow, too, so I'm more than happy to help you."

Ariel worked extra hard to cover the concierge desk and also to keep an eye on the goings-on in Willow. She poked her head in to witness a video in session. She heard a portion of Mr. Barbaria's convincing presentation of his merchandise and saw him introduce his pretty new assistant who would help take orders after the session and offer support with accessing Skylar's Web site.

Everything appeared to be on the up-and-up, but Ariel had a funny feeling that something not so pure and wholesome was bubbling under the surface. She decided to circle by the Security Office and chat with Ed and Randy to probe them about Ross and his business. As she approached the office, she could see the two in their comfortable guy mannerisms exchanging easy conversation.

"Hey guys, what's up?"

They turned their heads as she poked her head through the door to the office. "Not much," said Ed.

"What's up with you—anything exciting going on at the front today? By the way, where's Dina?" Ed questioned.

"Oh, she took a couple of days off. It's pretty quiet out front, but the ballrooms are really full and busy aren't they? Do you guys know Ross Barbaria, the guy in Willow very well? It seems he has quite a booming health business with the Skylar products."

"Nope, I don't know him," Randy confirmed; his voice laced with indifference.

"What about you, Ed?"

"Naw, I've just seen him doing his dog and pony shows and have delivered boxes to his meeting rooms, but I don't really know him other than that."

Baloney, you only raced out of The Cove with him for

something important the other night. Ariel kept her thoughts to herself. "He seems like a successful guy. I've made room deliveries and helped him with some of his business needs. I think I'm going to buy some of his nutritional supplements and see if they are any good. I'm going to help him with his shipments tomorrow."

She eyed Ed as she spoke. He just cocked his head and nodded slightly.

"Well, I better get back to the front; talk to you guys later." Before Ariel could turn away, the Security phone rang. "Ed here." Through the speaker they could hear a lot of commotion. The call had come from the pool area. "We have a 911 situation—come quick," a man's voice on the line commanded.

The three of them raced out of the back and down the side hall past the ballrooms to the pool off the south side entrance. The door to the pool was propped open, and the smell of chlorine and warm heavy air hit them as they entered. "Oh my gosh," Ariel gasped.

Reece was in water up to his waist, towing a woman's body out of the pool. It was too early to tell if she was still alive, but her skin was a ghoulish purple hue. He placed her up on the tile beside the pool and turned her on her side to expel water. He fished his fingers down her throat to clear her airway of vomit, then rolled her to her back and began administering CPR with alternate chest compressions and breathing into her mouth.

Ariel watched in horror. It seemed like an eternity, but eventually the woman gasped for air as oxygen filled her lungs. Slowly, the bluish-purple color was replaced with flesh-colored skin. The paramedics had arrived, and Reece turned his valiant efforts over to them. The police weren't far behind. Thank God.

Reece walked toward Ariel, dripping from head to toe. She put her arms around him.

"What happened?"

"I'm not sure. We were in a management meeting across the hall, and a woman came out screaming for help and that someone had drowned."

Ariel could tell he was a bit shaken. "Are you okay?"

"I'll be fine, but I guess I better go home and change." He towel dried his slacks, removed his wet shirt and tie, and slipped into his dry jacket and shoes that he had managed to remove before jumping into the pool. Ariel offered him an extra towel for his car seat.

The paramedics loaded the woman onto a gurney and whisked her to the ambulance as everyone's gaze followed them from the pool area. The small audience that was witness to the frightening situation was grateful for Reece's quick action and thankful that he had taken charge. Before he was free to leave, the police questioned Reece and made notes. At this point, it wasn't clear whether it was an accident or an attempted homicide.

---

32 – Suspicious Shipments

As they had discussed the previous day, Mr. Barbaria needed Ariel's help with the mailings generated from the seminar. He brought by two large boxes filled with an assortment of packages. The return address was stamped "Skylar Health" in California. The recipient addresses were blank and in need of labels. This time Ariel was familiar with the process. He provided a sheet with a list of names and addresses to where he wanted the items shipped. "People are really eating up these vitamins and nutritional supplements." He smiled. "Will you please get these ready so we can ship them first-class today? I'll check back in about an hour."

"I sure will." Ariel assured him they would be ready. She was perspiring underneath her mauve jacket as adrenaline coursed through her veins. She was about to do something that the United States Postal Service regarded as highly illegal. Scanning the list, she saw familiar out-of-state destinations. Fortunately, she had saved her computer work from the previous time and opened the folder and address document to check the names against the new list. Most of them appeared to be the exact same addresses. Thank goodness I won't have to retype all these. She printed them out and got busy matching and affixing labels. Knowing that he would be back in an hour to check the list and account for every package. She had to work quickly.

She opened the closet and rummaged around on the shelves looking for a bag. Perfect! On top of an unopened box of toothbrushes was a large, colorful satchel Dina had left behind. It was the kind you get for free when splurging on beauty products—usually perfume or makeup—that you really don't need, but the bag is so cool that you can't resist. This is great. It's big enough.

Just then, some friendly guests stopped by for information. "Hello there, can you please help us with some lunch recommendations?"

"Sure, what kind of food are you interested in—Chinese, Mexican, American, seafood?" Ariel brushed her hair back and pulled on her collar. "There are so many great restaurants right around here." The young woman looked at the older man.

"What are you hungry for?"

"Oh, anything except Mexican; what are you in the mood for?"

"Hmm, I'm not sure." The lady wrinkled her nose.

While they hem and hawed around, Ariel quickly offered a reference sheet of restaurants available in the nearby area. "Well, here you go. Please take this and I'm sure you'll decide."

Ariel didn't want to sound impatient, but dang, she had to keep moving; time was wasting. She glanced at the front desk. Troy and another gal were checking in new arrivals. Troy had no idea what she was up to and hopefully no one needed her or would miss her for awhile. The undecided couple thanked her and left poring over the choice of restaurants she had provided them.

After tucking the boxes of packages behind her desk, she glanced around and discreetly dropped two different sized packages into the pretty black and pink shoulder bag. She zipped it up, grabbed her purse and made a beeline for the south side door and around the side to her car parked in back. She knew that every entrance had camera surveillance, but thankfully Chuck and Randy were on duty today. They wouldn't think twice about her comings or goings. In fact, they probably were patrolling the hotel or just shooting the breeze in the back, unaware of activity on the monitors.

She started the engine, looked around, and threw her car into reverse. She couldn't sit in the parking lot to do her investigation. Making sure she wasn't followed, she drove to the nearby park. It was quiet, aside from a mother and her two children playing on the swings and a girl walking her dog. Ariel parked and pulled the two packages from Dina's colorful bag and stared at them. She really needed to hurry, but she had to think. *If there are just vitamins and minerals in here, I'm sure going to feel foolish.*

From the duplex, she had brought an assortment of empty bottles and jars of various sizes, a couple of bags of dried beans, a one pound and two pound bag of rice, glue, scissors, and clear packing tape. Whatever she removed from the packages she needed to replace with something of the same size and weight so Ross wouldn't be suspicious that the outgoing packages had been tampered with. It was also important that she keep any evidence.

Without further hesitation, she began to work her fingernail under the flap on the smaller package—a thick eight-by-ten-inch manila envelope with bubble-pack lining. Her heart was racing and her hands were shaking. She glanced around, all was quiet. No one knew she was here, or if they did, they could care less.

She really needed to work quickly. Careful not to tear the

flap, she continued gently peeling it open. Inside were two bottles of Skylar brand vitamins. She unscrewed the lid on the first jar and the mouth was sealed with a layer of protective wrap. The second jar revealed the same tight casing. The plastic jars were opaque so there was no seeing through to the contents. Her pounding heart sunk. *These are the real deal. Or are they?*

She had come this far. She proceeded to pull the plastic away from the mouth of the jar far enough to peek inside— looked like vitamins. The pills were blue and white. She again glanced at her surroundings—still all clear. She sniffed. It smelled like vitamins. She poured them into an empty olive jar and decided there weren't many vitamins for the size of the container. Upon closer examination, Ariel discovered it wasn't empty after all. Her breath caught and her eyes widened. There stuffed in the bottom was a clear packet of white powdery substance. She shook the bottle to loosen it so she could pull it out. Definitely not part of the health regimen. *Oh my gosh. I was right. I was right!* Her adrenaline went into overdrive. She returned the packet back to its hiding place and poured the vitamins over the top. She grabbed the second bottle to check its contents and found the exact same situation.

Rummaging through her box of assorted empty bottles, she found two of similar size. She quickly filled them with the dried navy beans and held the real vitamin bottles in one hand and the new pseudo-vitamin bottles in the other. Close enough she thought. She placed them in the mailing pouch and glued it shut with her Elmer's glue.

The second item she needed to promptly examine was a blue and white, heavy cardboard box, twelve by four by four inches. The box was designed so that two ends were secured with inserted cardboard flaps and one side was sealed with a strip of clear tape. This was going to be tricky. Tearing off the tape would result in a torn box, and Mr. Barbaria might see that. A better strategy was to slit the tape at the seam and place a new strip neatly over the top of the existing one. She needed steady hands for that, and she needed to hurry. Time was ticking. With the tape slit, there was no turning back.

She hurriedly pulled out the flaps and lifted the lid. Inside was a large plastic jar labeled chocolate protein powder. She unscrewed the lid and peeled back the plastic security wrap. The jar was filled with a light brown powdery substance. She rolled the powder against the side and shook it to see if any kind of packet materialized. Tentatively she poked her hand in the soft grainy substance and felt around like a kid trying to find the toy in a box of cereal. It was messy, and a dusty cloud plumed out of the jar. Finally, after a few seconds her fingers touched something plastic. She drew it out. Bingo!

Quickly, she had to replace the two pound jar that she would keep as evidence. She grabbed the two pound bag of rice from her box of paraphernalia, placed it in the blue and white Skylar box, and stuffed some paper around the sides to hold it in place. It would mimic the weight of the previous contents. She pulled a strip of clear packing tape, cut it, and carefully placed it directly over the existing tape to seal the box. Whoever received these packages would be in for a shock. She figured she'd have about two or three days before the shit hit the fan.

Glancing all around for anyone who might be watching and satisfied that all was well, she placed the jar of protein powder and two vitamin bottles with their illegal substances into the box of odds and ends and jumped out to safely store the stuff in the trunk of her car. She placed the packet and box with the bogus contents into the black and pink bag.

Gravel flew as she sped out of the park to return to the hotel. The digital clock showed she had been gone twenty minutes. She would have time to wash the dry chocolate from her fingernails and deposit the packet and box in with the other addressed packages and be ready for Mr. Barbaria to check them against the list.

A sigh of relief escaped Ariel's lips as she entered the hotel. She darted into the restroom to rinse her hands and then headed for her desk. She glanced around, but thankfully saw no sign of Mr. Barbaria. However, he'd be coming very soon to see that his precious cargo was shipped successfully. Someone else, a man, was approaching her desk. She smoothed her hair and straightened her jacket. The black and pink bag, she held close to her body. "Hi there, may I help you?" She skirted around to the back side of the desk and lowered the transport bag near the boxes of labeled packages. He was looking for Ontario. "It's on the north side of the atrium, just past Erie." She pointed the way, but he was in no hurry.

"Oh, thanks. I'm going to an insurance seminar. I'm early." He was a talker. Ariel began to get antsy. She needed to get him moving along as she had to make note of the addresses on the two packages she had tampered with before Mr. Barbaria appeared. "Well, I hope you enjoy your meeting. I need to make a phone call for a guest." She turned to pick up the phone. "Have a nice time." As soon as he walked away, she dropped the phone and grabbed the black and pink bag. He could be here any minute. She pulled up the address list on the computer and highlighted the two that were being shipped with the beans and rice—one to Texas and the other to Arizona. That should give her three days, but to play it safe she needed to be ready in two.

---

33 – In Love

Ariel could hardly believe what she had gotten into. She was going deeper and deeper as if into quicksand; she was being swallowed by a dark, thick force from which she could not escape. Danger and deception seemed to lurk around every corner and crevice of the hotel. She should have trusted her original instincts and run away. She recalled the day she came for the interview and was overcome with the creepy crawlies in the restroom when no one was there. But it was all too late now. She was involved, sucked into that inexplicable force to which there was no turning back. Yet somehow, she would muster the courage to forge ahead and do whatever it took to bring down the evil that thrived within the confines of the Capitol Plaza. Also, she fondly realized, had she not started working at this hotel, she would never have met Reece. It was surely fate, but hopefully not fatal.

Strangely, another woman had almost turned up dead. She hadn't been able to shake what had happened at the pool and the sight of Reece working fervently to bring the woman back to life and the obnoxious smell of chlorine that permeated his clothes when he emerged dripping from the water. Fortunately, the reports confirmed there was no foul play involved and the woman had experienced a seizure. She would not have survived had Reece not been there to save the day.

Reece was a blessing and a comfort. There was no doubt about it; Ariel was head-over-heels in love. But falling in love while plagued with the ugly truths she had uncovered was a real distraction and a burden that needed lifting. Euphoria and fear—what a bizarre emotional cocktail that she hoped her heart could handle. While her days were filled with foreboding feelings and paranoid thoughts, nights with Reece delivered the salvation she needed. Tonight was no exception and Ariel was grateful for the companionship.

It was late in the evening and a light snow was falling outside as Ariel arrived at Reece's place. He helped remove her wool coat and scarf and she pulled off her snow boots. Reece grinned at the sight of her soft flannel pajamas that were revealed. "I see you came comfortable, but let me assure you, I will take that to a whole new level," he promised as he took her hand. He ushered her toward the fireplace where dancing flames crackled and a thick down comforter was spread out to greet them. Two wine glasses and a bottle of wine waited. Ariel entered the magic realm of Reece Rhetlock. She looked up into his eyes and conveyed a gracious smile. He bent down to kiss her luscious lips.

The firelight gave their faces a warm, rich glow to match the warm glow they felt inside as they snuggled together and sipped Cabernet. Their newfound love created a harmonious, peaceful bond that belonged to them alone. They talked and teased and laughed at their own personal jokes.

As they had come to know more about each other, it was evident that his strength was her weakness and vice versa. They balanced each other perfectly—yin and yang—all that was complete. They had found such common ground and enjoyed mutual activities and interests. It was the proverbial match made in heaven.

Ariel felt safe nestled in Reece's strong arms. He caressed her hair and face. She marveled at his touch. It was gentle, yet strong. His hands massaged her neck, her back, her buttocks, and her thighs. She reciprocated the pleasure she was receiving and worked her hands through his hair and over his neck and back. They enjoyed the feelings they exchanged. The intensity mounted as their physical closeness, which started slowly and peacefully, grew frenzied as their desire blossomed. The heat from the fire and their passionate blaze burned as clothes were shed and their bodies melted together as one to share the ultimate earthly pleasure.

The passionate lovemaking left the couple in a euphoric peaceful state and their bodies were deeply relaxed. Eventually, weariness overcame them as the late night hours closed in. While Reece drifted of in a deep slumber, Ariel stared at the ceiling unable to sleep even though she was physically and emotionally exhausted. Thoughts of the day's events came flooding back—the risk of stealing Mr. Barbaria's product and learning her hunch was right. She wondered how everything would play out and prayed her decision and actions of earlier today didn't backfire. She couldn't take back what she had done and she was petrified of what lay ahead.

At the moment, she turned to look at Reece's peaceful body lying next to her. His strong facial features were relaxed; his breathing was slow and steady. What would he think if he knew what was going on? Would he scold her for putting herself in danger or would he praise her for her courage? Probably both. When she was with him, their newfound love trumped everything else. It was easy to forget the turmoil that plagued her mind. Now with him asleep and the only sound in the room the soft snores that escaped his lips, she was alone with her thoughts, and despite her exhaustion, Ariel's brain churned, trying to figure out how to handle the situation she had uncovered. *Should she call the police right now and just get is over with?* She pondered. *No, there was more work to do!*

In two or three days, everything would come crashing down. To be safe, she had to finalize a plan and be prepared for the fate she had created by stealing the packages that contained evidence against Ross Barbaria and his business, still safely stowed in the trunk of her car; she could drive straight to the police station tomorrow and turn them over as evidence and let the police begin their investigation. However, she still had many questions that she wanted to explore. She was convinced there was more to the story, and she wanted the police to have as much ammunition as possible to capture all the thugs involved. *How did the drugs get into the Skylar products—did they arrive at the hotel that way or was there an inside operation?* She would have to check out Mr. Barbaria's room, which might disclose further revelations.

Also, Slade was surely part of this ring and the missing woman had disappeared for reasons related to it. As much as she dreaded the thought, she somehow needed to scour Slade's hideout. She loathed and feared that man, but as fearful as she was of him, she also felt growing anger to think he had control over her, and that he was somehow involved with the missing woman who had worked for Mr. Barbaria. She instinctively knew that Mr. Barbaria was just one player in a web of many. She was sickened to think that maybe Ed was involved, which was why they left together in secret from The Cove.

As thoughts flickered in and out of her mind, slowly Ariel nodded off as her body turned limp. Hazy images floated in and out of focus. Her subconscious mind was at work on a plan. She was going to have to tell Troy everything. She needed his help. Suddenly, her limp body twitched temporarily spurring her back to life. Again her body relaxed, and she drifted off to sleep.

---

34 – Investigating

Troy was a nervous wreck. Ariel had explained all she knew about Ross Barbaria's covert operation—right under their roof! She was now on a dangerous mission. Her first undertaking was to sift through his room once he left for a night on the town. Ariel smiled as Mr. Barbaria passed by her desk in his polished and confident manner, on his way out for the evening.

"Have a nice time," she voiced in her most pleasant tone.

"Thanks," he said. "I will."

On the surface, she looked cool and calm, but inside, she was vibrating like a shivering Chihuahua. Once she was finished with a search of Mr. Barbaria's room, she was going to scour the engineering area and boiler room if she could ensure that Slade and Larry were not around. The thought of that really made her shudder.

Troy reluctantly handed over the key card to room 902. "Be careful," he warned.

"Don't worry; I'll be fine. In and out, ten minutes tops and he'll never know. But for heaven's sake, if for some reason he returns while I'm in there, call my cell." She patted the pocket of her mauve jacket to reassure herself that her phone and lifeline were there.

She was greeted with a very well-organized room. Once inside the suite, she quickly went to work, being careful to keep all contents in place. His suitcase in the closet was empty—she checked side pockets and zippers—nothing. Clothes were hanging—nothing in any suit pockets. The bathroom was clean and orderly. She felt around in the dresser drawers running her hands under his shirts, boxers, and socks searching for anything unusual. She pulled back the curtains to check behind them—clean.

Down on her hands and knees, she knelt to check under the king-size bed. It rested on an encased platform so that nothing could fit underneath. However, starting at the headboard end on the right side, she visually and manually checked carefully for any breaks in the wood casing and made her way slowly around the perimeter. To her astonishment, at the foot of the bed her fingers caught a loose plank that fell open when she wiggled it. In the absence of a flashlight, she pulled the lamp off the dresser and pulled it on its side to obtain a light source. There, hidden under the bed were several boxes. She pulled one toward her and lifted the lid. It was the size of a large shoebox. Her suspicions were confirmed. Inside were clear packets of white powder similar to what she had unearthed in the Skylar products. *So they do have an inside packing operation going on here!*

Now, extremely nervous, she quickly replaced the lid on the box, slid it back into place, and attempted to re-fit the wooden plank at the foot of the bed. The board didn't want to stay secure. It fell off and she had to try several times before it locked into place. She was sweating and felt drained. She returned the lamp to the dresser and shut off the light. She looked around to ensure things were as they should be and turned off other lights that she had turned on. She realized she had almost stopped breathing while snooping around and inhaled a much-needed breath of air. She cracked the door of room 902 open and peered around to make sure the coast was clear before slipping out.

Troy was anxiously waiting for Ariel to return to the front desk. He had chewed his fingernails to the quick upon hearing of her story about the drugs and Mr. Barbaria. When not checking in patrons, he paced from side to side, watching for any sign of Mr. Barbaria to come through the front doors. Even though he was long gone, Troy was scared to death he might return for some reason. What if he forgot something? If he showed up, he would have to alert Ariel and quick, he thought. He glanced at his big shiny watch. She had been gone for nearly fifteen minutes. She had promised it wouldn't take more than ten. What was she doing up there?

Finally, when Troy thought he couldn't take it anymore, he saw Ariel through the glass elevator being whisked to the first floor. She approached the front desk area with an anxious look on her face. She motioned him to come to the side door, and he quickly popped out to meet her. His co-worker, Malcolm, had the front desk covered. They both looked around for signs of anyone in the area. All was clear. "What did you find out?" he whispered.

"Promise you won't breathe of word of this." She swore him to secrecy. "We have a really big deal going on here. I found boxes of drugs under the bed, which has a secret compartment. He is using this hotel for drug trafficking, and he's repacking his products here. I know he has inside help. I'm sure that his assistant got in the way and I'm pretty certain that Slade took her out."

Troy's jaw with the dimple in the middle was literally hanging open, and his green eyes were focused intently on Ariel as she relayed what she had discovered. "We need to tell Security about this right now!" Troy's nerves were starting to unravel.

"Troy, calm down and listen to me carefully! We need to keep this quiet for another day or two. Also, I'm not so sure but what Ed and Slade aren't involved in this operation so telling Security is not an option nor is telling anyone else, because we don't know who all may be involved. The minute Mr. B. learns his drugs were tampered with, I'm sure they'll come after me, but I have a plan and I need your help."

Troy shook his head in disbelief. "Are you crazy? I am scared out of my wits right now."

"Well, hold it together, buddy, because I need you, and I have one more dangerous task to perform."

"Does Reece know about this?" he whispered as he glanced around. People were gravitating to the front desk, and Malcolm was going to need his help. He didn't wait for her to answer before he slipped through the door. He wished he didn't know all that he had recently learned.

Ariel returned to her desk and assisted some guests. Keeping an eye on the front, she waited for the opportunity to resume her conversation with Troy. When all was clear, she joined him again. She was ready to hit him with her next request. "I need you to find out where Slade and Larry are right now."

"Why?" Troy wrinkled his nose.

"I need you to make sure they aren't in the engineering office, but if they are, you need to come up with a reason to lure them away for awhile."

"Why? What in the world are you going to do? What are you looking for?"

"I can't tell you right now. Just help me get them out of there for a half hour."

"I . . . I can't do that. What would I say?" Troy stammered.

"Let's think. Hmm, think, think, think! Do you know of any

rooms that need repair?"

"No. I don't know of any."

"Well then, we have to make up something." Troy threw her a sideways glance with knitted brows as if she were out of her ever-loving mind.

"Wait a minute." Troy looked at her as if a light bulb went on. His green eyes twinkled. "Sometimes the banquet area or sales staff sends Larry or Slade on errands to pick up rental items or purchases from Home Depot or Menards. I actually think Slade is off tonight, so it's just Larry that we need to worry about."

"That would be great if Slade's not here. So we need to find out where Larry is, huh? Does Slade ever come in unexpectedly on his night off?" Ariel asked in a worried tone.

"I doubt it, but if he did, tonight would be the night with our luck."

Ariel shot him a frown and paused in thought. "Hey, I've got it, Troy! Why don't you go stuff a roll of toilet paper down the men's toilet, and then call Larry to report a clog." Ariel was half-joking and half-serious. Troy shook his head and released a short, high-pitched laugh.

"Oh Ariel, you are crazy. But that's funny. The problem is, Larry would have that resolved in less than ten minutes tops so, unfortunately, it wouldn't give you enough time to snoop around. Maybe we could get Reece to yank the whole damn toilet off the wall. Now that would be a whale of a clean up." Troy flashed a big grin.

"Oh geeze—so back to the errand idea. I'm starting to think it is about time to pull Reece into this mess. He would have the authority to send Larry out for something they might need in the convention area." Ariel combed her fingers through her bangs and blew out a heavy breath of air. "Gosh, though, I sure don't want to have to explain what I've dredged up here. I don't know what his reaction will be."

"I think it's best if someone besides the two of us know about this. We are going to need reinforcement when all this goes down. Actually, I think we should call the police now." Troy was as authoritative as Ariel had ever seen him.

"Trust me. There is more evidence to gather and I'm going to get as much as possible. There is still time," Ariel countered in her stubborn style. "I won't tell Reece everything. For now, I'll just tell him about finding the box of hair in the closet, which explains why I want to go look around. I'll tell him the freaky stuff now and all the other heavy stuff later."

---

35 – Searching for Evidence

As suspected, Reece was shocked by Ariel's story. She initially only shared her findings in the closet and he couldn't understand what else she needed to look for. In the end, Ariel spilled all the beans about the drugs, Ross Barbaria, Ed, Slade, and her ex. It took a while for Reece to comprehend the horrific happenings in the hotel. He asked Ariel many questions and had a hard time grasping what she had uncovered. Although nervous for her to continue her search, he finally caved in and supported her valiant efforts to gather additional information.

"I'm calling the police the minute there is any hint of anything going wrong," he promised.

Ariel's cell phone lit up, and she answered softly. "Yeah."

"He's outta here. Get in and get out of there quickly." Reece's voice on the other end sounded strained. He was not fond of this idea and was still trying to grasp the unbelievable account of Ariel's discovery. He had a whole new perspective on Slade Sobronski—what a sick son of a bitch. He tried to imagine what he would do to him if that bastard ever laid a finger on Ariel.

The minute she got the call, she was ready and waiting

Lora Lee Colter

near the entrance to Engineering and secretively slipped through the door. In the pocket of her mauve jacket, she patted the small flashlight and plastic bag that she had retrieved from her purse for this very adventure.

In the instant that she opened the door to the back boiler room, she wondered if she could even proceed. Her body was resisting this idea, and it was all she could do to put one foot in front of the other. As she edged into the large area filled with supplies and the hissing machines, she felt sick to her stomach as the memory of Slade flooded over her. His sickening words and smelly breath were vivid in her mind. She tried to shake the vision out of her recollection. She needed to work quickly and really wasn't even sure what to look for, but felt there was a good chance she might find clues to the woman's disappearance.

Although she had turned on an overhead light, it was dark in the spaces and crevices between the huge boilers and generators, and they cast shadows into the far corners. Switching on her flashlight, she pointed the beam toward the floor and swept it back and forth. There were fuzz balls and an accumulation of dust and grit that would be expected to appear on the floor of a boiler room where big machines cranked and churned. She circled the beam of light around the incinerator where signs of tiny scraps of trash and ash speckled the area. She studied the matter carefully. The shaft of light caught a glimmer of reddish string-like material. Ariel bent down and discovered it was a piece of hair—auburn red like the hair in the box in the closet. With the baggie inside out over her hand, she pinched the hair strand off the floor and pulled it into the bag. Suddenly she felt vulnerable and slowly looked over her shoulder to reassess her surroundings.

The red hair was evidence of something, although the real evidence was in the closet, or at least she hoped it was still there. She continued to sweep the light across the floor. It was interesting that directly in front of the incinerator, the dust seemed to have been swept away or it looked as if something had been dragged across that section of the floor. She got down on her hands and knees to look underneath the big furnace for anything else unusual. It was dark and dusty. She puffed on the dust to blow it away and puffed again as she moved along the perimeter. She found a dime. Running her hands underneath, her finger caught on a small rough object. She brushed it out into sight. It was the tip of a jagged, pink polished fingernail. Oh wow. She added the coin and fingernail to the plastic bag. This was evidence for sure. She could only image what might have happened here, and it scared the *bejeezus* out of her.

This discovery fueled her desire to find even more, and she skirted around to the back wall and squinted into the dim light cast on the cobwebs behind the incinerator. Lower to the floor, she peered for signs of anything out of the ordinary. There was nothing in sight, and the space was too small to get any closer.

Her eyes scanned over the remainder of the space and up toward the ceiling. It had rafters, but was too high for the beam of her flashlight to reach, although she could make out an outline of an attic type door. Unfortunately, there was no time and no means to investigate. She had been caught up in the sleuthing and temporarily forgot to be afraid. She jumped as her cell phone vibrated. It was Reece checking up on her. "If I didn't have to keep my eye on this banquet, I'd be there with you. Are you okay?"

"Yeah, I'm fine. I think I'll keep looking for a bit more."

"Larry is probably at Home Depot now loading up, and he'll be on his way back so you need to get moving and get out of there."

"Yep, just a few more minutes."

"Promise? Okay, come find me when you're done."

This was her only opportunity, and she didn't want to miss anything. She approached the closet, and this time the padlock was secure. Slade wouldn't let that mistake happen again. Ariel made another quick sweep around the room and poked around behind boxes and old furniture, but couldn't find anything else. She decided what she had found was better than nothing, even though she had hoped for something more profound.

As she finished with the back area and made her way toward the door out of the boiler room and to the front Engineering area, she was suddenly again struck with fear of what would happen should Larry or worse, Slade, find her on their turf without their permission or knowledge. She shut out the lights as she left and quickened her pace. The baggie in her pocket contained some evidence that might be useful, especially if that fingernail contained DNA evidence against Slade. She would place this along with the other evidence already safely tucked in the trunk of her car.

- - -

36 - Busted

Ross Barbaria clutched at his chest as he listened to the venomous voice being delivered through his cell phone. The message coming through the line was loud and clear and definitely poisonous. His heart was not taking this news well. Fear started at his core and spread like paint thinner through his chest and upper body. Toxic fingers of venom threaded through his veins, squeezing his oxygen supply. He couldn't breathe. He couldn't think clearly.

What had he just heard? One of his Arizona customers was in a rage. The male's voice on the other end pelted Ross with a string of expletives that would make a sailor blush. He heard certain words but not entire sentences. Where . . . delivery . . . what kind of a sick prank . . . a bag of rice . . . insane . . . trouble . . . hell to pay. The first time Ross had pressed the message button, he was so caught off guard he couldn't comprehend the news on the other end. He had to replay it.

Perspiring and nauseous, Ross did what he had to do. His fumbling fingers found his cell phone contact, Oscar Kaufman, and hit send. He wasn't sure how he was going to explain this, but he knew that fast action was imperative. There could only be one person responsible for this incomprehensive situation, and that was Ariel, that overly helpful concierge. He hoped against hope that they wouldn't be too late. They had to get to her, take care of her, re-coup the evidence.

Oscar was going to be furious. It was Ross who had decided to use Dina and Ariel to assist with his mailing. He should have used better judgment, but who would have thought either of them would have had any suspicions; definitely not that bimbo Dina. But Ariel was a different story. It turns out not so different from Ross's previous assistant who had to be hushed.

"Oscar here; what's up?"

Ross cut to the chase. "Uh, I'm afraid we've got a big problem. A delivery has been tampered with." Oscar's temporary silence on the other end was deathly nerve-racking. Ross waited for something, anything.

"What the hell do you mean? What is going on? Damn it!" Ross could hear something slam in the background, probably Oscar's fist hitting the wall.

"I just got the call now. A bag of rice was in the shipment rather than the usual product."

"Who's responsible for this bullshit?"

"I'm pretty sure it's that nosy concierge, you know, Jake's ex. She helped ship the packages a couple of days ago. It has to be her! Can you get Slade on her tail now?"

"Yer damn right I will. She won't see the light of day," he ranted. Then his voice became pensive. "Although, we better think carefully about this. The hotel is already under the spotlight with the earlier murder. Slade is going to have to make this look like an accident or burglary at her place; something of that nature. And if she's already gone to the police, we're soon screwed."

Ross shuddered. "She apparently hasn't alerted the police

yet or they would have pounced by now."

"If you have a stash under the bed or in your room, you need to get it back into secret storage on the double. When is the next seminar?"

"Tomorrow, which is why I'm still here and if I check out, that would raise a red flag."

"Don't worry; just sit tight. Triple S will get the job done. I think we're going to be fine. You're right, if she had gone to the police already, they would have swarmed the place by now. You're damn lucky, you son-of-a-bitch."

"Well, I don't feel lucky. I need to call back my customer and explain what happened and get his goods re-shipped. He's probably going to get all edgy and cancel future business with us, which is actually the least of our problems."

"Just take care of it," Oscar instructed. "And while you're at it, why don't you deliver the bad news to Ed and you two can take care of transporting the goods back to the safe. Also, make sure Ed stays on through the night if he's not already scheduled."

"Sure thing, boss."

"I'm calling Slade now with instructions to get to work, and I'll let Jake know what we are dealing with. He is going to go ballistic!"

---

37 – A Killer on the Hunt

The duplex on Plum Tree Lane was dark. It should be. It was 2:00 a.m. on a week night. Slick Slade Sobronski had a job to do. It was to be quick—in and out—a piece of cake, really. His gloved hands easily jimmied the patio door in the dark shadows at the back of the residence. He had parked up the street and quietly sauntered to the address of his next assignment. There was no one in the area, and all the homes were dark. This was a good sign. Apparently there were no night owls, and no one suffering with insomnia in this neck of the woods.

He was actually looking forward to this mission. He was going to make it a torturous process, and at the end of the day, simply make it look like a burglary gone bad. Ever since snooping Ariel had stumbled onto his goodies in the closet, it was all he could do to keep his distance and not hand her what she had coming. Now with orders from above, he had his wish. The only directions were to silence her quickly and find the evidence she had stolen before she went to the authorities. The *how* and *where* were left up to his skilled decision. He decided her place would be the most practical and he could look through her things. Although at her place, the roommate could potentially be a liability but that was a minor detail. He'd take her out, too, if necessary.

Slade was always prepared. He prided himself on the fact that he was always thinking. Except for the day he had left his private closet unlocked. That aggravated him to recall his foolish, carelessness. But now it was water under the bridge. He would have his day with Ariel. For this particular job, he didn't need a lot of tools. He had muscles and a brain. If his victim were asleep, it was just a matter of putting a pillow over her head. If things turned ugly, there were always knickknacks, artwork or a lamp that could be used as a weapon to strike with, but just in case, he had his nylon rope to use. He also brought along some meaty treats in his pocket in the event there was a dog to appease.

This could be quick and easy, but he wanted to have some fun, too. The lock popped on the back patio door, and he was instantly inside the great room. As usual, it was organized and free of clutter. He stopped and sniffed the air. It smelled fragrant and lady-like. His nostrils twitched, and a slow smile spread across his face. He took a deep breath. No growling dog attacked. It was extremely quiet. His eyes had adjusted quite nicely to the darkness of this hushed neighborhood. There were sparse street lights on Plum Tree Lane, just enough to give a soft glow, but nothing too glaring.

He fixated on the staircase to the upper level, which housed the bedrooms, but first decided to take a look around the lower level. He drifted into the kitchen and pulled open the refrigerator. It was well stocked with all the usual basics, and to his delight there were opened packages of sliced turkey and cheese. He helped himself. He washed it down with a swig of milk directly from the carton. Then, he pulled the back of his gloved hand across his mouth to clear the crumbs and wipe the milk mustache from his lips. *It's nice to have a snack before performing anything too strenuous,* he chuckled to himself. He glided out of the kitchen and down the short hall toward the door that led to the garage. He quietly turned the knob. To his satisfaction, Ariel's car was tucked away in its place.

After gaining a sense for his surroundings, he sauntered back past the kitchen and into the great room. He found the staircase and stepped lightly on the bottom stair step. The thick carpet masked all noise, and it was easy to move in silence. Slowly, he put one laced boot in front of the other as he climbed his way upward. Stopping at the landing, he listened for breathing or tossing and turning, but could hear nothing coming from either room.

Which was Ariel's, he wondered. First, he peered to the left into the dark room. Closer he crept. His ears strained, listening for any sound. His eyes narrowed as he attempted to draw light into his pupils. The bed was made. No one was there. He quickly retreated and retraced his steps toward the landing to the room on the right. He methodically eased his head around the corner into the bedroom whose windows faced the street. The foot of the bed was bathed in dim light from the street lamp. His eyes traveled from the footboard to the headboard. The covers were made up. There was no one there! No! Rage flared inside him. He had built himself up for the moment only to be deprived of his exploits. Oscar would not tolerate failure. It was up to Slade to preserve the secrecy of the operations. He vowed to find her. Like a fox on the hunt, he was driven.

Quickly he spun on his heel and fled down the staircase and out the way he had entered. In the dark shadows of the house, he remained concealed, scanned his surroundings and edged his way back to the street. Once in his car, he tried to collect his thoughts. Where would she be? Most likely with Reece Rhetlock. He would pose an additional threat, but he wouldn't worry about that now. He had to find her or his ass was grass.

Slade dialed Ed's cell phone. Ed answered, and a loud command blasted through. From the incoming number, he knew it was Slade.

"Get me Rhetlock's address. I hope you're at the hotel on the late shift tonight."

"I'm here. I wasn't scheduled, but when I got the awful news from Ross, I knew I had to cover tonight, so I sent Randy's skinny ass home. I heard what went down. Is the job done yet?"

"No, why the hell you think I'm asking for Rhetlock's place? You think I'm looking for a party?"

"Hang on." Ed searched the employee database and found the address. "He's on Parrot Bay Drive in the Parkview condos—1350, No. 7, in Waukee." Ed plugged in MapQuest and provided directions while Slade scratched the address on his hand with a ballpoint pen.

"It's not far. Just head west on University and hang a left after the Casey's store. What if the building has a security entrance? How the hell you going to crack through that?"

"I have ways." Click. The phone went dead in Ed's ear.

Ed couldn't wait to hear what happened. He was on high alert at the hotel and was on pins and needles. He was quite surprised to learn that Ariel was most likely involved with switching out the Skylar shipment. He and Ross had managed to get a cartload of boxes from under Ross's bed transported to the secret hiding place without raising suspicions. While Ed was stressed, it was Ross who was a complete basket case. He had returned to his room for a glass of scotch once the goods were safely stowed in the back storage room.

After providing orders to Slade, Oscar had notified Jake of the dire news Ross had delivered and the predicament in which they found themselves. Like Ed, Jake was in disbelief

Lora Lee Colter

that Ariel could have been involved. He felt a pang of heartache to think she was being hunted down like a wild animal, but knew business was business. Despite Jake's request to have Oscar get his plane ready so he could return to Des Moines, Oscar had not felt that necessary and instructed him to sit tight. "There's not a damn thing you can do here," he said. "I'll keep you posted. It shouldn't take long for Slade to take care of things."

Back in his room, Ross was writhing on the bed with chest pains and anxiety unlike anything he had experienced before. The two glasses of double scotch on the rocks had barely calmed his twitching nerves.

Meanwhile, Slade was fueled by adrenaline. He had turned into a robot with tunnel vision to complete the job as instructed.

This was definitely not a good day. The team of enterprising drug dealers faced their worst nightmare. And now, everything depended on Slade's ability to pull off a clean murder with no ties and to get his hands on the stolen evidence. If Ariel got to the police with her findings, Skylar Health and all of them were in jeopardy. Even if Slade pulled off an impeccable job, another missing woman from the hotel would raise a lot of red flags, and now, as Ed knew, Reece could be part of the equation. The sad truth was that if Ariel had told anyone about this, they could all go down the tubes regardless of whether she was disposed of or not.

---

38 – A Killer Down on His Luck

Slick Slade double-checked the address he had scribbled on his hand and cased the eight unit condo in the dimly lit shadows and determined that unit No. 7 was on the upper level. He was relieved to see that the building didn't have any security barriers. While he could pry through anything with the right tools and a little time, time was what he didn't have right now. The parking lot was devoid of activity, and all the lights in the windows were out except one sliver of soft yellow that peeked from closed drapes on the lower level. He ducked into one of the stairways between the units and dashed up the flight taking two stairs at a time. At the top, the two outer doors revealed No. 5 and No. 6. Damn it. The sands were sifting through the hour glass.

He retraced his steps down to the lower level and glanced around. He sprinted fifty feet to the other open stairway and raced to the top. There it was—unit No. 7. His eardrum was greeted with cold stone silence as he pressed his ear hard against the door. He tried to twist the door knob, but it was tight so he slipped the small tool out of his coat pocket and tripped the lock.

Easing the door inward, Slade peeked into the dark confines of the condo and moved discreetly toward the back where he suspected the bedrooms were located. He didn't take any chances with Reece involved and brought along his buck knife for added security, knowing this job most likely would result in a double homicide.

It was darkest in the short hallway, and he felt along the wall with his gloved hand until he reached the doorway that he assumed was the bedroom. A bedside clock illuminated the area just enough to cast a dim light over the bed. Covers were twisted and disheveled. The bed was empty. He slammed his fist hard upward into the door frame nearly cracking his wrist. Seething with anger, he whirled back through the dark hallway and out the door, slamming it behind him.

In a blind rage, Slade drove back to the hotel pushing the speed limit, but careful not to exceed it. The last thing he needed in his state of mind was to be stopped by a cop.

He parked by the employee entrance, ripped open the door, and blasted through the hanging weather strips. Ed practically crapped his pants. All had been quiet, and he hadn't seen Slade's figure approaching via the back door monitor. He jumped out of his seat from behind the glass windows of the office when he caught sight of Slade storming in and went to confront him. "What happened?"

"She wasn't there and neither was Rhetlock." The circumstances were growing ever grim, and Slade's agitation was escalating in his elusive attempt to find Ariel. "Get Troy's address. Better yet, get him on the line. As tight as those two girls are, he probably knows where she's at."

Ed released a short mirthless chuckle. "Yeah, and all you'll need to do is ruffle his hair and give him a wedgie and he'll probably give up all the information you need."

"And if not, I'll pull his manicured toenails out one by one," Slade responded in a flat tone.

As Slade's mind churned in a frenzied state, his phone

began to jingle. He clenched his teeth, and his jaw bone tensed. It was Oscar. "What the hell's going on?" he wanted to know. "You better tell me the job's done!"

"No, I haven't found her yet. She wasn't at her place and she wasn't with her boyfriend at his place, either. Ed and I are trying to figure out where she's at."

"Well you better find out fast, because I want her dead before daylight and its fuckin' 4:00 a.m. now so you don't have much time. Report back to me in two hours with some good news." The phone went dead.

Slade shot Ed a look of dread. Ed responded in a cool logical manner. "Honestly, I don't think it's a good idea to call Troy. He would tip her off that you are looking for her. He lives downtown somewhere, so you don't have time to mess around locating him."

Slade began to punch his fist into his hand. "I don't have any more time to waste!"

Ed offered ideas. "Okay, so, she isn't at home, and she isn't with Rhetlock, who, by the way, will be stopping in around six-thirty or seven as he does every day to check out his keys. Think about it. He can't be too far from here, and they are probably together. I'll grill him when he gets here. He won't suspect anything since we talk every morning."

"I don't have that kind of time. Hang on! You just said . . . they can't be too far from here. What if . . . Get me the room vacancy list and the master and *E* keys *now*. I'll betcha sure as shit, she is tucked away in one of these rooms—snug as a fuckin' bug in a rug."

As the Chief Engineer, Slade had access to the highest security level possible. The master key allowed access into any room other than those in which the deadbolt had been thrown. The *E* key was an emergency key that was capable of overriding even a dead bolt that had been clicked into place.

"If she's hiding out here, you better believe I'll find her," he snarled. Grisly features spread across his hard facial muscles, and his face contorted into an animal-like appearance.

Within minutes, Slade was in the employee elevator with a list of vacant rooms and keys in hand. In his jacket pockets, he still carried the tools of his trade. The elevator climbed to the top floor. He would methodically start at the top and work his way down. At this time of the morning, to his benefit, all was quiet. He promptly went to work to check the first room on the vacancy list. Slade's head throbbed and his stomach felt like an empty cavern. Through bloodshot eyes, he quickly scanned the room for signs of occupancy. To be certain, he checked the closet, the bathroom, and behind the curtains, even though it was unlikely anyone would have time to hide as he barged through the door unexpectedly. The first room was clean.

On to the next room, and the next on the list, he swept through the tenth floor without any luck. With growing anger and doubt, he had scoured floor after floor, reaching the sixth floor and then the fifth. Exhaustion was settling in. A little over an hour had passed and only an hour or so was left before daylight. He tried not to think of Oscar's wrath if he didn't execute the job.

On auto-pilot, he reached for the doorknob of the first room listed on floor five as vacant—again, nothing. How long would this hunt take? Slade's mind flashed back to childhood. He was ten or eleven and searching for kids in his neighborhood. His big back yard and the cemetery beyond was a perfect place for hide and seek. He loved the game— enjoyed being the hunter. The girls were easy to find because they hid together and giggled when they spied him approaching. Sometimes, after he reached the count of fifty and hollered "ready or not, here I come," he'd sprint around the front of the neighbor's house, through their garden and along the edge of the cemetery so he could covertly enter the back side of the graveyard. He would spot boys crouched behind stones or trees and stealthily sneak up from behind and yell "gottcha." They would jump, gasp, and say something like, "Geeze, Slade, you scared the crap out of me." Their startled reactions were priceless. He felt smarter and superior in his strategy. Not only was he an expert hunter, but he was clever in choosing his hiding spots and was tough to track down.

Slade had fond memories of his childhood growing up with his mom, dad, and a younger sister and brother. That was, until the summer between his freshman and sophomore year in high school. It was a hot summer evening when news broke that his dad had run off with the banker's wife. His mom, the banker, and their entire small town were shocked to pieces. He still remembered it as though it were yesterday. His mom pulled up to the Grill 'n Chill in her white convertible as he sat with his friends laughing, telling stories, and slurping frosty shakes with not a care in the world. She called out, "Sladee, come. I need to take you home." He could tell by the tone of her voice that something was terribly wrong. He rose and turned to wave at his friends as he half trotted to the car. The moment he got close, he saw the raccoon eyes of dark smeared makeup and tear streaked stains on her face.

"What's wrong, Mom?" he said, in a choked voice. He knew it was something terrible. He had never seen her like this.

"Where are Charlie and Maggie?"

"The kids are fine; they are with the neighbors. It's your father—seems he's disappeared with that despicable Sonya Murray, the banker's wife." Slade couldn't have felt any different had an iron fist drove into his stomach. It was a punch in the gut he'd never forget or forgive.

As it turned out, scheming Sonya had managed to funnel millions into a private account and she and his dad just disappeared into thin air and undoubtedly reinvented a new life of leisure in some tropical paradise. Slade felt duped and betrayed. It was a real scandal, and man, did that ever make him furious. Ever since that night, he wanted to hunt down his father and beat him senseless. Although he was at an all-time low point after the life-altering news broke, he tried to stay strong for his mom and be the man of the house. However, as if things weren't bad enough, his mom remarried a no-good arrogant ass of a man once the allotted time had passed to declare his dad divorceable. Slade couldn't understand why his mom chose to bring that no-good loser into her life and trade her oldest son for that creep. Things really got ugly after his step-dad moved in.

Although Slade was an intelligent kid and was capable of good grades, he no longer applied himself in school and joined a rough crowd. Half the time, he didn't even bother to come home. He just didn't give a rat's ass anymore. The fork in the path had presented itself and he took the wrong turn, although at the time it seemed a logical choice.

While reliving his unfortunate childhood memories, he completed three more room searches. At the fifth door on level five, he was unexpectedly caught off guard. The master key neatly tripped the lock, however this time the deadbolt had been thrown. Someone was inside! He pulled out the E key to release the deadbolt. His senses piqued, and he quickly asserted his killer instincts—his breathing slowed and his movements softened. He could see the dark and quiet room as the door swung in ever so slightly. The safety latch was in place, which required his special tool. Snap, it was open.

His eyes adjusted to the darkness, and he could see a quiet shape under the covers of the king-size bed. No stirring, only soft breathing. After all he'd been through, he felt no need for fun and games; the time was here. He would make sure the last thing Ariel saw before the life drained out of her pain-filled body was his face. She would have no doubt that she messed with the wrong crowd.

He expertly pulled the buck knife from his pocket, flipped the blade out, and approached the slowly breathing form barely stirring under the covers. Drawing the knife high, he brought it down in one swift motion tearing through the thick blankets into flesh; he drew back and stabbed at the torso— one, two, three more times. There was no fighting chance, just the immediate sounds of deep sucking air and gasping. Slade snapped on the lamp switch and pulled the covers away from the face and leaned in close to reveal his victory, but rather than triumph, he instead was sickened at the sight. Not because of the blood and gore, but because this was not Ariel. It was some poor sap who was in the wrong place at the wrong time.

"Holy shit." Slick Slade Sobronski grabbed at his head and dug his fingers into his hair. In a broad sweeping motion, he flung the lamp off the bedside table. He tried to grasp what had just happened. Was the room number on the list wrong? In his sleep deprived and stressful state did he mistake the room number as a vacancy. He did not make mistakes!

A complete numbness swept through his tired body. Not that he felt a sense of loss because he had taken another life, but because he was not accustomed to feeling a loss of control. This scene completely caught him off guard and flared an anger in him that was hard to manage. He struggled to pull rational thoughts into focus and out of the disorientation that flooded his mind. *You have to find Ariel; you have to keep moving. Call Ed,* a voice inside him urged. He pulled his cell phone out of his pocket and found Ed's cell number.

"Ed here. What's up?" He heard Slade exhale a heavy breath on the other end of the line.

"You need to get your ass up to room 505 on the double and clean up a mess. Get the foot locker out of the back engineering room and grab some cleaning supplies. I have to keep moving. I'm half done and haven't found that bitch yet."

"What the hell are you talking about?"

"There was someone inside a room that was supposed to be vacant, and it's not her." Slade's nervous and irritated voice forged on. "The person is dead. Stuff the body in the foot locker and clean things up. Wear gloves," he instructed. Ed was speechless. "Did you hear me?"

"Uh, ah, I heard you but I don't believe it. Are you sure it's not Ariel?"

"Yes, I'm sure. Now step on it." Slade cut the phone call and turned away from the lifeless body in the bed of room 505.

Ever since that concierge had arrived at the hotel there was nothing but trouble. Boy, he couldn't wait to slice her neck. He exited the room and continued his vigilant and exhausting search. He had to find her sooner or later. Around the perimeter of the fifth floor, he stormed, checking room after empty room. With each search, he invested less time and energy—just a quick entrance and then out.

He was drained and not thinking clearly, especially since this horrific error. He had been up twenty-four hours straight, and his body was full of tired, nervous tension. His muscles felt like knots twisted to the breaking point, ready to snap at any second. Atop his frazzled body, his head felt sluggish. He had a vision of his brain enveloped in mold—greenish black and fuzzy—the kind that sprouts in containers of food forgotten at the back of the refrigerator.

As exhausted as Slade was, and as bad as his foggy head hurt, he fought to remain composed and knew how important it was not to draw attention to his activities. He had to appear nonchalant. Early risers were beginning to stir as he reached and searched the lower floors. He couldn't believe he was to the third floor and had nothing to show for his hard work. Could he be wrong about Ariel's whereabouts? She just had to be here!

---

39 – Careful

Reece kissed Ariel goodbye. It was time for him to get to work. He held her close and prolonged the departure. "Be safe, my love."

Ariel gave him a tight hug, drawing into his strong body. "Don't worry. You know I've got everything I need for the police. I'm calling them the minute I'm out of the shower. It's time to take these nasty weasels out of operation."

"Lock the door and keep your phone close. I'll give you a call once I get everyone in banquets rolling this morning. I love you."

Reece gazed down into Ariel's brown eyes, full of determination, the corners rimmed with lines of exhaustion. He brushed her hair off her forehead to plant a gentle kiss and then squeezed her hand. "Bye for now, and be careful. I can't imagine what's going to happen when the police hear about all this. The hotel will be surrounded with cops and media in no time—like ants on a popsicle stick."

Ariel threw her arms around Reece and gave him one final hug before he departed. "Talk to you soon." She closed and secured the door after him. A quick call to work let her boss know she would be running late this morning. She started the coffee pot and looked forward to a warm shower to reinvigorate her tired body.

The Security area was empty as Reece arrived to collect his keys. That was unusual. Instead of waiting, he decided to make his way down the back hallway to see if by chance his office was already unlocked and open for him. He couldn't take his mind off the revelations Ariel had shared the night before and the potential danger she was in until the police were contacted and on the premises. He would hurry and get some work done and give her a call to make sure she was safe.

His office door was shut and locked. Damn. *Where is Security when you need them?* Reece wondered. The guys in blue didn't typically stray too far from the office during the 6:00 a.m. time frame when the majority of employees arrived and clocked in for the early shift. Reece turned and crossed the back hallway. He cracked a door and poked his head into the banquet area, which was dark and quiet. He pulled the door shut and made his way to the bright noisy kitchen. He said good morning to the kitchen staff and servers who were getting started for the day. "Have you seen anyone from Security this morning?"

"Nope, the office was empty when I got here," replied the kitchen manager as he shook his head. "Kind of strange, huh?" He was busy pulling big pots off the storage shelf. Reece stopped long enough to exchange some small talk and pour a cup of freshly brewed coffee.

"Well, I better keep moving to see if I can find someone. I've got to get my keys." He exited the kitchen and strode down the north hallway toward the atrium en route to the front desk to have Security paged.

---

40 – Big Trouble

As she waited for the water to warm in the shower, the familiar ringtone alerted her of an incoming call. It was Troy. She greeted him with "Good morning, Sunshine. Are you on your way to work?"

"Yes, I'm on the freeway close to Eighth Street. Don't you sound chipper this morning? This is a big day. Have you called the police yet?"

"Nope, just getting ready to get in the shower right now. I'm calling as soon as I'm dressed."

"Well for crying out loud, don't dilly-dally," Troy scolded.

"Don't worry. I'm ready and I've got as much evidence as I'm going to get."

Troy sighed. "Oh, this is going to be huge. Are you scared?"

"No, well, okay, a little bit. I wonder what kind of state Ross is in as I'm sure by now he knows a package was tampered with, and I bet he is livid and on the war path."

"I'm just glad you're in a safe place. I'll be at the hotel soon before the police show up." Just as Troy was ready to say good-bye, Ariel let out a gasp.

"What is it?" He heard a scream and the sound of her cell phone ricocheting across a hard surface. "Ariel, Ariel. Oh, my God, Ariel," he shouted but there was no response. All he could hear was muffled noise and the sounds of a struggle. Troy's heart didn't just skip a beat; it felt like it skidded to a stop. His phone was frozen to his shaking hand as he strained to hear what he could only imagine was happening on the other end.

Morning traffic was heavy on 235 westbound and he accelerated, erratically weaving in and out of the traffic flow. His mind was numb. "Ariel, can you hear me?" He continued to plea for a response to no avail; he could not get her to answer. Finally, coming to his senses, as hard as it was to end the call, he broke the connection and dialed 911.

A sleepy sounding woman answered after what seemed like an eternity, "911, what's your emergency?"

"Oh my God, send someone to the West Des Moines Capitol Plaza Hotel immediately. He's going to kill her—room 210. Hurry, lady, hurry!"

"Calm down; who is going to kill who?"

"My friend, she is being attacked right now. I could hear her scream, her phone hit something and then there was no response. She has evidence and was going to call the police," Troy blurted out in breathless gasps.

"What is your name, sir?"

"Troy. I work at the front desk at the hotel. I'm on my way there now. Please send the police before its too late."

"Okay, the police will be there in five or six minutes."

"Thank God. I'm going to try to reach her cell phone again. Good-bye."

---

41 – Perilous Encounter

Ariel was utterly caught by surprise—like a deer in the headlights. The only thing imaginably worse would have been if she was standing there stark naked. She had been sure of her plan and only within minutes of calling the police. Unfortunately, she had been overly confident, feeling secure and concealed on the second floor of the hotel with the safety locks in place. How did he know she was here, and how did he possibly get in? With the shower running and the distraction of conversing with Troy, she didn't hear anything suspicious in order to prepare herself or call 911. She was a prime target—exposed and completely blind-sided by the most disgusting excuse for a human being she knew. Slimy Slade was advancing with a knife directed at her, and she could tell by the look in his eyes that he wanted to slash her to pieces.

The soles of her feet felt like they seeped glue, rooting her to the spot in which she stood. There she was in her robe, just inside the doorway of the bathroom. He stalked toward her, a menacing grin across his stubbly face. She gasped in horror and fought that frozen sensation. His movement, her own movement, everything seemed to play out in slow motion. She saw her arm extend and her fingers flex outward to grab the only thing in eyesight that was within reach, a can of hairspray at the edge of the sink. At the same time, she hurled her cell phone, which she held in her other hand, at Slade. It appeared to whirl across the room in a slow, spinning motion and glanced off the side of his head before it hit the wall and finally clattered to the tile floor. Troy's voice trailed through distorted space and time as the situation took on a surreal effect.

Slade's face revealed only minor irritation in response to the offensive cell phone attack, and slowly his hand rose to massage the spot on his forehead where the phone had landed an unexpected blow. Unfazed, he didn't break stride and proceeded to her like a robot fixated on its target.

With both hands firmly around the can of hairspray, Ariel aimed and pressed down hard on the nozzle. A plume of stinging aerosol mist met his eyes in a nasty assault. It caught him by surprise, and his free hand flew to his face. In a split second, Ariel released a primal scream and kicked the hand that held the knife. The knife with its extended, shiny blade released from his grip and spiraled across the room. Again she sprayed and kicked, planting a foot firmly to the groin area. Slade howled in pain and folded over, giving her a chance to skirt around him as he brought his head down between his knees.

Despite the agonizing pain, he wasn't about to let her get away and just as she shot past him, he threw out a solid elbow that caught her square in the ribs. It knocked the wind out of her, and she stumbled to the floor. Within a second, he was upon her from behind and expertly flipped her over to her back with a hard thud. His hands reached for her neck. She screamed and kicked with all her might. The only advantage she had was that he was exhausted and a bit disoriented by her attack. His eyes still burned from the chemicals that saturated them and numbing pain throbbed through his lower extremities. Throughout the struggle, she pressed her feet hard against the floor to scoot herself closer to the door, clawing and scratching like a savage animal.

It seemed like an eternity since Slade appeared out of nowhere, but she guessed it had only been minutes. Her original dream-like state of mind was now replaced with a fight-or-flight mentality that created an adrenaline rush like Ariel had never known. She felt sharper and stronger than ever. She tried not to think what would have happened had he still held the knife. She guessed she would have been dead by now.

Ariel proved to be a handful for Slade as she continued to unleash her wrath, wreaking havoc against his tired and run-down body. Skin peeled away from his arms and face as her fingernails raked deep into his flesh at all angles. The searing pain fueled his anger. Due to his size and strength, he managed to maintain control of the situation. Slowly but surely, he was able to overpower her. His hand encircled her neck. "This is it, bitch. You should have kept out of everyone's business." The stench of his breath was nauseating.

At that moment, Ariel knew what an insect in a spider web must feel like—not at the first touch of the silky threads of the web, but after the struggle and strategy to break free. Sensing the web turn sticky and feeling new strands shooting from the spider to wrap tighter around the body, the prey would slowly succumb to the inevitable.

As the grip around Ariel's neck grew ever tighter, she fought for air and struggled to maintain consciousness. The room was spinning and fading in and out. Eventually blackness enveloped her.

---

42 – To the Rescue

After calling 911, Troy managed to redial Ariel's number while dodging in and out of traffic in the westbound lane. "Pick up, pick up. Come on." Her phone rang with no answer. In the distance, he could hear siren's wailing. Oh why hadn't he programmed Reece's number into his cell? Instead he dialed the front desk.

The Night Auditor, at the end of his shift, answered the phone on the second ring. "Good morning, Capitol Plaza Hotel—West Des Moines. May I help you?" Ron Wickers jerked wide awake as the voice on the other end streamed through in a panic.

"It's Troy. The police are on the way. Get to room 210 now!" His voice was powered with an authoritative command.

Ron was trying to wrap his head around the information being directed at him. "Wha—huh—what do you mean?" He was in shocked disbelief.

"It's Ariel—go help her. Run."

Ron threw the phone down and raced out from behind the front desk. A startled guest jumped back as Ron flew past headed for the side stairs. He pulled the two-way radio off his belt clip. "Paging Security—all Security to second floor—room 210." There was no response from Ed, the lone hotel security guy on duty. He was busy in the boiler room, dealing with the dead body he had transported from fifth floor. He was cursing Slade at the moment and in a quandary, wondering what to do.

Reece was just crossing the atrium and saw the commotion upon nearing the front. He dropped the cup of fresh, hot coffee he held in his hand and instantly broke into a sprint to see what had Ron in a panic. He caught up with him as he reached the doorway to the stairs.

"What's wrong?" Reece demanded to know, even though in his gut he felt like he knew the answer.

"Room 210," Ron huffed as he grabbed the door to the stairs. Reece, in his haste and overly energized state, pushed Ron out of the way with his strong forearm and rushed the stairs two at a time, propelling himself upward by grabbing the handrail as he went. He had to get to Ariel.

Was it his imagination, or were sirens wailing in the background? He would never forgive himself if he was too late. He should have immediately checked back with her, or not even left her in the first place. *This couldn't be happening,* he thought with dread.

He couldn't afford to lose the best thing that had happened to him in a long time, and Ariel had so much to live for. She didn't deserve to die. He sprinted. He had to rescue her.

---

43 – Ariel's Heroes

Reece could not believe his eyes as he blasted through the door where he had just minutes before kissed his beloved Ariel good-bye. She lay motionless on the floor in her soft robe, with Slade atop her, his grimy hands squeezing her delicate neck. Slade's head snapped toward the sound of the door banging open as Reece barreled through.

Adrenaline coursed through Reece's veins. "Get off her, you bastard," he bellowed. In one swift motion, he dove at Slade knocking him off Ariel. He jumped to his feet shaking in both fear and anger as he stared into the eyes of a murdering, soulless monster. Reece was no longer the suit wearing yuppie he had made himself out to be. He was transformed into the tough, fearless military man and fighter of times past—times he had left behind a few years prior.

Before Slade could rise, Reece hauled him up by the collar and in a quick single jerk of his hand pushed his face down hard to meet his knee and snapped him back up, launching him onto the bed like a rag doll. Not letting up, Reece grabbed the phone, ripped it from the cord, and smashed a powerful blow square to his startled face with a bone-cracking sound. Slade rolled off the bed in an attempt to escape toward the door. Still fueled by rage, Reece jumped over the bed and grabbed Slade around the neck from behind, squeezing and choking. Slade continued to struggle but grew weaker as the life was leaving his body. It was then that Reece turned his head toward Ariel. She was not moving. The sight of her fragile beauty snapped him out of his hell-bent fury. He released the death grip from Slade's neck. Slade was motionless, but still alive.

Ron arrived on the heels of Reece and stood in the doorway in disbelief. The sirens grew louder, and it sounded like the police had arrived at the hotel. "Go get help!" shouted Reece. Ron turned and raced off to get their assistance. Thank God, they had arrived. Reece leaned over Ariel's limp body and pressed his head to her heart. He felt for a pulse on her red and bruised neck, but felt nothing.

Behind him, he heard a familiar but hysterical voice. "Reece, is she okay? She has to be okay." Troy quickly dropped beside him and watched as Reece searched for signs of life and began to administer CPR.

After the darkness had cleared from her frightened mind, Ariel felt extremely light, fresh, and free, as a swooshing corridor of air swept her upward, like the rush of a stream toward a brilliance of blinding light. As she rose higher, a kaleidoscope of colors shimmered all around her. She experienced peace and tranquility unlike anything she had ever known. A rainbow appeared behind the yellow-white light. The gentle, but swift stream of air that propelled her upward, was heading toward the brightest end of the rainbow.

After what seemed like several amazing minutes, Ariel was suddenly sucked quickly downward, and the heavenly out-of-body experience was over. She felt heaviness and pain. She tried to lift her eyelids.

Reece was alternating chest compressions and mouth to

mouth breathing. He was frantic, but knew his performance could mean life or death, so he focused intently on his rhythm and counting. Miraculously, before long there was a faint flutter of her lashes, and her eyelids slowly parted. She looked through blurry eyes as two faces came into focus, and she realized the two men she trusted most were at her side.

"Ariel, oh Ariel, are you okay?" Reece raised her up by the shoulders and pulled her close.

She started shaking. "Where is he? Is he gone? He was going to kill me."

"Don't worry, my love. He will never hurt you again."

Reece glanced over at Slade who was beginning to raise himself on one elbow. "Don't bother getting up, you sack of shit." Troy feeling confident, with Slade down and Reece there, hopped up and placed two swift kicks to his ribs. Slade let out a howl and fell back to the floor. "Take that you ghastly beast."

As if on cue, Ron appeared back at the room with two policemen to finish up where Reece and Troy left off. In unison, Reece and Troy both said, "He's right there," as they pointed to Slade groaning on the floor. "Get yer hands above yer head, now!" With guns drawn and pointing directly at him, they cautiously approached Slade who painfully raised his arms. The big burly cop expertly handcuffed him and brought him to his feet as his rights were read to him.

The other officer, of slight build, began a pat down from top to bottom. Just as he finished the body search, a ringing sound emanated from the phone he had pulled from Slade's pocket. He pushed the button to receive the call and put it on the speaker. A gruff voice came through. "I need a status report, and it better be good." Oscar Kaufman's demand came through loud and clear.

The officer responded. "The status is that your friend is in handcuffs." There was dead silence on the other end. "This cell phone is being confiscated for call history evidence. Thanks for calling." The officer smiled and shook his head, suspecting correctly that the voice on the other end belonged to a partner in crime. How did they get so lucky?

"Get him outta here!" the burly officer commanded. By now the paramedics were streaming through the doorway and onto the scene. Ariel pushed herself away from Reece's chest where she had buried her face. Despite Ariel's refusal to receive help, they looked her over and checked her vitals anyway. "I'm fine, really. I have some evidence for the police. There's been quite an operation going on in this place."

Ariel's anger overtook her fear and pain. She rose and looked at Slade as the two officers led his slumped and defeated body toward the doorway. She tried to look him in the eye, but his bloody gaze was directed to his feet. "You know, Slade, you are a disgusting low-life scum-bag who deserves to be punished for the rest of your miserable life. Good riddance to rubbish. Go rot in jail."

"We'll have an officer conduct a full report, but we need to get this character safely out of here and under lock and key." She breathed a sigh of relief and dropped her head to Reece's chest again for comfort. He stroked her hair.

Moments later, back-up officers were there to listen to Ariel's account of what had happened and take notes. Troy fetched a glass of water and handed it to her, which she gratefully accepted. The brewed coffee no longer sounded good.

Ariel sat on the edge of the bed beside Reece, who held her hand, and recounted the attack and the events that had lead to her assault. When she had completed the story of finding the box of hair in the boiler room, Slade's threats, and the discovery of the drugs in the mailings and in Ross

Barbaria's hotel room, she went to the closet and pulled out the box that contained the two Skylar packages, the baggie with the swatch of auburn hair, the coin, and the pink fingernail tip she had found. "Here's the evidence I've collected. I was actually ready to call the police this morning. Thank goodness everything worked out."

She looked at Reece; her eyes displayed eternal gratefulness. She then turned to Troy and thanked him for calling the police. "I owe you both my life," she said as they simultaneously leaned in to give her a body sandwich. She knew then who her true heroes really were and always would be.

---

44 – A Gruesome Discovery

The officer who took notes pulled out his radio and instructed other officers, who by now had converged on the hotel. "We have one suspect in custody. Get access to the engineering and back boiler room pronto. There is a closet that needs to be searched. And we have a guest room that likely is housing another suspect. If what our witness says is true, you will find major evidence in both those locations."

Troy stepped up to render assistance and resume his duties of the hotel. "Tell them I'll meet them at the front desk." He let go of Ariel and paused, then spun on his heel with renewed energy.

A duo of uniformed officers rushed through the lobby and Troy intercepted them and flagged them to follow. He led them through the atrium toward the back south hallway and to the door of the engineering area. They quietly pushed the door inward and Troy pointed to the back boiler room. In single file, they entered.

It wasn't clear who was more startled, the police and Troy, or Ed as he was caught struggling with a foot locker near the incinerator. Troy was astounded, and his hands flew to his open mouth. "Ed?"

"West Des Moines police—hands up." The two officers drew their guns and approached him slowly, eyeing the trunk. "What's going on here?" Ed was speechless. "What's in the box? Open it up," one of them instructed. Ed stood there dumbfounded. "Open it up!" The request was much bolder this time. Ed didn't comply, so the other officer tentatively raised the lid.

There stuffed in the box was a middle-aged man in an undershirt and briefs. Dark crimson stains oozed from rips and tears in his white cotton shirt. A blanket was wrapped around his lower torso. Troy and the officers were not prepared for what they saw. Troy's mouth gaped open, and he quickly turned away. It was incomprehensible: a bloody body in a trunk. Even more incomprehensible was that a reliable hotel security guard was about to dispose of the human remains.

While the three were gawking at the mind-boggling view, Ed took advantage of the small window of opportunity of having the attention shifted away from him. He slowly edged backward, closer to the mammoth machines that towered behind him. A few more steps back, and suddenly he bolted into the shadows and disappeared out of sight.

The officers reacted quickly and swung into action as Ed ducked out of view. Their guns drawn, the pair forged onto the vacant spot that just seconds before had showcased their suspect.

He had disappeared. Upon rounding the back side of the incinerator, they were greeted with emptiness and silence. They looked at each other in puzzlement and scanned the area. There were no visible outside doors, however closer scrutiny of all surfaces revealed the outline of a square trap-door in the floor, just the size for someone to drop through.

"We need some flashlights, quick," instructed one officer to Troy.

"I'm on it! There should be some in the other room." Troy hoped he could quickly locate them. The officers were hesitant to proceed without a light source, as the opening was black as a tar pit. A dank smell wafted from the hole.

"Calling all units: we have a suspect on the run—he's underground. Make sure the building is surrounded."

- - -

45 – Progress

Inside room 902, Ross Barbaria pushed the send button on his phone to accept an incoming call from Oscar. Hoping for good news that their troubles were finally over and the girl was disposed of, he was caught off-guard by Oscar's harried voice. "The police have Slade! I don't know where the hell he is, or what exactly is going on, but when I called him to get a status check, an officer answered his phone and said he was in handcuffs. The last time I spoke with him was around 4:00 a.m. and he had not found her at either her place or her boyfriend's."

Reeling from the information, Ross's chest pains flared with a vengeance. At that moment, a strong rap at the door practically put Ross's heart out of commission.

Officers, escorted by Ron, the Night Auditor, were outside the door. "Police. Open up!" Another rap on the door of 902 was met with silence. Ron slid a key card into the slot and the door parted, but was stopped by the flip lock. With guns drawn, they shouted again. "Open the door, now!" There was no response. The policemen wasted no time in ramming the door with their shoulders. It didn't give after two tries. "Go for it." One said to the other, and a gun shot blasted through the lock. A curious patron from next door poked his head out and quickly ducked back inside when he saw the police firing at the door next to him.

Ross was crumpled on the floor near the bed, holding his hands over his chest. One officer held a gun to him while the other marched to the bed and kicked the bottom panel loose from beneath. Down on his hands and knees, he searched the cavity, but it appeared clean and empty. "Where did you hide the evidence?" he asked in a stern tone. Ross didn't answer. The officer began searching the bathroom, dresser drawers, and closets. He hauled a big suitcase out of the closet and on the handle hung a blue and white Skylar Health tag. "So you must be involved with the Skylar Health business?" Ross gave up no information. "We have some evidence in our possession with this same name and logo. Isn't that interesting? We need to take you in for questioning. Get on your feet, buddy." His rights were read to him as handcuffs snapped shut over his trembling wrists and he was led out of the room and through the lobby to another waiting cop car.

By now, guests were congregating in the lobby and peering down from every floor to see what the commotion was about. Similar to the behavior that the snowstorm had provoked, some people embraced the action and wanted to see everything that was going on, and others wanted to flee. For now, the hotel was on lock down until the police had things under control. There was another suspect on the run and until he was caught, no one was going in or out.

The entire hotel was surrounded with cop cars, and it looked to be under siege, just like a scene right out of one of the *CSI* episodes. This was big news for a quiet city in the Midwest. Inside, the police worked to get people back into their rooms and lock the doors. As word spread that one suspect was still on the loose, the hallways quickly became deserted as people heeded the warning. For the few people who had planned to check out and had left their rooms locked with the key card inside, the police had them safely corralled in the lounge area near the front. All employees on duty were called to the front for their own protection and to be accounted for.

In no time at all, the media were on sight with cameras rolling. Frank Scaglione, the handsome and competent captain of the West Des Moines police department, took center stage. He spoke in a clear, deliberate voice to share what he knew of the events leading up to the arrest of two men inside the hotel and the ongoing search for a third. Two of the men worked at the hotel and another was a frequent guest.

He explained there was evidence of drug trafficking, conspiracy to commit murder, murder, and attempted murder, along with a number of other charges. "In time, we will determine how many other parties are involved, but it is believed this crime ring may have far-reaching connections and we will piece together that puzzle. A young woman who works at the hotel as a concierge is credited for gathering much of the evidence that will be used against these men," Captain Scaglione reported. "This is an ongoing investigation, and I can provide no more details at this time. Thank you."

- - -

46 – Underground

Troy returned with two powerful flashlights and handed them to the officers who were anxiously waiting at the mouth of the gaping dark hole into which their perpetrator dropped just minutes earlier. They had bent down low to listen for any sounds that might direct them once they descended into the darkness. It was quiet as a coffin.

The light sources exposed a ladder hanging down to just a few inches above the cement floor. Although the depth appeared to be only about six feet, they opted for the ladder just in case their perceptions were off. No need to risk twisting an ankle or snapping a wrist by jumping. Once underground, they swept the high beams of their flashlights across the expanse of the dungeon-like space. There were multiple layers of various pipes and tubing that crisscrossed into the ceiling overhead, connecting water, electrical, and gas supplies to the water tower, boilers, and heating units. Massive cement footings were positioned about every twelve feet to support the vertical load above. This made for several hiding spots to conceal their escapee. The two walked in unison, spread far enough apart to keep the light span as wide as possible. They each held a flashlight in one hand and a gun in the other.

"Do you see anything?" Troy lay flat on the floor with his head hanging down into the darkness.

"Nothing yet," one replied. Troy watched as the flashlights grew dimmer with each step they took. He could hear them instructing Ed to come out of hiding. "We know you're down here. Come out with your hands up. There is nowhere to run."

"Ed—come out of there! It'll be better if you come out now. They'll shoot you." Troy's voice reverberated off the empty walls and echoed back to him. He placed his forefinger to his teeth and began to chew a nail as he waited. He could not believe what was happening.

The pair continued on course, heading toward the far reaching corner of the darkness. When they had traversed the fifty-some yards of the basement and reached the west wall, they turned to the right and made their way back on the far side of the unexplored area. They continued in a steady pace with their flashlight beams sweeping around them. It was impossible to see behind the four-foot-by-four-foot cement footings as they passed. "He must be on the move, sneaking from spot to spot as we approach."

"Yeah, if that's the case then we'll just get more back-up down here and some spotlights. We'll light this place up like a Christmas tree if we have to."

"Well, the good news is, I don't see any exits for him to get out of here, unless it's the same way he got down. I'm calling for back-up now to cover the opening and assist us."

"Yeah, go ahead and do that. I'm afraid that since we haven't found him yet, we will just be playing a game of cat and mouse with this loser."

Troy had reluctantly relinquished his post when instructions were ordered for all hotel employees to report to the front lobby. "Hey guys, I have to go," he hollered as he saw their lights at the far end heading back. "Still nothing?"

"Nope."

At the time Troy departed, Ed was still MIA.

Before long, four additional officers arrived with mega-watt floodlights. By this time, the two officers had completed their search from end to end and came up empty handed. "Hey, glad you're here. He's hiding. We need those big-ass lights."

One officer stayed at the opening to be sure he couldn't escape that way. The other three lowered themselves and the spotlights into the space below and flipped the switches. Suddenly the place was as bright as a day at the beach. Shadows from the footings cast angles around the large cavernous space, but there was no way Ed could hide now.

"Okay, team, line up, and we'll flush this no good thug outta here." Five members of the West Des Moines police department spanned into formation across the breadth of the hotel underground and broke out in synchronized stride, guns drawn. They were ready to capture their man. "Come out with your hands up!"

Nothing but silence and emptiness met them as they navigated toward the far wall. Finally reaching the end, the only thing they had flushed out was a scared rodent. They looked at each other in puzzlement.

"There's no way he could have gone anywhere!" said one of the officers that had been on the scene since the beginning.

"Maybe he's hiding in the pipes in the ceiling. Let's check that out as we walk back." All eyes focused upward and they began a steady pace back.

Reaching the opening and the officer on guard who waited there, they had uncovered zip, nada, nothing. It seemed as though Ed had disappeared into thin dark air.

"It sounds like this is a job for the bloodhounds. He's somewhere down here."

"But where?"

"That's for the dogs to figure out."

Two officers went to fetch Troy who was confined to the front lounge with the rest of the patrons and employees. They needed help to locate anything that would contain Ed's scent. "Let me take you to the Security Office where Ed spent most of his time. Let's see what we can find." Happy to be needed, Troy strutted off with the uniformed men on his heels.

In the Security Office, Troy spotted a navy suit jacket. He lifted it off the back of the chair and there like a sign from God himself was a gold name tag with Ed spelled out in black letters. "Here you go. This should have plenty of Ed's smell on it!" Troy was delighted he was able to give the men what they desperately needed. One of them grabbed the jacket and the two raced off toward Engineering and the back boiler room where the dogs waited.

Andy and Barney sniffed excitedly as the jacket was rubbed in front of their wet black noses. They were ready to get to work and were carefully lowered underground. The minute their paws hit the cement they were tugging at their chains. With noses to the floor they sniffed and rooted, moving their heads from side to side. They were on a reasonably straight path toward the west wall. Upon reaching the wall, they temporarily sniffed, turned to the right and went about ten feet. It was there they went crazy, pawing at the area and raising themselves up on hind quarters. It suggested this was the place Ed vanished.

Officers stormed the area with flashlights to scrutinize the floor and wall. Close examination revealed that a secret door panel allowed passage to the other side. Pressing on the cement bricks, one officer finally found the lever that released the latch.

With guns drawn, the officers formed half a circle around the door that was about to open. The dogs were straining at their harnesses, ready for action. As the door swung in, the illumination of the lights exposed a small room with many boxes, but no Ed. A ladder on the wall drew their eyes upward to a rectangular outline. One of the officers clamored up the ladder and pressed the door upward. His head popped through the opening, and he found himself surrounded by party decorations, tables, chairs, and shelving that held linens, candles, and supplies. He was in a storage area. "Lift the dogs up here. We need to stay on the trail."

---

47 – Grand Finale

The dogs picked up the scent immediately and led the team out of the storage into the back hallway toward the Security Office. At the door of the office, they went nuts. However, it was not surprising since this would be where Ed's scent would register the strongest. It was his territory. As Andy and Barney were pulled away and redirected, they followed their noses and made a beeline toward the door of Housekeeping. Inside, dryers were running and a Stevie Nicks song droned in the background.

The dogs lurched forward toward the laundry bins and began to bark and paw at one in particular. Officers surrounded the hamper that held the dirty linens and bed sheets. "It's the end of the line Ed. Come out with your hands up." Slowly the pile shifted and Ed rose from the laundry, a dirty white napkin draped across his head. They had never seen a man with such defeat in his eyes. What an ordeal.

"You are under arrest. We have the rest of your scumbag friends already in custody."

As Ed was led through the lobby in handcuffs, people cheered and clapped. He lowered his head in embarrassment and anger. Troy called after him. "Why, Ed, why?" Ed didn't respond and only stared at the floor as he was led straight to the cars with flashing lights that were parked outside. His dream of service with the FBI was over. Ariel, leaning into Reece for support, watched with saddened relief as Ed was led away. It was difficult to make sense of all that had happened in the past few days.

Residents of the greater Des Moines community were shocked as the news spread like wildfire. By the time the investigation was well under way, evidence linked and implicated five men: Oscar Kaufman, the leader, Jake and Ross, the drug traffic operations coordinators, Ed, the security guard, and Slade, the hotel's chief engineer.

Involved since the hotel was constructed, the team had contributed personal finances to add the secret room under the back hall storage area and to install additional, but unnecessary spy cameras that were used to monitor activities around the hotel. Jake, as the general contractor of the building project, managed to coordinate the extra installations and cover the expenses without drawing any attention to excess building costs.

Ariel was sickened to think that her ex-boyfriend and other men of acquaintance were involved in such heinous and evil activities. She hoped they were convicted in a swift trial and locked up forever. It was scary to imagine what they would do to her if they had another chance, and she was sure Slade wouldn't mess up a second time to finish what he hadn't accomplished on the first go-around.

Fortunately, Reece was there for her, to comfort and protect her. She also would always have her friend Troy, who she knew would watch her back. Out of this ordeal, she was certain they would remain friends forever.

Epilogue — Endless Possibilities

Ariel pushed aside thoughts that a witness protection program might become a reality some day, in the event that one of the five men she sent to prison would receive early parole or escape from prison. But the truth was, she had never been happier. The horrible events at the Capitol Plaza were finally over—mysteries solved. She had cracked the case wide open with the support of her friend Troy and the wonderful new man in her life.

She looked over at Reece as they drove south on I-35 and exited toward the airport. The sunroof was open, sunshine poured over them in brilliant light, and a warm, soft breeze ruffled their hair. The grass was exceptionally green on the rolling hillside beneath a beautiful blue sky scattered with little puffs of white, soft clouds. It was finally springtime in Iowa after a long, cold winter. In her state of euphoria, everything seemed more alive, sharper, and brighter. She placed her left hand on top of Reece's and stared at the sparkling diamond that rested on her finger.

There was a lifetime of endless possibilities ahead. For now, a vacation was in order. When they returned, there was a wedding to plan and a little girl for Ariel to meet. Ariel savored the moment and relished life which she knew was forever full of miracles and mysteries.

CPSIA information can be obtained at www.ICGtesting.com
Printed in the USA
LVOW081354121012

PP7146600001B/1/P